JUN 1 8 2015

D1505239

PLAYED BY THE BOOK

Center Point
Large Print

Also by Lucy Arlington and available from
Center Point Large Print:

The Novel Idea Series
  Every Trick in the Book
  Books, Cooks, and Crooks

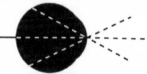

**This Large Print Book carries the
Seal of Approval of N.A.V.H.**

Large Type
Collection
M
ARL

9052222s1

PLAYED BY THE BOOK

Lucy Arlington

CENTER POINT LARGE PRINT
THORNDIKE, MAINE

This Center Point Large Print edition
is published in the year 2015 by arrangement with
The Berkley Publishing Group,
an imprint of Penguin Publishing Group,
a division of Penguin Random House LLC.

Copyright © 2015 by Lucy Arlington.

All rights reserved.

This is a work of fiction. Names, characters, places, and
incidents either are the product of the author's imagination
or are used fictitiously, and any resemblance to actual
persons, living or dead, business establishments,
events, or locales is entirely coincidental.

The text of this Large Print edition is unabridged.
In other aspects, this book may vary
from the original edition.
Printed in the United States of America on permanent paper.
Set in 16-point Times New Roman type.

ISBN: 978-1-62899-592-3

Library of Congress Cataloging-in-Publication Data

Arlington, Lucy.
  Played by the book / Lucy Arlington. — Center Point Large Print
edition.
    pages cm
  Summary: "Lila Wilkins, literary agent and murder magnet, is planning
a book signing garden party. But things aren't coming up roses when she
has to weed out a dangerous killer"—Provided by publisher.
  ISBN 978-1-62899-592-3 (library binding : alk. paper)
  1. Literary agents—Fiction. 2. Murder—Investigation—Fiction.
    3. Large type books. I. Title.
  PS3601.R545P57 2015
  813′.6—dc23
                                                    2015010049

To my readers.
Your loyalty and support has allowed
Lila's story to continue.
Thank you.

PLAYED BY
THE BOOK

Chapter 1

I WAS COMPLETELY ENGROSSED IN reading my latest proposal, a cozy mystery set in a charming English hamlet, when a couple of specks of dirt fell across my paper. I looked up just in time to see a blue ceramic pot coming down fast.

"Dead," Bentley bemoaned, setting the pot down with a thud on my desk and sliding it under my nose. "Dead as a doornail," she added for emphasis.

I brushed away the stray soil and examined what looked like a brown stick with a pair of shriveled leaves. "Did you water it?"

My esteemed boss, Ms. Bentley Burlington-Duke, founder and president of Novel Idea Literary Agency, hardly ever looked perplexed. Even though she now resided in North Carolina, Bentley maintained her Manhattan façade. At this moment, however, she stared down at me with a strange, quizzical expression. Then, she took the diamond-studded readers that dangled on a bejeweled chain around her neck and placed them on the end of her nose, giving the plant another inspection.

I cleared my throat. "Water?" I asked again.

"Well, of course I watered it," she replied indignantly.

I stuck my finger in the soil. Dry as a bone. "And, what year was that?"

Her eyes shifted a bit before she started backtracking. "The problem is that plants need a lot of nurturing and I'm just not the nurturing type. Unlike you—you're a nurturer. And, you have a green thumb." She pointed out the rhododendron that I'd received from my son, Trey, last Mother's Day. The vine was practically taking over the top of my file credenza.

"Anyone can grow a rhododendron," I said, wondering what it was she had in mind this time. In the course of my employment I'd carried out my share of minion duties: fetching her coffee, catering to her most demanding authors, and unpacking hundreds of boxes of books. Was she going to add nursing a dead stick to that list? "They grow like weeds," I continued, hoping to distract her. "Which, speaking of weeds, you wouldn't think much of my gardening skills if you saw my flower beds. They're a mess."

She folded her arms and stared down her regal nose at me with a stern look. "That simply won't do, Lila! You'll need to whip them into shape right away."

I did a double take. "Huh?" The truth be known, I'd intended to create a charming English garden after moving into my little cottage. But after a nearly fatal encounter with a murderous woman in that garden only two months ago, I got the shivers every time I even thought about touching the very trowel or rake that had been brandished against me. Was Bentley, in her own way, suggesting I move on from that trauma? I looked at her imperious posture and suspected a less nurturing motive. I asked hesitantly, "Why's that?"

"Didn't Franklin tell you?"

Franklin was Novel Idea's nonfiction agent. A mild-mannered, older gentleman whom I'd grown quite fond of over the past year. "Tell me what?"

"Well, you know Damian York's book, *Perfect Outdoor Spaces*?"

I nodded. Of course I knew about it. *Perfect Outdoor Spaces* had been the main focus of our status meetings for the entire past month. Its author, Damian York, was one of Franklin's newest and most promising clients. As the host of a popular public television series, he was quickly becoming a rising star in the home and garden entertainment industry. Not only that, but Damian was a homegrown celebrity, born and raised in nearby in Dunston, which is partly the reason he chose Novel Idea Literary Agency to represent the first in his series of gardening books. Lucky for us that he did. *Perfect Outdoor Spaces* was destined to be a bestseller.

Bentley lowered her voice and spoke deliberately. "You're going to help Franklin host a signing for Damian's book during Inspiration Valley's Annual Garden Walk."

I leaned back in my chair and drew in my breath. "Isn't that just two weeks away?" Flyers for the garden walk were plastered in the front window of every business in town. I was kind of flattered that she'd ask me to help a senior agent plan a signing for such an important client, even though it was on short notice. I could see her point, though. The garden walk was the perfect venue for an author like Damian York. I'd already planned on attending the walk and was hoping to talk my boyfriend, police detective Sean Griffiths, into taking a day off from work to accompany me. So, it really wasn't that big of a deal to line up a simple signing.

Bentley smiled slyly. "Which should be plenty of time for you and Franklin to put together a dinner event."

I lurched forward. "A book signing *and* a dinner event?" Sure, I'd planned many events like these, but never two at once and with so little time.

Bentley had taken to pacing in front of my desk, her well-manicured hands gesturing as she talked. She had that intense look she often assumed when she was scheming a new plan. "Yes, of course you'd have to plan a dinner event. Half of his book features outside dining areas." Her eyes lit up. "I can just imagine how you'll set it up. An afternoon signing, perhaps set in a garden, followed by a meet and greet dinner where Damian can interact with . . . oh, let's say . . . a hundred of his biggest fans."

"A hundred?" I croaked. I'd retrieved a legal pad from my top drawer and was frantically jotting down her expectations.

She continued on, her wide-leg trousers flowing gracefully as she paced. As usual, Bentley looked cool, fresh, and perfectly put together. The outfit she was wearing probably cost more than I earned in a month. "Yes, I can see it now. It'll be the perfect fusion between rustic and elegant—earthy tablescapes and candlelight . . . well, you can figure out the details," she finished with a final wave of her slim hand. "Just make it fabulous. Oh, and of course, you and Franklin will need to coordinate all your plans with this year's garden walk chairwoman, Alice Peabody."

I jotted down the name.

Bentley continued, "She's the president of Inspiration Valley's garden club, the Dirty Dozen. She'll be coming by to look at your gardens the first part of next week."

"What?"

"That's why you need to get that garden of yours into tip-top shape; you're garden number thirteen on this year's garden walk. The original entrant had some sort of family emergency and had to withdraw from the lineup."

I could feel my eyes bugging out. "But . . ."

Bentley wagged her finger at me. "No buts, Lila. We need the garden club to help facilitate this event. In this business it's all about paying it forward. You scratch their back and they'll scratch yours."

Oh yeah, well, my back isn't itchy, I thought, struggling to maintain a civil attitude. This was not part of my job description. I'd happily weed through thousands of queries, prune hundreds of manuscripts, and nurture several promising new authors; but keeping a real garden trim and neat? Well, that was asking too much.

I held my breath for a few counts and then released it slowly, relenting to the fact that I was stuck. Once Bentley set her mind to something there was no dissuading her. So, instead of arguing, I simply nodded in agreement.

It's true that Bentley could be a taskmaster, but despite my sometimes overly demanding boss, I loved my job as Novel Idea's newest literary agent. After being laid off from the *Dunston Herald*— a daunting situation for a forty-five-year-old divorcée with a son heading to college—I'd taken a chance and responded to the agency's help wanted ad. After cutting my teeth on a few hundred query letters, and bringing *The Alexandria Society*, a blockbuster novel written by Marlette Robbins, to the agency, Bentley had offered me my dream position. I'd been assigned to mysteries, from cozy and romantic suspense to hard-boiled and soft-boiled, which gave me the daily thrill of traipsing through manuscripts looking for the next bestseller. Sometimes I just couldn't believe my luck. After all, what other job would pay me to travel in my mind's eye to exotic locations, meet captivating characters, and ride the roller coaster of fast-paced plots with twists and turns so unexpected that they kept me spellbound until the last page?

Bentley made her way to my office door. "Oh, and Lila, be prepared to discuss your plans at Monday's status meeting. We're all here to help you in any way we can. Have a good weekend," she added as she breezed out of my office.

I shoved aside the dead plant she'd left behind and collapsed on top of my desk. "Impossible," I muttered. I sat there for a second, my mind reeling with doubt. How could I possibly pull together an event of such magnitude in two weeks? Not to mention, tame my unruly flower beds. *Impossible. Absolutely impossible.*

A quote from Mark Twain popped into my head. "There are thousands of excuses for every failure, but never a good reason." I sat up and repeated the quote out loud, drawing inspiration from Twain's wisely spoken words before snatching up my legal pad and heading to find Franklin.

I was in such a hurry, I didn't bother to look before entering the hallway and ran smack-dab into one of the other agents, Jude Hudson. "Oops! Sorry," I said, stumbling backward.

He reached out to steady me, placing his hands on my shoulders. The unexpected contact kicked my heart rate into high gear as his sculpted arms revealed themselves under his snug and immaculately tailored shirt. Much to my annoyance, I still hadn't been able to shake the spark left over from a kiss that we'd foolishly shared during my first month at the agency.

"No problem. Running into you is always a pleasure," he said playfully, keeping his hands in place and holding me at arm's length. As always, his eyes kind of shimmered when in close proximity to any woman (how *did* he do that?) but this time those sparkly chocolate brown eyes studied me with concern. "You look stressed."

"Bentley just dumped a load of work in my lap," I replied, shaking off his hands and reminding myself that I was a one-man type of girl, and that man was definitely Sean.

A swatch of dark wavy hair fell over his forehead as he lowered his gaze. "I'm sorry to hear that. Is there something I can help with?"

"There might be." I was touched that he'd offered. "I'll be discussing it at Monday's status meeting. I may need to delegate a few tasks for a meet and greet dinner I'll be planning for Damian York."

"Count me in," he said, throwing me a wink.

Then with a mischievous grin, he reached down and snatched up my left hand. "I see there's no ring on that finger yet. If Griffiths doesn't put one there soon, I might just take care of it myself."

"Give it a break, Jude!" I said, ripping my hand away and stomping down the hallway. I knew he was only kidding, but I just wasn't in the mood. Truth be told, his words hit on a nerve. It'd been a couple of months since I'd overheard Sean ask Trey for his permission for my hand in marriage —a wonderfully romantic gesture that sent me into an immediate tizzy. Ever since, I'd fantasized about my dream wedding—a literary-themed wedding: simple glass candle votives arranged on stacks of vintage books, copies of Browning's love poems splayed open for guests to read, and my treasured copy of Austen's *Pride and Prejudice* prominently displayed next to the wedding cake. Why, I'd practically planned the whole wedding in my mind, everything from my bouquet—roses much like those that must have grown in the Capulets' garden where Romeo stole away to speak to Juliet—to my dress, which of course would be a 1920s flapper-inspired gown, reminiscent of *The Great Gatsby*. The only problem was, Sean still hadn't popped the question. To make matters worse, Sean's new promotion from officer to detective was keeping him so busy we'd barely had any time together, which was just going to get worse now that Bentley had given me all this extra work.

I knocked on Franklin's door harder than necessary and walked straight in, not even waiting for his invitation.

"Bentley talked to you?" he asked with a sheepish look.

I nodded, walking over to his wall that displayed all his clients' framed book covers. I located Damian York's cover, which showed a table set for two in a romantic English garden, with candles flickering inside hurricane glass and paper lanterns strung on overhead branches. For one wistful second, I thought of how such a table would be a perfect setting for a proposal, then I snapped back to reality. "Yes, Bentley talked to me." I pointed up to Damian's framed cover. "She wants a signing for *Perfect Outdoor Spaces* followed by a dinner for a hundred of his fans." I rolled my eyes up to the ceiling. " 'Rustic but elegant,' I think she said. And, of course, she wants everything to be *fabulous,*" I added, waving my hands in a mock gesture.

Franklin shook his head. "Oh my, she's been scheming again. I'm sorry, Lila. I should have warned you."

I looked across the desk at my friend. Franklin Stafford was one of the sweetest men I knew, the definition of the term "Southern gentleman." I could never be angry with him. "It's okay." I sighed. "If we divide and conquer, I think it'll be doable."

He seemed relieved. "I have to admit, I'm not the best at planning dinner events."

I took out my legal pad and started adding to my notes. "Okay, then. I'll handle the dinner if you want to take on the book signing. Bentley has a garden venue in mind."

Franklin nodded. "She told me as much. I was thinking the Secret Garden." The Secret Garden, in keeping with Inspiration Valley's literary theme, was the perfect name for the local nursery, which was located on Sweetbay Road just past the railway station. Its enchanting acres were surrounded by a hand-stacked stone wall covered in trumpet vines. Patrons entered through carved wooden doors under a double-arched gate covered with pastel climbing roses and made their way around the nursery's beautifully orchestrated settings on pea-gravel pathways defined with colorful beds of perennials.

I jotted it down. "Perfect! That would work for both the signing and the dinner. I could arrange to have a large tent brought in and set up in the gardens. It would be a lovely location."

"We should do flowers on every table," he added.

"Wildflowers, perhaps." Field lilies, hibiscus, and mallow popped into mind, but I couldn't quite picture them all together. I made a note to check with Damian to see which flowers would suit both the book and the occasion. Or perhaps my friend Addison Eckhart, manager of the Secret Garden, would give me some advice.

"Yes, and we'll use some of the repurposed containers that he suggests in his book." Franklin's voice rose an octave as he described his ideas. "I like the idea of tinted mason jars or vintage boxes and tins. It adds a sort of an earthy charm, don't you think?"

I started to reply, but he jumped back in with more ideas. "Oh, and I saw in his book that Damian likes to fill small metal buckets with a mixture of herb plants and place them on the table where guests can clip fresh herbs if they want. Isn't that clever? As for the other containers, we could pop by Beyond and Back to see what they have."

Beyond and Back was a new home décor store that sold gently used home decorating items. "Good idea," I agreed, then went on, tapping my pen excitedly as another thought came to mind. "You know, I bet we could get How Green Was My Valley to cater the event with a fresh-from-the-garden menu."

"Damian would love that," Franklin agreed. "His book features several ideas for hosting garden-to-table dinner events featuring in-season vegetables."

I sat up a little straighter, making a note to read the book right away and check out some of those menus. "Speaking of Damian, when's he coming into town?"

Franklin's face brightened. "I'll be picking him up tomorrow. I reserved a room for him at the Magnolia Bed and Breakfast."

"Good, that's the best place in town." It wasn't always that way, though. Mother had told me that when she first moved to the area, called Illumination Valley at the time, the Magnolia Bed and Breakfast was nothing more than a dilapidated old Victorian, close to ruin. Not much more than a hangout for freethinkers and New Agers. Illumination Valley had practically dried up during a hard-hitting recession. That's when Bentley came onto the scene, establishing her agency in the center of town. The success of the agency soon carried the town out of its slump. Then, jumping on the bandwagon, the town reinvented itself, changed its name to Inspiration Valley, and adopted literary-like themes for many of its small businesses.

Franklin nodded. "I'm anxious for you to meet him. He's simply . . ." A hint of red showed in his cheeks. "Simply bigger than life."

I couldn't help but smile at Franklin's enthusiasm over his client, wondering if it was only a professional interest or something more personal. He must have realized his description of Damian was a bit overzealous, because his eyes grew wide and he suddenly took interest in tidying up his desk. A while back, I'd stumbled upon a secret Franklin had worked hard to keep from his friends and coworkers. And, while I'd discovered the truth about Franklin's love life, I'd never talked about it with anyone, including him, out of respect for his privacy.

When he finally spoke again, his tone was all business. "I'm afraid that you'll have to do most of the initial planning for this event on your own, Lila."

My brows shot up. It was unlike Franklin to skirt responsibility.

"I'll be spending most of tomorrow with Damian and Ruthie Watson from Sherlock Holmes Realty. Damian is moving back to the area and is looking for a large piece of land to build a home. He wants me along for a second opinion."

"Really? But what about filming his show? Doesn't he do that on the West Coast?"

Franklin's voice was tinged with excitement as he began to explain. "That's just the thing. He's planning on building a home that will showcase his design ideas. It'll be like a live-in set for his show. In fact, Damian says that if he finds the perfect spot, he may be able to talk the network into doing a spin-off show that features the construction of his new home and the expansive gardens that will surround it."

"What a great concept," I commented, thinking of all the possibilities for Novel Idea and the Valley's art community. "Ruthie will find him the perfect place. She's the agent who helped me buy my cottage." I remembered that tumultuous time like it was yesterday. Trey and I had been living in nearby Dunston at the time when a combination of events—me losing my job and Trey, along with several rowdy buddies, causing a boatload of damage to Dunston High School's football field —forced me into selling my home. Luckily, my mother let us move in with her. Finally, after I landed my job at Novel Idea Agency, I was able to pay off my debt and save enough for a down payment on my dream home—a charming butter yellow cottage with periwinkle shutters.

"That's right. You're over in Walden Woods Circle—a lovely location," Franklin complimented me. Although, thinking of my cottage and my unsightly flower gardens brought on a whole new level of anxiety. Now that Bentley had added me to the garden walk, I was going to have to face down my garden with its tangled mess of weeds, overgrown perennials, and the attention-starved primroses. I started rubbing at a kink that was forming in my neck.

Franklin must have picked up on my stress. "Don't worry, Lila. I know this seems over-whelming now, but it'll all come together in the end. It always does."

I nodded, still working on my neck. For some reason, I had an uneasy feeling. Perhaps I was just leery of this current disruption to the prosaic rhythm my life had assumed over the past couple of months. The monotony of late was a welcome change from my first year in Inspiration Valley, which had been tainted with more violence than I'd ever experienced while living in Dunston.

I shuddered at the memories, although those days were behind me. Thankfully, ever since the deathly events at this spring's Taste of the Town, my steady and uneventful routine had brought back a sense of harmony to my life. Except for the fact that my relationship with Sean was in some sort of weird funk, things were on the upswing: After a successful freshman year at UNC Wilmington, my son, Trey, was on task, working hard this summer as a barista at Espresso Yourself; my wacky mother, the Amazing Althea, local clairvoyant and tarot reader, was behaving herself; my best friend, Makayla, was hopelessly in love; and my professional life had never been more stimulating or rewarding.

I sighed and put on a smile. My apprehensiveness was silly and completely unfounded. "You're right, Franklin," I said, trying to relax. "This event will be like a walk in the park . . . or should I say garden." I giggled. "After all, it's just a signing and dinner. What could possibly go wrong?"

Chapter 2

STILL, MY UNEASINESS GREW. EVEN AS I headed back to my office to wrap up my work for the day, I couldn't shake the feeling of dread that had settled over me. Instead of dwelling on it, I busied myself with the manuscript I'd started on before Bentley's interruption. It was the first of a proposed English cozy mystery series. It featured a feisty female pub owner who, after ferreting out a local murderer, served up a little justice with her whiskey and beer. The author had done such a lovely job of describing the quaint English hamlet and developing its quirky inhabitants that I never wanted the story to end. That's the thing I love most about a well-crafted story: The story line and characters stay with me even after the last page.

In this case, the author's talent had given me a much needed reprieve from my current worries. So much so, I'd decided the uneasiness I was feeling was all in my imagination. I was just stressed after being caught off guard by the extra workload, a problem which could be easily solved.

I glanced over at my desk phone. It was time to call in the big guns.

"Hello, Mama. Are you busy this evening?"

"Of course not, hon. You and I have plans."

I searched my brain. "We do?" I knew we'd discussed trying out the new Italian restaurant in town, Machiavelli's, but I didn't recall setting a date.

"Yes, I knew that you would be needin' me, so I cleared the whole evening. It was in the cards."

Aw . . . I should have seen that coming. My mother, the Amazing Althea, made her living by reading palms and tarot cards. And not a bad living, at that. Although I'm not sure if her clients referred to her as "amazing" because of her fortune-telling or her baking skills, because every person who came by her home for a reading was treated to a slice of her famous banana bread. Althea's banana bread had become legendary in these parts.

"So, what is it we're doing?" she asked.

I sat back, enjoying the moment. "Why don't you tell me?"

"Don't get ornery with me, Lila Wilkins! You know darn well the cards don't tell me every-thing."

I stifled a chuckle and got on with the reason I'd called. "Actually, I need a favor."

"Uh-huh."

"Can you take your truck by the Secret Garden and pick up a few items for me? I'll throw in a pizza and beverage of your choice." I needed to strike a bargain because there was very little I could haul on my Vespa. My sporty yellow Vespa

26

scooter was great for jaunting back and forth to work and easy on my gas budget, but not always the most practical mode of transportation, especially when it came to things like grocery shopping. Although, I'd been known to use packing twine laced through the bars of the rear seat rack to haul home sizable purchases from the monthly artisan fair.

"Well, if you're planning on invitin' my ol' friend Jim Beam, then we've got a deal." My mother had enjoyed an ongoing relationship with Mr. Jim Beam for as long as I could remember. I was just sure her veins flowed with the stuff by now.

I finished the conversation by giving her a list of things I needed and agreeing to meet at my place around six o'clock. That would give me enough time to run by and pick up her "friend" and still get home in plenty of time to change and call in a pizza order.

Sean was next. I dialed his cell, but had to leave a message. He'd been hard to reach lately. Since major crime incidents had been on a decrease, his sergeant had allocated Sean's time to assisting the specialized narcotics unit. Narcotic trafficking was on the rise in Dunston due to an uptick in gang activity. The city's department was dedicating half its force to trying to get the situation in check before things spiraled out of control. As a result, Sean had been working a lot of overtime. I couldn't even recall when we'd last had an evening together.

Frustrated that he wasn't available—yet again!—I gathered my stuff, took one last glance at the dead plant Bentley had left behind, and flipped off my office light. On the way down the agency's back stairs, I decided to take a detour by Espresso Yourself.

Walking into Espresso Yourself was like walking into a feast for the senses. The first thing that always hit me was the spicy blend of coffee, cinnamon, and chocolate. Then my eyes would alight on all the artistic creations displayed on the walls and shelves, their textures and colors stealing away my imagination. All that, combined with the soft whirring of the espresso machine, piped-in acoustic guitar music, and the sound of the owner's—Makayla's—melodic laugh were enough to abate my strongest worries. I could already feel my shoulders relaxing.

As Makayla greeted me from behind the counter, I noticed her chocolate-colored skin was practically glowing. Probably the effects of a blossoming relationship with the local bookstore owner, Jay Coleman. He'd wooed her last spring by slipping anonymous love poems into her tip jar. Then he finally revealed himself as her secret admirer in the most romantic gesture I'd ever witnessed. It started with a single violinist and a rose at Espresso Yourself and ended in a dozen roses, and that many or more musicians later, at the Nine Muses fountain, where Jay serenaded her with a touching rendition of "The First Time Ever I Saw Your Face." They'd been seeing each other ever since, and I'd never seen my friend happier.

She gave me a once-over, shook her head, then turned back to her machine. "You've been working too hard, I can tell. Looks like you've had a bad day," she said over her shoulder. "Let me get your usual."

I sidled up to the counter. "Thanks, I could use a boost, but make it a small cup. I won't be here long. I really came by just to ask Trey a quick question."

"Sure, let me get your coffee and then I'll get him. He's in the back working on today's dishes."

I laughed. "He does dishes?"

She glanced back over her shoulder again, her fern green eyes twinkling. "He's a wonderful worker, Lila. I just don't know what I ever did without him."

I beamed. "Just what every mother wants to hear." Over spring break, Trey had stepped in to help Makayla during the busy Taste of the Town events. He'd done such a good job, Makayla offered him summer employment, a real boon to a college boy.

"So what's going on tonight? A date?" she asked.

My shoulders slumped. "No, afraid not. Work stuff."

She slid my cup across the counter. "Work stuff? On a Friday night? Something big going on?"

Before answering, I let my nose hover over the rim, closing my eyes and inhaling one of my favorite smells. "You ever heard the expression 'Where flowers bloom so does hope'?"

Makayla smiled. "Lady Bird Johnson."

I nodded. "Well, I'm changing it to 'Where weeds grow so does despair.'"

Makayla tipped her head back and laughed, a sound that always reminded me of wind chimes. "Having garden problems?"

"Garden problems, work problems, boyfriend problems . . . you name it, I've got it."

She leaned over, resting her chin in her palm. "Oh boy. That bad, huh? Tell me about it."

I waved it off. "I'm just tired. Sorry." I suddenly felt bad for unloading.

"Don't be. What's going on?" For being in only her midtwenties, Makayla possessed the confidence and diplomacy of a much older woman. Since I moved to Inspiration Valley, she'd become my dearest friend and best confidante.

I drew in a deep breath and began giving her a quick rundown on my latest project. "And, I was hoping to have some time with Sean, but he's tied up with work, and now it looks like I'll be swamped for the next couple of weeks," I finished.

My friend straightened up and smiled. Pointing

to herself, she said, "Girl, you are now looking at your official decorating committee. All you have to do is tell me what you want and I'll see that it gets done. Jay will help me and Trey can cover for me here if things get too crazy."

I shook my head. "Oh, Makayla, that's too much. I can't ask you—"

She reached across the counter and placed a graceful hand over mine. "Don't argue. What are friends for?" She beamed. "Besides, I'm a huge Damian York fan. It'll be the perfect opportunity to meet him in person."

My eyes slid over to a set of bookshelves that Makayla kept full of worn paperbacks so that her customers could help themselves. I made a note to myself to bring down Damian's new book for her to display. Not only would it be a nice gesture, but it would provide some extra exposure, since practically everyone in Inspiration Valley got their caffeine fix at Espresso Yourself. "And Jay? How's he going to feel about being volunteered for all this?" I asked. Not only was Jay Coleman the proprietor of the Valley's only bookstore, the Constant Reader, he was also one of the agency's best clients. Just that past spring, Jay had signed on to write the sequel to *The Alexandria Society*. The first book, a bestseller, was created by Marlette Robbins, an extremely talented local who'd lived his final years as a recluse before his unfortunate death.

A broad smile played across her face. "Are you kidding? A new author in the area, and a celebrity to boot? Think of all the possibilities for Jay and his bookstore."

"Okay, then." I gratefully relented. "You're hired. We'll have a meeting of the heads early next week and get everything planned out."

"Everything what?" I looked over to see Trey coming out of the back. He had on an apron and a long dish towel draped over his shoulder. He looked so young and vulnerable that I fought hard not to jump up and hug him. I stayed put, teasing him instead. "If the girls could see you now."

He snapped the towel in my direction and flashed a good-natured grin. "What's up, Mom?"

"Are you hungry?"

His dark brown eyes lit up. "You bet!"

"Careful now," Makayla warned. "She's setting a trap."

Trey eyed me suspiciously. "A trap?"

Makayla and I exchanged a glance and laughed.

"No, not really," I replied, feeling a sense of warmth at my son's youthful gullibility. "I thought maybe I could make you a trade. Your muscles for a couple of large pizzas."

His chest puffed out at the compliment, but he remained hesitant. "What exactly do you have in mind?"

Makayla turned over the *Closed* sign in the front door and busied herself with wiping down tables.

"I need you to help me remove those three hawthorn bushes in the back garden."

He stared at me blankly.

"You know, the ugly brown bushes under the windows," I explained.

"Oh sure. Why?"

"Our house has been added to the Annual Garden Walk and we need to spruce things up a bit."

"The Annual Garden Walk? Us?"

"I know it sounds crazy, but it's something I have to do for work. It's important, Trey." When I purchased my charming little cottage on Walden Woods Circle, I'd harbored fantasies about converting the gardens into a scene worthy of the great Impressionists: van Gogh's soft irises, Matisse's dahlias, and splatterings of Manet's pastel roses. Unfortunately, life—and a few bad memories—had got in the way. What I had now was something that might inspire a painting more along the lines of Munch's *The Scream*.

Trey shifted his feet, dipping his chin and shoving his hands into his jean pockets. "Is anyone else coming to help out?"

"Grandma."

The corners of his mouth tipped upward and his brown eyes gleamed mischievously. "In that case, throw in a couple more pizzas and I'll see if I can round up a few friends to help. I'll tell them to bring their shovels."

I couldn't hold back any longer. I leapt from my chair and engulfed my son in a huge bear hug. Not an easy feat since his normally thin frame had filled out during his time at college. "You're the best, Trey, you know that?" I said, planting a kiss on his cheek and ruffling his chestnut brown hair.

He stiffened, immediately wiping his cheek and mumbling something under his breath as he disappeared back into the kitchen area. I stared after him affectionately before draining the last bit of my latte and bidding Makayla good-bye.

Talk about good timing—the pizza and the extra help arrived simultaneously. After filling the stomachs of Trey and three of his buddies, I put them to work digging out the roots of the damaged shrubs. I planned to replace them with a combination of spirea and barberry. I was thinking that the deep red barberry foliage would contrast nicely against the light green leaves of the Gold Mound spirea.

As they dug away, I got to work on weeding my flower beds. I hadn't made it far when my efforts were interrupted by the sound of my mother's truck rumbling down the street. Her turquoise 1970s C10 pickup, complete with Patsy Cline blaring out the windows and two magnetic signs boasting *Amazing Althea's Psychic Services*, always seemed to announce her arrival with an air of slightly eccentric flamboyancy. Well, maybe more distinct than "slightly."

She climbed out, tossed me a wave, and shouted, "Come give me a hand unloadin' this stuff, boys. Show me what you're made of." She slammed the door and moved around to the back of the truck to open the tailgate.

"Holy crap!" I heard Trey exclaim from his digging site.

I spun around to see him stooped over, staring at something in the ground.

"Mom, come here!" he added, waving frantically.

Both my mother and I rushed to his side, pushing our way through his huddled friends. "What is it, darlin'?" my mother asked, wrapping a protective arm around Trey's trembling shoulders and peering down at the upturned earth.

Although she didn't have to ask. It was obvious. Trey's digging had unearthed a skull—a human skull.

Chapter 3

AFTER THE GRUESOME DISCOVERY, THE first person I thought of was Sean. Not only because he was a police officer and I knew the authorities should be informed, but because the sight of the skull completely unnerved me. I needed him there. So I borrowed Trey's cell phone and after a few shaky attempts, managed to dial Sean's number. For the second time that day, I couldn't reach him. Half disgusted, I hung up without leaving a message and dialed 911.

As I waited for the call to be picked up, I glanced over at my mother. She seemed as upset as I was. Trey, on the other hand, now seemed okay. He and his friends had moved away from the hole and were huddled together talking. Bits and pieces of their conversation told me they were speculating about the origins of the skull.

"Ma'am?" I heard the 911 operator on the other end. "What's your emergency?"

"We've dug up a dead body in our yard," I replied, cringing. Couldn't I have thought of a better way to put it? "I mean bones. Actually a skull. I think it's a human skull. Can you send the police to look at it?"

I glanced back over to where my mother was hanging on my every word. Even from where I was standing, I could see that she'd begun shaking. I gave the 911 operator my address, disconnected, and went to my mother.

"Mama? You all right?" I placed my arm around her shoulders, her trembles unnerving me. My mother was the strongest person I'd ever known. She was my rock, always there to see me through the difficult times: my divorce from Bill, Trey's adolescent stunts, losing my job, and even all the craziness that I'd been through since moving to the Valley. It just wasn't like her to be so shaken. "What is it?" I asked again.

"Oh, Lila. I'm losin' my touch, that's what." She pointed down at the skull. "Somethin' as awful as this . . . well, I should have seen it comin'. I should have been able to warn you."

"Don't be silly. How could you have possibly predicted that we'd dig up a skull this afternoon? Besides, it could be a hundred years old, for all we know." Although, even as I said it, I knew that probably wasn't true. My cottage was built in the 1960s during the Illumination days when all the houses on Walden Woods Circle were built as rentals for a New Age retreat site. Since the town's reinvention, they'd been renovated and turned into quaint little cottages. Unless my house was built on some sort of ancient burial ground, this body was probably buried sometime in the last thirty to forty years. The thought of it made my stomach churn. My eyes darted to my neighbors' homes and then back to my own. Could this be the remains of the previous owner, or someone who lived nearby? Why would it be under my hawthorn bushes?

"Lila, don't go tryin' to sugarcoat this." She shook off my arm. "It's simply a fact that I'm losin' my abilities. This poor soul, lying right under my nose and I didn't even sense it?"

We both looked down at the skull and then backed away. I glanced around at my garden, once a place that I dreamed about renovating, a space full of hope and marked by ambitious goals. It was quickly becoming my least favorite part of my home. I let my eyes wander to the maple tree in the corner of the yard where, just a couple of months ago, I'd had a confrontation with a ruthless murderer. In a small way, today's project was a step toward reclaiming the sense of tranquillity that I'd once felt about my garden— before a killer's abhorrent actions had tainted it with dark memories. Now, I had to wonder if I'd ever feel at peace again in my own yard.

My mother had started pacing, a worried expression on her face. "Oh, hon. It's not just this thing today, there's been some other things, too. Like, just yesterday Fannie Walker came by for a readin'. She comes by every year about this time to have me predict whether or not her roses will take a prize in the garden walk competition. For the past ten years, my predictions have been spot-on, but this time when I laid out the cards they were all a mumble jumble. I couldn't make neither hide nor hair out of them." Her shoulders shriveled inward. "Then, of all things, I forgot to add the baking powder to my banana bread batter. It came out as flat as a pancake. Why, I don't think I've ever messed up a batch of banana bread."

That *was* troubling. My mother was a banana bread artisan, her baking skills finely honed over the years. Even as a youngster, I was fascinated by watching her expertly whip together ingredients without even using a measuring cup: "A pinch of this and a smattering of that," she used to say, her graceful hands flying over the bowl. Then, for my seventh birthday, she got me a miniature-sized apron and a tiny loaf pan of my own and invited me to bake with her. It was one of the best memories of my childhood. In fact, that little apron still hung on a hook inside my pantry and I couldn't look at it without recalling Mama's hands guiding mine as I practiced cracking eggs over the banana bread bowl.

"How am I gonna to take care of you all if I don't have my gift?" she continued, still pacing. "You know, Lila, some people take care of their loved ones with their physical strength, some with their money, some with their smarts. Well, I ain't never been big on any of those things, but I've always had my gift. It's how I care for y'all."

Her words struck a chord and caused me to

dip my head in shame. I'd always been half embarrassed by my mother's gift; I'd never stopped to think of it as the way she'd shown her love all these years. Isn't that the way it always is with parents and children? Trey had always hated my worrying and fussing, but I'd been telling him all this time that it was just the way I loved him. Why had it taken me so long to realize that my mother's often dramatic predictions and warnings were the way she loved me?

I looked over at her, really looked at her, and noticed that the fine lines around her eyes were deeper than I'd remembered. "You haven't been feeling ill, have you?" I asked, but before she could answer, the first of the police cars pulled in front of my house. I gave her a little squeeze and a peck on the cheek. "Take the boys inside, Mama, and get them some soda or something. I'll be in as soon as I'm done out here. We'll talk more then."

She successfully herded the boys back into the house just as the two officers approached. The first, a young guy with close-cut dark hair, a strong jaw, and an enthusiastic bounce in his step, shot me a quick greeting before placing gloves on his hands and stooping over the hole to examine the skull.

"My son was trying to pry out the roots of that hawthorn bush when he dug it up," I told him. "It looks human, so I called right away."

Both of the officers were kneeling now, peering down into the hole with interest. "Did you dig up anything else, ma'am?" the other officer asked. He was much older than the first guy, maybe in his midfifties, with a round shiny head and robust stature.

"No. That's it; just the skull." Thank goodness. The skull was bad enough. I was probably going to have a whopper of a nightmare as it was.

The officers remained silent as they stood and began examining the rest of the ground around the hole.

"How do you suppose it got there?" I asked.

Neither one of them answered that question. Instead they began asking questions of their own, like: *How long had I lived in the house? How old were the hawthorn bushes? Did I know the previous residents?* All questions that gave me the willies yet simultaneously incited my sense of curiosity. Nonetheless, I did my best to answer their questions and was still doing so a half hour later when Sean arrived on the scene.

He crossed the yard quickly, approaching with a concerned look. It had been a few days since I'd seen him and I wanted nothing more than to run into his arms, but the presence of the other officers made any display of affection seem inappropriate. "One of the guys recognized your address and called me," he said, standing next to me and placing his hand on the small of my back. Then looking at the officers, he asked, "What's going on?"

After getting the initial rundown, Sean sent me inside the house while he remained outside to assist the officers. Once inside, I found the boys in the family room playing video games, eating cold pizza, and finishing the last of the soda. I was glad to see they were carrying on, seemingly unfazed by their macabre discovery. Although I had no doubt that once word got out, I'd be spending most of tomorrow fielding questions from their concerned parents.

I worked my way around them and back to the kitchen, where my mother was. She was at the table, a set of tarot cards laid out in front of her. "Come over here and look at this, darlin'," she beckoned.

Glancing over her shoulder, I saw that she'd laid out several cards. I wasn't an expert on tarot reading, but I did recognize one of the cards, the Magician, sometimes known for his deceptiveness. "Who are you reading?" I asked.

"You, sug. And, the cards are finally speakin' to me."

I breathed a sigh of relief. "Well, that's good, isn't it? That must mean that you're not losing your touch, right?"

She glanced up at me, her eyes dark with concern. "Hon, there ain't nothin' good about this. Nothin' at all."

I sighed, pouring us each a finger of Jim Beam before taking up the seat across the table and sitting back to indulge her latest prediction. I'd spent my whole life torn between brushing off my mother's so-called gift as an eccentric obsession and being amazed by her sometimes uncannily accurate predictions. Tonight, I knew I had to appease her fears over losing her gift. Because in the big picture, it didn't really matter if my mother's abilities were real or not, they were what made her the Amazing Althea, an identity that she'd be lost without.

I remembered a line from Patrick Rothfuss's book, *The Name of the Wind*: "It's like everyone tells a story about themselves inside their own head. Always. All the time. That story makes you what you are. We build ourselves out of that story." That was so true of my mother. And I, for one, loved the quirkiness of her personal story and never wanted to see the identity she'd built torn down by her own doubts or that of some naysayer.

So we sat together, our heads bent over the table, sipping Jim Beam and trying to reason with the cards. "It just doesn't seem right, sugar. Either I am way off, or you're in serious danger. You see the Magician? The way he's reversed like this tells me that there's going to be some trickery comin' your way."

I chuckled, trying to lighten the mood. "Well, that may not be all bad. Actually, that could mean anything." I rolled my eyes upward, trying to come up with something plausible. "Like, maybe Trey's going to try to pull something over on me. Boys his age can be so mischievous. Or, maybe one of the other agents at work is going to play a prank on me. Probably Zach. You know how he is. Or maybe—"

My mother placed a wrinkled hand on my arm, her eyes boring into mine. "No, darlin'. This is more serious than all that. I can feel it."

As if on cue, the front screen door slammed and heavy footsteps brought Sean into the kitchen. His face wore a troubled expression. I stood and went to him, this time wrapping my arms around his neck and leaning in for a hug and quick kiss.

After we separated, he placed a hand on my shoulder and spoke with a concerned tone. "The forensic pathologist has determined it's a human skull. He can't really tell much more until we have more of the skeleton. So we're sending for an anthropologist to come and unearth the rest of the remains. He'll be able to determine the age of the bones, whether it's male or female, and maybe even the cause of death. I should be able to tell you more later."

I rubbed my fingertips against my temples where I could feel the beginning of a dull ache. "All I really want to know is who that poor person was and why they're buried in my yard."

"That's what we're going to try to determine,"

he replied, his demeanor shifting noticeably. I recognized the change in his expression. He was wearing his she's-not-going-to-like-this look. I'd become quite familiar with this look over the past year or so. After all, I'd seen it quite a few times. The first time was when he came to my home in Dunston to inform me that Trey and some of his friends had landed in trouble. Then, more recently, I noticed "the look" when I came home from work to find he'd halfway burned down my kitchen in an ill-fated attempt to make a romantic dinner for our nine-month anniversary. And lately I'd seen that very look every time he had to cancel a date due to some sort of work demand.

I narrowed my eyes. "What is it that you're not telling me, Sean?"

He drew in a deep breath, shifting again and staring down at my glass of Jim Beam as if he'd like nothing more than to have a stiff drink. "This whole thing might become a little disruptive," he finally said.

"Disruptive? What do you mean?"

"Well, this process could take several days and the anthropologist will have to excavate other parts of the backyard, maybe even the whole yard. I don't know how much they'll actually dig, but it'll be inaccessible for a while. Hopefully they won't find any other skeletons buried out there."

I swallowed hard. Not because I couldn't tolerate a little inconvenience or because I was worried about my garden. It was the thought that there might be more remains in my yard. One skeleton was enough. In fact, no one deserved that type of treatment. To simply be discarded after death, their remains destined to spend eternity lying in anonymity, with not even a simple stone to mark their death or an epitaph to commemorate the life they lived. It was almost too much to grasp. I rubbed at my temples some more. Then another thought snuck up on me. The garden walk! There was no way I'd be able to participate now. I swallowed hard again. How was I going to break the news to Bentley? She'd be fit to be tied once she found out that her plans were going to be waylaid by a police investigation. I decided to wait until Monday morning to tell her.

I glanced back down at my mother, who was gathering her cards and preparing to leave. "Believe me, hon, this is only the beginnin' of your troubles," she warned.

Great. Like I didn't already have enough troubles.

"If you knew what was good for you, Lila," she continued, "you'd pack up a few things and come on over to my place to ride out this wave of trouble comin' your way. I'd be happy to take you and Trey in for a while. It would be like old times."

She was referring to the time last summer when Trey and I lived with her while I paid off some debt and saved for the down payment on my cottage. It had been a wonderful time for all of us and I was still grateful that she'd been there for me. But I wasn't going to let my current troubles send me scurrying from my home. Besides, Trey and I had such busy schedules, we'd drive her crazy with all our comings and goings. "Thanks, Mama, but I'll be fine."

She nodded, her eyes moving between Sean and me with a wistful look. "Well, okay then. I'd best be gettin' on home and leave all you young people to your fun." She chuckled, but I could detect a pinch of sorrow in her tone. I wondered if there was more to her request than just offering us a safe haven. Perhaps she was feeling lonely and wanted the company. I guess I had been neglectful of our relationship lately. I made a note to make more time for my mother.

Unfortunately, there wasn't much fun to be had amongst us young people. Right after mother left, Sean begged off, saying that he needed to check in with the anthropologist again and then needed to return to Dunston to interview a suspect in a drug case he was working. He did, however, ask me to dinner the following evening at Voltaire's, the Valley's best French restaurant. Since Sean was more of a James Joyce Pub type of guy, my heart fluttered at the mention of Voltaire's. Was he planning to finally pop the question?

Despite a headache and the constant noise

emitting from the family room full of boys, the possibility of Sean's long-awaited proposal carried me through the rest of my evening. It wasn't until later that night when I was lying in bed that my thoughts returned to the skull in my garden and my mother's predictions. There was only one thing to do: Find out more about my home's previous owners. And I knew just where to start. I planned to stop by Ruthie Watson's office at Sherlock Holmes Realty first thing in the morning.

Chapter 4

WALKING INTO SHERLOCK HOLMES REALTY was a bit like walking into the real Holmes residence, or at least what my mind's eye conjured Sir Arthur Conan Doyle's famous 221B Baker Street residence to look like. Ruthie, whom I knew to be a devoted Holmesian, had painstakingly converted what was once a run-of-the-mill reception area into a nearly perfect reproduction of the famous sleuth's sitting room. She'd nailed the look, too. Right down to the deep red, embossed Victorian-era wallpaper and a dark-walnut-paneled fireplace flanked by high-back wing chairs. She'd even managed to find a replica of Holmes's famous wicker chair, which she'd offset with a small, round coffee table. Only, instead of a calabash pipe and magnifying glass, the table's top sported several full-color pamphlets of property listings.

"Ms. Watson is with a client, but she should be available in a couple of minutes," the fresh-faced receptionist told me before pointing to a side table set with coffee and rolls.

I meandered toward the refreshments, taking special notice of a few framed *Strand Magazine* covers that dotted the wall above the wainscot. They featured illustrations of Sherlock Holmes by the famed Sidney Paget. I was impressed. Not only with the extent of Ruthie's collection, but with the fact that she'd assembled a goody tray full of treats for her customers. I recognized one of my favorites: raspberry cream croissants from Sixpence Bakery.

I was just about to pop a piece of the buttery roll into my mouth when a ruckus arose from down the hallway.

"That woman doesn't have any right to my father's land!" an angry male voice bellowed, followed by the low murmur of Ruthie's voice. I couldn't discern her words, but could tell she was trying to smooth things over. "This is ridiculous," the man continued. "I'll not have her messing up this deal!" This final statement was punctuated with a door slam and heavy stomping. A young man with dark, disheveled hair burst into the waiting area, stopped short, and regarded me with a wild look in his eyes before hightailing it out the front door. Through the window, I saw him straddle a motorcycle, kick-start it, and peel out of the lot, fumes flying from his exhaust.

The receptionist and I exchanged a look. "Who was that?" I asked.

"Grant Walker," she replied, fanning herself with a pamphlet. "Isn't he something?"

"Something?" I echoed. Then it dawned on me what she meant. Of course, this twenty-something gal noticed a guy like Grant Walker. Even I, who was old enough to be his . . . well, his older sister at least, noticed his brooding good looks in the few fleeting seconds I'd seen him. However, it was the snap of anger still glittering in his eyes that had me concerned more than his high cheekbones and those delicious telltale bits of whiskers that bespoke any male's manliness.

"He's about as hot as they get," she went on, still fanning and sporting a wicked little grin.

I nodded, thinking Grant Walker was hot, all right. Hotheaded. I was secretly glad I had a son and not a daughter. I wouldn't have to worry about her getting mixed up with a guy like him.

"Tina, why didn't you tell me Lila was here?" We both looked up to see Ruthie approaching. She looked professional in her A-line skirt and button-down blouse, her trademark gold magnifying glass pin displayed on her lapel.

"I just arrived," I said, falling in step behind Ruthie as she led me back to her office.

"What brings you here?" she asked, indicating one of the visitors' chairs. She scooted behind her desk and plopped into her own chair.

I studied her over a stack of papers. Her usually bright face appeared drawn and sallow. "Everything okay, Ruthie?" I couldn't help but ask, especially after hearing her previous client's outburst.

She sighed. "Just tired. Seems it's one thing after another these days." She shrugged and changed

51

directions before I could ask her what she meant. "Are you here about Damian York's property search? I thought he was Franklin's client."

"Oh, he is. No, I'm here about something else. Something personal."

She pursed her lips. "Don't tell me you're thinking of listing that cute little cottage I sold you?"

I shook my head. "Oh no. I love the place. I just came in to ask you a couple questions about its history."

"Its history? Why? Is there a problem?" She started fidgeting with a pen, tapping it a few times before sticking it behind her ear. I noticed a hint of gray along the edges of her normally twice-a-month salon shade of auburn.

"No, no problem really," I replied. *Unless she'd consider a skeleton in the yard a problem.* "It's just that we were doing some landscaping yesterday and we may have unearthed a gravesite."

"A gravesite!"

"Not really a gravesite, but a skull. Just one, though." *So far.* I had a bad feeling that our archaeological discovery was going to lead to something more ominous. Or maybe I was just allowing my mother's grim predictions to give me the willies. "For the life of me, I can't remember anything about the people who owned the place before me."

Ruthie briefly paused before pushing away

from her desk, the wheels of her chair squeaking as she rolled toward a large file credenza. She pulled out the drawer and walked her fingers across the tips of the manila files. "Here it is. Let's see."

I watched her shuffle through a stack of papers from what must have been the file on my home. "That's right. The Cobbs. Peggy and Doug Cobb," she said, leafing through a few more papers. "Actually, the original title was owned by Illumination Valley Rental Company. The Cobbs purchased it in the early '80s. Eighty-four to be exact. Prior to their owning it, the property served as a vacation rental owned by a property management company."

"But the Cobbs owned it until I purchased it?"

Ruthie nodded. "Yes. They were an older couple. And, if I remember correctly, Doug was quite ill when they listed with me. They'd already vacated the property and were living in Dunston. I think Doug was in a convalescent home there."

What she said made sense. I did remember the cottage was empty when I first saw it. Plus the inside had an air of seniors about it at first—that mix of menthol combined with Jean Naté and a musty dust that dim eyes can't always see to clean. "Do you know if Peggy is still alive?"

Ruthie shut the file. "No idea. I only met with them a few times. Enough to sign the initial paperwork. I remember Doug was too ill to make it to the closing, so they signed before a notary and appointed a power of attorney."

I tried to remember back to the closing. It was such a hectic time, with starting a new job and living in my mother's house. All I could remember was Ruthie handing me the keys and telling me the cottage was finally mine.

"Too bad about the skull," Ruthie was saying. "It'll depreciate your home's value, you know."

My stomach lurched. I'd already felt a bit guilty for thinking of the inconvenience my yellow-ribboned crime scene garden would be to me personally instead of the greater concern of knowing someone died in my yard—or at least was cast off like refuse in my garden. Now Ruthie's ever-so-practical mind gave me yet another reason to be selfish in my appraisal of this turn of the spade: the financial impact. "Really?" Interest rates were dropping and I was hoping to refinance and take some cash out to purchase a vehicle for the upcoming winter months. I'd made it through the previous winter on my trusty Vespa, but had to borrow my mother's truck several times when the weather was at its worst.

"Most certainly," she postulated. "After all, would you want to buy a home where a dead body was found in the yard?"

Ruthie's words rang through my mind as I maneuvered my banana yellow scooter over cobblestone side streets on my way to the Secret Garden. She was correct about one thing: Who in their right mind would buy a house where human remains had been found? It was just my luck that this had happened to my charming little cottage. There was only one way to make peace with this situation and with myself. I needed to find out who the remains belonged to and lay their memory to rest. Whether that would help remove the stigma on the property was beside the point; this person needed to be respected, even in death. Not to mention my mother would be infinitely relieved as well, allowing her to feel better about the spirit world that had failed to prepare her—or me—for this event. I resolved to look up Peggy Cobb, the first chance I got. But, for now it would have to wait. Thanks to Bentley, my schedule was full for the day.

I pulled through the stone gate that marked the entrance to the Secret Garden. I'd phoned ahead and made arrangements to meet with Addison Eckhart to discuss Damian York's pending signing. I hated to do business on a Saturday, especially since it was Addison's busiest day of the week, but with my looming deadline, there was no choice.

I spied Addison as I was parking my Vespa under the shady branches of a magnificent magnolia. I cut the engine, lowered the kickstand, and took a second to inhale the lemony scent of the tree's showy white blooms before heading over to where she was tending a colorful display of potted flowers.

"Lila," she called out as I approached. She was wearing a wide-brimmed hat to shield her already freckled face. Addison had recently been promoted from the gift shop manager to general manager, a job I thought she was well suited for, and I was glad to see her obtain it. Especially after the misfortune she'd experienced last year when a member of her family was incarcerated. "Just in time," she continued. "I've been thinking of your venue and I know the perfect spot to hold the dinner and signing."

I followed her around the corner, over the pea-gravel pathways through the various themed garden areas to a tall green hedge. "You'll love this," she assured me as we walked the length of the privet hedge until we came to a white trellis covered in climbing roses. "This is the entrance," she said, opening a small gate, pushing aside a stray rose hanging low overhead, and walking through the enchanting entryway to the open yard beyond.

"Oh, Addison! This is perfect!" A neatly mani-cured lawn, anchored by two grand willows, led to a large stone patio shaded by a rustic pergola covered in wisteria vines. "I've been to your nursery at least a dozen times, but didn't know this was here."

Addison shrugged. "We use it mainly for weddings, baby showers, and such. Do you think it'll be big enough to accommodate a hundred guests? We can only fit eight or nine round tables on the patio area, but I thought we could place some tables on the lawn, too. There's a service road behind the back hedges, so the caterers can easily access the area."

I nodded. "I'm sure we can make it work. I'm thinking we should place Damian's table on the right side of the patio, directly under the main timber of the pergola," I started, temporarily side-tracked by a group of chatty, hatted women who pushed past us and headed for the pergola. One of them was carrying a covered tray, another a pitcher of sweet tea and a stack of plastic cups. They headed straight for one of the tables on the patio without bothering to even glance our way.

"Don't mind them," Addison said, waving their way. "It's just the Dirty Dozen."

I tried not to laugh. The garden club's name always reminded me of a war movie with the same title. Only that movie featured a squadron of a dozen miscreant commandos. A sharp contrast to the Aunt Bee look-alikes who were passing around cookies and iced tea.

Addison squinted their way. "Cute name for a garden club, isn't it? They hold their monthly meeting here every third Saturday of the month."

I could imagine they had a lot to discuss with

the garden walk coming up. "Actually, I'm glad they're here. I need to coordinate a few things with them for the signing. Which one is Alice Peabody. Do you know?"

She pointed to the hefty woman with a smart-looking blue hat perched on her well-coiffed head. "Watch out for that one; she's as prickly as a cactus."

"Thanks for the warning." I cringed inwardly, wondering how the prickly Mrs. Peabody was going to take the news about my yard being unavailable for the garden walk.

I firmed up a few more details with Addison and excused myself, making my way toward the cackling ladies. I could hear snippets of their discussion as I approached: "I think it's a wonderful idea to ask him to judge the contest." And "Of course it is, think of the notoriety we'd receive." One contrarian added, "I don't know. I think we should stick with Professor Jackson. He's a horticulturist, after all."

The gals were caught up in such a frenzied discussion, they didn't notice me until I cleared my throat a couple of times. "Excuse me, ladies. I'm Lila Wilkins with Novel Idea Literary Agency."

Finally they looked up.

"I'm sorry to interrupt your meeting, but I thought since you're all gathered here, I'd take the opportunity to introduce myself and perhaps discuss a few points about the upcoming events." I smiled around the table. I definitely had their attention, though they held back smiles, waiting, I guessed, before making their decision about me. I continued, "My boss, Ms. Bentley Burlington-Duke, has assigned me to coordinate Damian York's author event with this year's garden walk." I let my gaze settle on Alice Peabody. "I believe she's discussed the event with you, Mrs. Peabody."

Mrs. Peabody shifted her girth and eyed me curiously. "Are you number thirteen on the garden walk?"

I hesitated, trying to think of just the right words. "Yes, my garden was assigned to the final spot on this year's walk, but—"

"Do you grow roses?" one of the ladies interrupted.

"Roses?"

"I've won the van Gogh competition for the past three years and everyone knows my roses were the deciding factor," a dark-haired woman added with a competitive gleam in her eye. I knew she must be Fannie May Walker. Her reputation for rose cultivation was well-known, even amongst brown-thumbed gardeners like myself.

I shook my head. "I'm not really into roses."

A collective gasp sounded from the table.

"I mean, I can't grow roses. Of course, I *like* roses. Who doesn't?" I backpedaled, wondering how this conversation had gotten so off track. I attempted to swing it back to the author event. "Anyway, I'm working with one of my colleagues, Franklin Stafford, to plan an afternoon signing and meet and greet dinner for Damian York."

"We were just discussing Mr. York," Alice Peabody interjected. "Do you think that he'd be available to judge this year's garden walk competition? We've always used a retired horticulture professor as our judge, but some of us think he's become biased toward certain gardeners." Her eyes slid toward Fannie May as she dished out that last comment.

"Uh . . ." I didn't know what to say. Damian wasn't actually my client, so I couldn't speak on his behalf. "I'd have to check with my colleague Franklin Stafford about that. It's possible, I guess." These ladies were all about roses and not much else. I didn't think I'd accomplish much by discussing the garden walk weekend's events with them as a group. I'd be better off approaching Alice, the group's president, alone. I glanced at my watch. "How about I discuss it with him and get back to you on Monday, Mrs. Peabody," I said, looking pointedly at the club's president.

She agreed and we made plans to meet for lunch at Catcher in the Rye. I bid the rest of the ladies good-bye and scurried off to run other errands. I still needed to stop by the catering division of our local grocery store, How Green Was My Valley, and discuss menu ideas, plus get home in time to find something special in my closet to wear for my dinner date with Sean.

Before ducking back through the trellis, I glanced wistfully at the charming patio area. I could just envision Sean and me exchanging our vows under the sweet-smelling wisteria, followed by an extravagant lawn party. It would be just like a garden party in one of my favorite books, *The Great Gatsby*: linens flowing in the breeze, dainty teacups, and women in cloche hats and men in derbies. I, of course, would wear something reminiscent of one of Daisy Buchanan's flapper-style gowns, along with a wide-brim hat and a simple bouquet. A quote from the book jumped into my mind: "In his blue gardens men and girls came and went like moths among the whisperings and the champagne and the stars." Yes, I thought, a lawn party would be a perfect way to celebrate our vows.

Chapter 5

THE REST OF MY ERRANDS TOOK LONGER than expected—probably because I had my mind full of things like Duesenbergs, gauntlet gloves, and parasols instead of table settings, menus, and serving plates. It was difficult to concentrate on a garden-themed dinner extravaganza for Damian and a hundred of his closest admirers while also envisioning my own gala and ever-so-tasteful wedding details. I'd have to review my notes and follow up with the caterer later to be sure I hadn't mixed my Gatsby flapper fringe into Damian's recipe for angel hair–nested shrimp.

At the moment though, I needed to focus on getting ready for dinner with Sean. I hastily shuffled through my closet, trying to find the perfect outfit. I'd been so busy, I hadn't been able to figure out what I was going to wear tonight. I chastised myself for not having one of those little black dresses that women are always talking about. The type of cover-all-occasions dress that could be dressed up or down depending on the event. I *so* wanted everything to be perfect for tonight, but all I could find was business wear, and Voltaire's was an evening-wear type of establishment. For all the changes my life had seen in the last year—new job, new house, new love in my life—my closet had seen little of the effects. I'd never been a fashion maven even as a young girl, and my job with the *Dunston Herald* for twenty years as a Features writer hadn't required much. Just clean and presentable pantsuits or modestly knee-skimming skirts with easy-to-iron blouses in solid and subdued hues. I always felt a writer should kind of blend into the woodwork a bit, make the interviewee feel like the centerpiece. I guess that attitude had flowed into my being a literary agent as well. The authors —and their plethora of fascinating characters— were the stars of the show. I was just their humble servant. And judging from what I saw in my closet, a bit too humble. Didn't I *ever* go out? Ever get dressed to look beyond *presentable?* Sean, with his detective's simple suit attire, probably hadn't noticed I rather mirrored him in my plainclothes approach to dressing. Well, this evening deserved something much better!

Finally, in the back of the closet, I uncovered a deep blue wraparound dress that I'd forgotten about. It was an ultrafine wool, very soft to the touch, the kind of material that sashayed as I walked. The deep V-neck was edged with just a hint of matching lace. Very classy—and sexy—I assured myself. Paired with strappy sandals and the right jewelry, it'd be perfect. Next, I worked my shoulder-length, nut-brown hair into a glamorous twist, letting a few loose tendrils curl around my neckline, and added a little extra eye-liner for what I hoped was a sensuous evening look.

I stepped back and studied my reflection. All I needed now were some accessories. I took a pair of pearl earrings out of my jewelry box and had started putting them in my ears when I recalled they were a gift from my ex-husband, Bill. A throwback to our happier times when he actually gave me gifts. That was before he decided to roll that year's Ms. Tobacco Leaf up tight in our bedroom sheets. I shuddered and quickly removed the pearls, reaching for another pair of earrings. No reason to chance jinxing this new chapter in my life with past relics. I sighed. I was starting to think like my mother.

I heard the front door open. "Mom. You in here?" Trey called out from the other room.

"Don't go anywhere, Trey," I yelled. "I'm going to need a ride from you."

I could hear him knocking around the kitchen while I touched up the dress and finished getting ready. Ten minutes later, I strutted out of my bed-room and found Trey nestled in the family room recliner, eating a sandwich. My grocery budget was twice as high since he'd been home on summer break from UNC Wilmington.

"Mom! You look awesome!"

I held out my arms and twirled, striking a little pose. "You think so?" I asked, trying to milk the compliment.

"Yeah. Why so dressed up?"

"I have a special dinner tonight with Sean."

My son's face lit up. I knew he was thinking the same thing I was. *Tonight is the big night. Sean is finally going to pop the question!*

Trey had been good about keeping Sean's confidence the last couple of months, but I knew he was anticipating the engagement almost as much as I was. I'd never let on that I'd overheard Sean ask Trey's blessing on the proposal he'd planned. Now we both beamed and I could only hope my grin didn't give away the reason for my excitement. "Sure, hold on. I'll grab my keys." He disappeared and returned a minute later, keys dangling from his hand. "Why isn't Sean picking you up?"

I stole one last glance in the hall mirror and fixed an unruly strand of hair. "Apparently, he could only get reservations for six. He's going to drive straight over from work. I told him I'd meet him there." I patted his shoulder on the way out the door. "Thanks for the ride, Trey. You're saving me from showing up with helmet hair." As much as I loved my Vespa, there were distinct times it wasn't appropriate.

He flashed a grin, which faded the moment we stepped out the door. "When are these people going to finish digging in our yard?" he asked, his gaze fixing on the official vehicles parked in front of our house. Various teams of investigators had been excavating in our backyard ever since our gruesome discovery. The entire circumference was taped off with yellow crime scene tape.

I let out an exasperated sigh and opened the door of his vehicle. "Not soon enough, that's for sure," I answered, moving a pile of junk and settling into the front passenger seat. Trey had scraped together enough money from working at Espresso Yourself to buy a used Honda. The thing was nearly as old as he was, but still ran relatively well. Better, anyway, than the car I didn't have. I thought back to what Ruthie Watson had said about the dead body depreciating my home's value and glanced back over my torn-up yard. There was no way I could apply for a refinance with my yard looking like a construction site. Guess it was going to be another long winter without a car.

Our resident skeleton monopolized our conversation on the way to Voltaire's. Apparently, word was out in the village and Trey had spent his workday fielding questions from curious coffee drinkers. "A lot of people wanted to know if it was another murder," Trey said, keeping his eyes on the road as we turned onto High Street and worked our way past Jay's bookstore, the Constant Reader. I could almost imagine him inside at his counter, putting the final touches on his manuscript, in between waiting on customers. Jay's sequel to *The Alexandria Society* was in the editing phase of publication and would be released right after the first of the year.

I turned my focus back to Trey. "Another murder? Why would they jump to that conclusion?"

"You have to admit, Mom, you've been sort of a magnet for murder since we moved here."

"A murder magnet! Honestly, I don't know where you come up with these things. Right up here," I said, pointing to the turnoff. *Great. Now the townspeople were beginning to think I'd brought some sort of curse over the Valley.* "What did you tell them?"

He shrugged. "Not much. Just that the cops are still looking into it."

"There could be any number of reasons why that skull was in our yard, Trey. We don't even know how old it is. It could be from some ancient tribe that roamed the area hundreds of years ago." I was glad to see we were pulling into the lot at Voltaire's. This conversation was putting a damper on my mood.

"Cool, like a prehistoric man or something."

"Exactly," I said, opening the door and hopping out onto the pavement. I turned back and leaned into the car. "Be careful driving. Sean will give me a lift home."

He nodded, a little grin tugging at his lips. "Have fun, Mom." I stared at him for a second. An unexpected emotion welled inside me. All these years it had been just Trey and I. Now we were getting ready to welcome another man to our family and I had Trey's unconditional support. All of a sudden he looked much older to me than his nineteen years. I fought back the tears threatening at the edges of my eyes. When had my son grown to be such an honorable man?

"Mom? What's wrong?"

I forced a smile. "Nothing, sweetie. Absolutely nothing."

It took my eyes a few moments to adjust to the dim lighting inside Voltaire's. I was hoping Sean would be waiting for me, but the maître d' met me inside the entrance instead. He addressed me with a somewhat put-on French accent. Actually, I knew the accent wasn't sincere; I recognized him as a former employee of the James Joyce Pub, not a European transplant. "Monsieur Griffiths sends his apologies. He's running a little behind schedule, but will be joining you soon." He guided me to our table, pulled out my chair, and placed my napkin in my lap. "He's preordered the wine. I'll have the sommelier bring it to your table at once."

I suppressed a giggle and fingered the crisp linen napkin on my lap. Any urges I had to feel annoyed at Sean for being late were subdued by the romantic ambience and outstanding service. The last time I'd been here was for a Taste of the Town event our agency sponsored to garner publicity for our cookbook authors. Dominic, the owner of Voltaire's, had generously allowed our agency to use the restaurant for a cooking demonstration after a murderous explosion killed one of our guest chefs and devastated the kitchen at the Marlette Robbins Center for Arts.

At the time, Voltaire's spacious interior was arranged with the tables facing the bar where our celebrity chefs demonstrated their talents. Tonight, the room was arranged to take advantage of the view. Voltaire's was located in the hills on the edge of town, allowing for a beautiful vista. My eyes scanned the sweeping view of Inspiration Valley to where it rolled away in a series of greenish blue ridges and then eventually rose again to the more rugged, hazy mountainsides on the other side of the Valley. I was touched that Sean had arranged, and probably paid dearly, for the best table in the restaurant.

"Lila?" A voice came from behind.

I turned, surprised to see my coworker. "Franklin! What are you doing here?"

He turned to the man standing next to him. "This is Damian's first night in town. I thought I'd show him what our valley has to offer in fine dining."

"Well, you've definitely chosen a good restaurant. I'm just waiting for Sean. He seems to be running late."

Franklin made a quick introduction. "Damian

York, this is Lila Wilkins, one of our agency's most highly regarded agents."

I could feel my cheeks brighten with pleasure from Franklin's compliment. I stood and held out my hand. Damian provided a charming smile to go along with his firm handshake. This guy was much cuter in person than on television. Not just cute, but devastatingly handsome: dark hair, strong chin, and what looked like an even stronger body, judging by the filled-out width of his precisely tailored suit jacket.

"You'll be seeing a lot more of Ms. Wilkins," Franklin continued. "She's helping coordinate the dinner and signing."

Damian dipped his chin. "I'll be looking forward to it."

Me, too, I thought, then checked my reaction. What was wrong with me, all googly-eyed over some celebrity? I was meeting my future fiancé in just a few minutes. "Actually, I'm glad I've run into you, Mr. York," I stated, willing my mind back to business. "I met with the ladies of the local garden club this afternoon. I'm afraid they've pegged you as this year's judge for the Van Gogh Garden Award."

"The van Gogh award," he echoed, a hint of amusement showing in his dark eyes.

Franklin spoke up. "It's an annual award for the best garden on the garden walk. The ladies in town take it quite seriously."

Damian shrugged. "Sure. I'd be glad to help in any way I can."

The impatient maître d' cleared his throat, obviously disgruntled about being waylaid on his way to show the men to their table.

Franklin straightened his shoulders and motioned for Damian to walk ahead of him. "Looks like our table is waiting. We'll discuss all the details Monday morning, Lila. Enjoy your dinner."

I watched them move to the back of the room and then resettled in my chair. A server walked by. The pleasing scent of garlic and the sweet tang of lamb cooked in wine drifted from his sizzling tray and caused my stomach to grumble. Outside, the sun was starting to set over the horizon, casting a warm glow over the Valley and causing the shadows to stretch and thin out. Much like Sean's tardiness was stretching and wearing my patience thin. I took another sip of my wine and glanced at my cell phone. What was going on? He was already thirty minutes late.

I dialed his number, glancing over my shoulder to where the wine waiter was on standby, bottle in hand. I motioned for a refill. Finally, Sean picked up on the other end. "Where are you?" I found myself nearly hissing into the phone before realizing it was his voicemail, not his actual voice. Irritated, I disconnected without leaving a message.

My waiter must have sensed my mounting anger, or perhaps he could hear my stomach growling, because he appeared at my side bearing a basket that smelled like a French boulangerie. I'd just popped a piece of buttery roll in my mouth when my phone buzzed. I swallowed hard and pounced on it.

"Hello," I whispered.

It was Sean. "I'm sorry, Lila. I'm tied up at work."

I paused a moment, gathering my composure. "I understand." I used my best ever-so-understanding-almost-fiancée-of-a-hardworking-cop voice. "So when will you get away?" I asked sweetly. When my question was answered by silence, my ever-so-understanding tone slipped away like a tossed bridal bouquet through the hands of a predestined old maid. I shook my head, but the image of a flowerless old maid stayed with me. "You mean you're not going to make it?" The question came out louder than I intended. I drew curious stares from every direction.

"I'm afraid not. I'm sorry. We've made a major breakthrough . . ."

I blocked out his words, shutting my eyes and attempting to stay calm.

"I've already talked to the restaurant and paid the bill," he was still explaining. "You can order anything you want."

"By myself?"

There was a long pause on the other end. I was so disappointed. I didn't know what to add, so I simply said good-bye and quickly disconnected. So much for me becoming the ever-so-understanding fiancée of a hardworking cop this evening. Maybe this was a wake-up call for me. I picked up my almost empty wineglass, tossed back the dregs, and held my hand over the rim as the sommelier approached again. "No thank you," I said, suddenly feeling conspicuous as the only loner in a room full of couples.

Unsure of what to do, I took another roll, letting my eyes roam the nearby tables. Next to me was a gray-haired couple, eyes locked in a comfortable gaze that can only be developed over years of devotion. A few tables over was a young married couple, looking a little uncomfortable in this fancy setting, or perhaps worried about the kids they'd left at home with the babysitter. And, if I bent my neck, I could just barely see to the back of the room where Franklin was seated with Damian York, his wide shoulders swaying as they carried on an animated discussion.

My head snapped back at the sound of the waiter. "I've been informed that your guest will not be accompanying you this evening. Do you wish to order?" In other words, either order or leave so I can get a full-meal-eating customer seated at this table. It was Saturday night, after all, and a line of waiting patrons filled the restaurant's vestibule.

I could feel the eyes of the other patrons boring into my back. My cheeks burned hot as I realized even the waiter's attitude toward me had shifted. Was that pity or curiosity I saw in his eyes? Perhaps he pitied this poor woman who certainly must have some sort of flaw that her date chose work over enjoying a four-star dinner in her company, or maybe he was just curious to see if I'd stay behind, order the most expensive meal on the menu, and stick it to the louse who abandoned me. While the second option sounded appealing, I ultimately decided that anything I ate would sit on my stomach like a rock. So, I answered with a soft, "No thank you," placed my folded napkin next to my plate, rose from the table with as much dignity as I could muster, and headed for the exit with my chin high.

I'd gone as far as the front vestibule before it hit me that I didn't have a ride. I ducked back into the restaurant and asked the maître d' to phone a cab. Then I returned to the vestibule to wait. And wait. Forty-five minutes later I was still waiting.

"What are you still doing here, Lila?" Franklin asked. He and Damian must have finished their dinner.

"I'm afraid Sean couldn't make it. I'm waiting on a cab."

"Oh my." Franklin wrung his hands. "This won't do."

Damian rested a hand on his shoulder. "Don't

worry, Franklin. I know you have another engagement to get to; I'd be happy to give Ms. Wilkins a ride home."

"I don't think that's necessary. My cab should arrive at any moment." Although, deep down, I knew there was a possibility it wasn't going to arrive at all. I could call Mama, but I hated the idea of her driving all the way out here. Trey was out with friends, so I didn't want to cut his evening short. Of course, there was always Makayla, but . . . "Actually, I'll take you up on your offer, Mr. York. And thank you."

"Damian, please."

I nodded and followed the men out front to where the valet had parked two vehicles at the curb. The first I recognized as Franklin's conservative four-door, the second was a dark model luxury vehicle. I couldn't begin to imagine how much a rental like that must have set Damian back.

Damian bid Franklin good-bye and stepped in front of me to open the door, allowing me to slide easily into the buttery soft leather seats. "Thanks again for the ride," I said after we were down the road a ways.

"My pleasure. Besides, I'm interested in hearing more about this garden competition."

I felt myself relax in this charming man's presence, in the luxurious seats and on a subject much nearer to my heart right now than Sean. "I hope you don't mind. The garden club ladies are huge fans. They'll be delighted that you've agreed to judge this year's entries." I chuckled. "I have to warn you though, they're quite competitive."

He quirked a smile. "It should be interesting."

"'Interesting' is one way to put it. There's a rivalry between the garden club president, Alice Peabody, and last year's contest winner, Fannie Walker. She grows prize roses." I noticed he flinched at the mention of roses. It was good to know someone else, even an expert gardener, struggled with the darn things. "Don't worry, though. As I understand it, the competition is more about overall garden design than any single plant."

He glanced my way and then refocused on the road. We rode quietly for the next few miles. As we neared the edge of town, I directed him to my turn. "I live in an older part of Inspiration Valley. Back in the day when our town was known as Illumination Valley, my house was a rental cottage," I explained. "Oh, but you're from this area, aren't you?"

"Yes, but I haven't been back in years."

"You don't have family left in town?"

He shook his head. "My father's around, but we're not close."

"I'm sorry," I mumbled. The car grew uncomfortably quiet and I searched for something else to say. Luckily, we were almost to my home. "It's up here on the right."

He pulled into my drive, his jaw gaping. "This is your house?"

I winced. When I accepted his ride home, I didn't think about my yard. With mounds of upturned dirt and sprawling crime scene tape, it looked like a cross between a postapocalyptic world and a mass murder scene. *How embarrassing.* "Please excuse my yard. It doesn't normally look like this. We're . . . uh . . ." I struggled for an explanation. I could say we were undergoing some massive landscaping project, but landscapers didn't use yellow tape marked *Crime Scene*. Besides, even if he overlooked that, he'd probably want to know more about it. Landscaping was his specialty, after all. Finally, I settled on the truth. "My son and I were digging up our old hawthorn bushes and we found a skull. Can you imagine?" I made a wide sweep with my hand, indicating the entire yard. "Next thing I knew, the police were digging up the whole place. It's horrible, isn't it? I'm not sure how we'll ever get it back to normal."

He was oddly quiet. Even in the darkness, with only the lights of his dashboard to illuminate his expression, I could tell he'd gone white as a ghost. I could understand. I felt the same way about the idea of someone being abandoned in an anonymous grave. I attempted to move the topic along. "Maybe if you get some time, you could give me some landscape pointers?" I prodded.

Yeah, like "Quit finding dead bodies in your yard."

He shook his head and looked at me. "What was that?"

"Pointers," I repeated. "I was saying that maybe you could give me some tips for landscaping. I have no idea where to start after all this."

He recovered and shook his head. "I can imagine how overwhelmed you must feel. What's that saying? 'It's so good, but terrifying to stand in front of a blank canvas'?"

My eyes widened. "Very good. I believe it went: 'It's so fine and yet so terrible to stand in front of a blank canvas.'" He shot me a look, but I couldn't tell if it was appreciation of our shared love of reading or surprise at my having corrected him. Which I instantly realized hadn't been necessary or polite, for that matter. "A habit from being an agent, I guess. I'm into the exact wording of things." I tried to cover myself. "I think one of the famous French Impressionists said that about painting."

"Cézanne, actually." This time I recognized his expression: pleasure at our shared knowledge. "A habit from my planning landscapes: I always know the source of my planting inspiration."

"Well, Cézanne nailed exactly how I feel about my yard. I haven't a clue where to start."

He shot me a sly grin. "You're not alone. And,

I'm glad. It's people like you that make it possible for me to earn a living."

I laughed, thanked him for the ride, and slid out the door, thinking it was going to be a pleasure to work with Damian York these next couple of weeks.

Chapter 6

I SPENT ALL DAY SUNDAY DREADING Monday morning's status meeting and facing down Bentley with the bad news. Sure enough, she wasn't taking it well. "What do you mean, you have to withdraw from the garden walk?" She'd yanked off her reading glasses and left them to dangle from a chain as she paced the conference room. "I thought I explained to you the importance of representing our agency."

"You did, but—"

She placed both hands on the conference table, leaning in to emphasize her point. "Lila, there are no 'buts' in this business. You just do it. You want to be a team player, don't you?"

I glanced around the table, looking for some support from the "team," but didn't find any. Franklin was doodling on his notepad. Jude Hudson seemed half asleep; apparently this little bit of drama wasn't enough to hold our agent who represented thrillers and suspense. Zach Cohen was tapping his pen annoyingly and staring out the window; Zach was Novel Idea's youngest agent and also the least attentive at any meeting. And Flora Merriweather was busy knitting her latest project.

Vicky Crump, our ever-efficient office administrator, was the only attendee who seemed genuinely tuned in to the meeting. Unfortunately, judging by the sharp look she was giving me, she wasn't going to be one of my supporters. She probably thought I was trying to shirk my responsibilities, an inexcusable action in Vicky's dutiful mind. Squirming like a naughty school-girl, I refocused on Bentley and tried a different approach. "It's impossible for me to have my yard ready in time for—"

"Nonsense!" Bentley interrupted again. "Nothing's impossible with determination and hard work." She'd clenched her fist and taken on a look that I recognized as her demented-coach look. She usually assumed this posture right before launching into a fervent pep talk, designed to inspire and enthuse—or perhaps terrify—delinquent members of her literary agency team.

"Now, hold on!" I blurted, louder than intended. "I was only doing what you asked, reworking my garden, when we found a skull buried under some of the bushes. Now the police have cordoned off my yard and I can't do anything about it."

Bentley stood motionless, her eyes locked in a weird raised-brow expression. Somewhere in the background, I heard Franklin's pencil tip break and a hollow pinging sound as Flora's knitting needle hit the floor.

It was Zach, our slightly hyperactive sports and

screenplay agent, who finally broke the awkward silence. "Wowsa! Another murder? Why, death practically follows you around, doesn't it?" He was leaning over the table, bug-eyed and practically licking his lips in anticipation of more details. "Spill, Lila. Who was murdered this time?"

I stuttered for a moment, my eyes darting from one agent to another. "Who says it was murder? There could be any number of reasons why a skeleton might be buried in my yard. Like maybe the house was built on an ancient burial ground or . . . or anything, really."

"Oh, come on!" Zach just wouldn't let it drop. "You're practically a murder magnet."

Oh no. There was that term again—murder magnet. First Trey, now Zach. Or maybe the whole town had dubbed me the local murder magnet. Heaven forbid.

Zach continued, "There was the poor guy who ended up dead the first week you started working here. Then it went downhill from there." He started ticking victims off on his fingers. "One of our own agents, an editor from New York. Boy, too bad she decided to do business with us, huh? Then there were the two murders during the Taste of the Town event . . . um . . . Am I forgetting someone?"

"The writer from Dunston," Flora answered bitingly. "How could you forget her?" Flora flushed from ear to ear and began fanning herself with today's meeting itinerary. "Dreadful, really dreadful."

"This just won't do," inserted Bentley. She was back to pacing. "If this trend continues, we may develop a reputation as a . . . a . . ."

"An agency of death," Zach finished, his hand sweeping before him as if proposing a brilliant subtitle to his latest book acquisition. Bentley shot him a look that could very well peg him as the next murder victim.

"Give it a break," Jude grumbled. "None of those things were Lila's fault."

"That's right," Franklin hastily interjected. "In fact, because of Lila's quick thinking, several ruthless murderers have been brought to justice. Personally, I'm grateful she's kept our little burg safer, and at great personal expense, I might remind everyone." He must have been referring to my own close scrapes with death.

Bentley's expression loosened and she let out a long sigh. "Yes, I'm sure we're all grateful for Lila's contributions to making our little corner of the world safer, but let's get back to the topic at hand, shall we?" Just like that, she repositioned her reading glasses and started scanning the itinerary, all dead bodies swept under the rug. Her callousness never ceased to amaze me. After all, it was her literary events that always seemed to land me in these compromising, even danger-ous, positions. And what did I get? Not so much as a "thanks for taking one for the team, Lila."

"First item of business is the garden contest," she continued. "Since Lila's yard is off-limits we'll need a replacement entry." She peered over the rim of her glasses and scanned the table. "Any volunteers?"

Vicky Crump's hand shot straight up. "I'd be glad to offer my humble garden as an entry," she announced, looking quite proud of herself. I eyed her straight posture and impeccable appearance and imagined her garden was as neat and prim as they came.

Bentley's face brightened. "Wonderful! Thank you, Vicky." She beamed as she marked that item off her task list. "Lila, inform Mrs. Peabody of the change," she said to me.

Great. Now I have that to look forward to. I glanced at Vicky's smug expression and scowled. This whole fiasco with my yard could have been avoided if Bentley had asked Ms. Perfect in the first place.

"Next item," Bentley continued. "The venue for Damian York's dinner and signing." Bentley sat down and indicated that Franklin and I should take the lead.

I gathered my notes and moved to the front of the conference table. Using a large whiteboard, I outlined tentative plans for the signing and dinner, with Franklin jumping in from time to time with his own points. To my delight, the rest of the agents listened enthusiastically, each taking on a piece of the action. Jude stepped up right away, agreeing to coordinate, with Vicky's help, a small marketing campaign with media announcements, flyers, and ticket sales for the dinner. Zach, who had fancied himself in charge of media relations for the Taste of the Town event, where two ill-fated visitors had met their demise, offered no resistance to Jude taking that role. Instead, he promised to be on hand to direct traffic and parking at the Secret Garden the night of the event. Franklin was thrilled that Makayla and Jay had agreed to take over the task of setting up the dinner, and planned to contact them right away with his visions for decorating. Flora graciously offered to meet with Nell of Sixpence Bakery to coordinate the design of a special cake. That really left me with only the planning of the menu, and Paul Cohen, the catering director at How Green Was My Valley, had already given me some great suggestions. Feeling a little bad about my earlier sentiments, I smiled around the room at my coworkers, even Vicky. Say what you want about Bentley—she may be an exacting boss, even onerous at times—but she'd assembled and trained one of the best literary teams around. What other group could pull off an event of this magnitude with only a couple of weeks to prepare?

With our tasks assigned, Bentley quickly

wrapped up the rest of the meeting and the group dispersed to their respective offices. I was looking forward to a little quiet time to finish the last chapters of the cozy English mystery I'd started on Friday. That wasn't to happen, though, because Flora was waiting for me in my office.

She immediately drew me to her ample bosom. "You poor dear. You must be simply shocked. Why, I can't imagine the horror of discovering a buried body. And in your own yard, even."

Pulling back, I mumbled an appropriate reply and stole a longing glance toward the partially read manuscript that was stacked neatly on my desk, waiting for my return. Part of my joy at my relatively newfound career as a literary agent was the escapism that reading manuscripts allowed me, and I knew it. Right now, aside from really enjoying this writer's understated descriptions and depth of emotions at every turn of the page, I knew part of me longed for a few hours, at least minutes, of escape from buried skulls and planning menus for a hundred guests. But life— and death—outside of the printed page existed and demanded its own due time. I forced a smile and reluctantly motioned for Flora to take one of my guest chairs. I sat across from her in the other.

"It *was* a shock. But these things happen more often than we realize. Trey looked it up on the Internet. I guess there was a couple up in Canada who discovered the four-hundred-year-old skeleton of an aboriginal woman in their yard." What he also told me was that the poor couple got stuck with five thousand dollars' worth of bills to cover the cost of the assessment, excavation, and relocation of the historic discovery. It'd be just my luck that I'd have to foot the bill for this whole fiasco. Then again, if our skull wasn't designated as historical remains, but was simply an unmarked gravesite, wouldn't I *want* to make sure the poor soul had a proper burial in a real cemetery? And, how much would that cost?

"So, you think the remains belong to an ancient skeleton?" Flora continued.

I shrugged. "Hard to say. I haven't heard anything from Sean yet." Of course, I might have heard something if I'd bothered to answer his calls. As it was, I was giving him the cold shoulder. A part of me, a large part actually, felt as if I'd been stood up on our date, hence he deserved that treatment. The fact that he was a cop and had higher priorities than our personal relationship, well, that only added to my plethora of mixed emotions. And it was, admittedly, another reason I'd have rather thrown myself into reading a manuscript for the time being. "I did check in with Ruthie over at Sherlock Holmes Realty. She said that a couple by the name of Cobb owned the cottage before me. Uh . . . Peggy and Doug, I think she said." Flora's jaw drooped and her shoulders seemed to crumble. "You know them?" I asked, wondering what brought about her sudden change in demeanor.

She quickly straightened her shoulders and adjusted her blouse. "Well, I have lived here practically my whole life. Guess I've come to know everyone."

"What do you know about the Cobbs?"

She fidgeted a little more with her blouse while her eyes darted around the room. "Well, I know Doug took ill. I believe he passed."

"Ruthie told me the same thing. I thought I'd try to track down Peggy, though."

Her nostrils flared. "Why in the world would you do that?"

I flinched, taken aback by the zealousness of her response. "I thought the previous owners might know something more about the history of the place. Like if there had been a family burial plot on the property or something. The skull was in my yard. Seems only right to figure out why, doesn't it?"

She wiggled in her seat, crossing and uncrossing her legs before responding. "Sure. I guess. It wouldn't be something *I* would do, but then again, you're more of the curious type."

This conversation was getting weird. After all, she was the one who came in asking me about the skull. What did she expect? I wondered what was really eating at Flora. She wasn't acting at all like herself. Then it dawned on me that maybe the fact that Doug Cobb had passed on, leaving his wife alone, might have triggered this reaction. "Is everything going okay, Flora? How's Brian been?" Brian was Flora's husband, a bit older than Flora and, according to her, the standard by which she gauged the heroes in the romance books she agented. Which made me want to giggle, considering she represented quite a few erotic romance authors. On the other hand, she also represented children's books. Flora loved children. "Is everything okay with your nieces?" Sadly enough, Flora and Brian were childless, but she doted on her sister-in-law's children.

She stood and waved off my questions. "Yes, yes, yes. Everything's okay. You'll have to excuse me, Lila. I'm just a bit tired today. I stayed up late last night working on my knitting project." Flora supported many children's causes, the latest being Knitting for Noggins, which was an organization that collected hand-knitted caps for children undergoing cancer treatment.

I stood also, placing a hand on her shoulder. "Don't you dare apologize!" I gave her arm a quick squeeze. "You're the nicest person I know, Flora. I appreciate you being concerned about my situation. And, by the way, thanks for volunteering to see Nell about a cake."

Her face brightened a bit. "My pleasure. I think I'll stop in on her this afternoon. I was thinking about picking up some dessert for after dinner tonight. Brian just loves her red velvet cupcakes."

With that, she was off without any further trace of agitation. I stared after her, glad that her mood had improved and even happier that I was free to delve back into my mystery. I still had over an hour before I needed to be at Catcher in the Rye to meet Alice Peabody for lunch. Plenty of time to get through the last pages. And, if the rest of the story captivated my attention as well as the first half, I'd be making a phone call to one talented author later this afternoon.

Only . . . I was just a few pages along when I heard a quiet knocking sound. I looked up to see Sean hovering by my office door. "Can I come in?"

He must have felt guilty. Sean, ever the authoritative type, usually didn't ask permission to enter a room; he'd just give a perfunctory knock and walk right in. I decided he wasn't going to get off so easy today. What did he think, he could just waltz over here and pour on a little charm and everything would be okay?

"I'm sorry. I'm busy *working*," I said, turning my attention back to my mystery.

He walked in anyway. "Look, Lila. I get it. You're still hot about Saturday's dinner. I'm sorry. Something important came up at work and I couldn't get away."

I glared up at him. "You stood me up. I felt like a fool all dressed up with no date."

He reached a hand across the desk. I sat upright and placed my hands on my lap.

"I tried calling," he said.

I knew as much. I'd been ignoring his calls for almost two days and a tingle of guilt fluttered in my throat for that, admittedly, selfish reaction. I mean, it was foolish (he could have had information that would ease my mind about the skull-in-the-yard fiasco); immature (he *had* called at the restaurant and explained already); and likely reflected the jealousy of a woman who wanted a man who placed her above his career. Which I was. I felt the fight drain out of me and realized I needed to meet him halfway. I knew Sean loved me and that I loved him. That should be enough.

He sighed. "Can we try again next Saturday?"

"Try?" I nearly screeched. Sean blinked in surprise at my reaction, oblivious to the impact that one word had. *Unbelievable.* Obviously, with that operative word, every date with him, let alone my life with him, would be contingent on whatever case he happened to have at the time. I tightened my lips and rolled my eyes sideways. "Well, I don't know. I'm awfully tied up with work. One of our clients is in town and I'm busy trying to coordinate a dinner and book signing with him. Damian York. Do you know who he

is?" Just in case he didn't, I pointed to Damian's book on the corner of my desk, his handsome face shining forth from the cover.

Sean glanced at the cover and did a double take, noticeably grimacing. "That's your client?"

"Well, technically he's Franklin's client. But I'm helping Franklin with the event, so I'll be working closely with Damian." I sighed. "I just don't know how much free time I'll have." I was playing one of those female games I detested, but I couldn't help myself. He wasn't the only one in this relationship with career obligations. Plus a tiny part of me thought the threat of another man might propel him into an immediate proposal. At least I wouldn't have to wait to *try* to get that proposal on a date.

I didn't need to wonder. Instead of dropping to one knee, Sean stood. "Never mind, then. But before you get back to work, you should know that they unearthed the rest of the skeletal remains."

He had my full attention. "And?"

"They don't know the exact age, but the anthropologist says the bones belong to an adolescent female."

"Oh no!"

He nodded. "She's been buried in your yard for approximately thirty years. We went through the missing persons records from that time, but didn't find anything." He paused, his gaze holding steady on mine. "There's more, Lila. It appears there's evidence of a basilar skull fracture involving the temporal bone."

"Meaning?"

"It's likely she was murdered."

Chapter 7

AS I WALKED DOWN LAVENDER LANE FOR my luncheon appointment, I was impervious to the warm rays of the sun and the light breeze perfumed by flower blossoms wafting from the terra-cotta planters that lined the sidewalk. Usually I reveled in the colorful displays of spiky red cordyline, crisp white lobelia, and wave petunias that spilled onto the walkway; but today my head was filled with macabre thoughts of crushed skulls and nameless entombments. I felt an overwhelming sense of pity for the poor young woman found in my yard, her life brutally taken and her body so disrespectfully discarded. Had her loved ones been searching for her all this time? Were her parents holding out hope that their daughter would return one day, unharmed, the happy young girl they'd lost so long ago? Had a boyfriend believed she'd just abandoned their love and lived his life alone and heart-broken all these years? It was almost too much grief to consider.

Not even the usually comforting aroma of baking bread or the welcoming smile of Big Ed, Catcher in the Rye's owner, could lift my sour mood. "A bad day?" he asked, adjusting a bandanna that covered his large bald head.

Despite his lack of hair, everything else about Big Ed gave the impression that he was much younger than sixty-something, especially his warm eyes and wide grin.

I forced a smile. "I'll be fine, thanks, Ed." Glancing around, I asked, "Have you seen Alice Peabody? She's supposed to meet me here." No sooner had I uttered the words than the door flew open and Alice tumbled inside, looking bedraggled and flustered. "Mrs. Peabody? Are you okay?" I asked, shocked with the woman's appearance.

Her hand flew to her disheveled hair and pushed a few loose strands back into place. "Why, yes, of course. Why do you ask?"

I shrugged, trying not to stare at her dirt-stained slacks and untidy blouse. She must have been working in her garden and lost track of time. "I haven't ordered yet. What would you like? My treat."

While she studied the chalkboard menu, I went ahead and ordered my usual sandwich—the Hamlet, which was rye slathered with Dijon mustard and piled high with Black Forest ham, Havarti cheese, and juicy fresh tomatoes. Alice finally settled on the Van Gogh—turkey, creamy Brie, and thinly sliced apples with honey mustard on a French baguette. "The Van Gogh, huh? A precontest ritual?" I asked.

She stared at me blankly for a second before

catching on. "Oh yes." She smiled tightly. "The van Gogh award. Maybe I'll finally receive the recognition I deserve this year."

I did a double take, surprised by the vehemence in her voice. I decided to let the touchy subject drop. Instead, I suggested we look for a place to sit. Monday's lunch hour was always busy at the popular sandwich shop and only a few tables were open. The one we headed for was quickly scooped up by someone fleeter of foot, but the outside seating area had only a couple of customers, so we set our jackets out on chairs and headed back to await our orders. I glanced down at my name card. I usually loved Ed's practice of assigning customers a name card displaying a picture of a famous literary or film character that suited the customer, instead of simply giving out numbers. But today my picture was of Groucho Marx, complete with bushy eyebrows and smoking cigar. I frowned. What was Ed trying to say? That I was a quick-witted funny person like Groucho had been? Or that I was grouchy and needed an eyebrow wax?

Alice must not have liked her card, either. She gave it a quick once-over and grimaced. "I swear, I don't know why this man doesn't just use numbers like everyone else."

I shrugged. "Part of his charm, I guess. Who'd you get?" But I needn't have asked. All of a sudden Ed bellowed out, "CRUELLA DE VIL!"

I stifled a chuckle, and so did the rest of the customers in line, as Alice stepped forward, slapped her card down on the counter, and snatched her bag. Suddenly, I thought being Groucho wasn't such a bad thing after all.

A peeved Alice headed for the outside eating area while I waited for my order to come up. I leaned one hip against the counter and folded my arms. "Cruella De Vil?" I asked with a grin. "Isn't that a little much?"

His mouth tightened into a thin line and he shot a baleful glance toward Alice as she made her way to the patio door. One of his workers slid an overstuffed brown bag his way. Ed picked it up and read the tag. "MOTHER HUBBARD!" he shouted, holding the bag out for a young mother with three tagalongs. "Still waiting on that Hamlet," he shouted over his shoulder. Turning back to me, he said, "Sorry for the wait. New guy in the back." Then he hitched a thumb in Alice's direction. "As for Cruella, watch yourself, Lila. She *is* a cruel devil. And she'll stop at nothing to get what she wants."

I swallowed hard. Big Ed wasn't usually so acrimonious. First Addison at the nursery and now him. I agreed that Alice Peabody seemed a little crusty around the edges, but how bad could she really be? I wanted to ask him more, but another bag came down the line. "Here you go, Groucho. Enjoy," he added with a wink.

I took my bag and made my way to the patio, where Alice sat at the shady table we'd chosen. She'd already unwrapped her sandwich and was munching away. "I've got good news and more good news," I started, settling across from her.

She swallowed and took a quick sip of soda. "And what might that be?"

"I spoke with Damian York yesterday and he seems on board with the idea of judging this year's van Gogh contest."

Alice's eyes popped. "Really? Well, that is good news, dear. I can't wait to tell the other ladies."

"Now . . . about the dinner and signing," I said, taking advantage of the moment. I pulled a notebook out of my satchel and ticked off the agency's plans for the event. Surprisingly enough, Alice agreed to the entire agenda. Which was good news, considering the Annual Garden Walk was completely under the Dirty Dozen's dominion. "I'm thinking, if we work together, we can aid each other's events," I continued. I reached back into my satchel and pulled out one of Damian's books. "Our agency would like to offer a signed copy of Damian's book to each member of the Dirty Dozen, plus complimentary tickets to the dinner."

She eyed the book like it was a snake ready to strike. "And what do you want in exchange?"

I took a quick bite of my sandwich, mulling over my reply while I chewed. "Not much, really. We just need a little help to get the word out about Damian's events. We're on a time crunch. I'm wondering, have you finalized the design for the brochure map for the garden walk?"

Alice brushed a few crumbs off her blouse. "No, I haven't. I'm on my way to the printer's right after lunch. Thanks to your agency agreeing to take a spot on the tour, we now have a full schedule. You see, each board member is assigned an entry, but we save the thirteenth spot for a local business. Our little way of saying thank you for supporting the Dirty Dozen. Last year, that spot was awarded to the local printer's wife." She leaned in with a surreptitious gleam in her eye. "He gave us a substantial deal on printing the brochures, you know? And the year before it was the hardware store. They gave our members wonderful discounts on gardening tools. This year"—she gestured my way—"it's your agency, of course. We do so appreciate the fact that you've coordinated the event for Damian York, who's perhaps the most prominent name in outdoor design, with our Annual Garden Walk. Not to mention that now we know that he's agreed to judge our competition," she added with a tiny squeal.

"That brings to mind my other tidbit of good news. You see, there's a problem with my yard. I'm afraid I need to withdraw from the garden walk."

Alice about choked on her drink. "And you call that good news? Who will I find as a replacement at this late notice?"

I held up a hand. "Let me finish. As a representative of our agency, and in an effort to show her support for the garden walk, our office manager, Vicky Crump, has graciously agreed to step in for me. She's happy to have her garden featured as the final stop on this year's tour."

"I'm sure she is," Alice interjected, pursing her lips and folding her sandwich wrapper into a tidy square, running her fingers over the creases until they were razor sharp. I couldn't tell if she was happy with the prospect of Vicky's garden on the tour.

"I haven't seen Vicky's garden," I continued, in my most convincing tone, "but I'm sure it's wonderful. Everything she does is so . . . so perfect."

"Yes, I know. Ms. Crump used to be a member of the garden club."

"Used to?"

"Well, as you can imagine, disagreements often arise when a large group of women try to run a successful club like ours. That's why we've limited the board to just twelve members, hence the name, the Dirty Dozen. And every year we vote on standing board members."

I tried to smile politely as Alice explained the inner workings of the Dirty Dozen. As I listened, though, a couple of reasons why an avid gardener like Vicky would no longer belong to the Dirty Dozen popped into my mind. Either she lost a vote to get on the board or she preferred to enjoy gardening without dealing with snarky women like Alice Peabody.

"Of course," she went on, "every garden walk entrant is automatically eligible for the van Gogh award, and the winner of this prestige automatically secures a lifetime membership as a board member. Only two members hold a lifetime membership: Doris Mosby and Fannie Walker."

I could see why the van Gogh award was so important for the garden club ladies. The winner won the opportunity to bypass the annual vetting of the board. "So, those two are the only ones who have *ever* won the van Gogh award?"

"Well, in the past ten years or so. There have been others, but they've either moved on or passed on. Doris won about seven years ago. Since then Fannie has been on a winning streak. But I think her luck is about to change." A conspiratorial edge to her tone made me feel more like I was at a clandestine meeting with one of the characters in the mystery book awaiting me on my desk than at a lunch with a garden club member.

I tried to lighten the tone with a little smile. "Oh yeah? How's that?"

"Well, she's had the judge in her back pocket, of course. But since Damian has agreed to step up and judge the competition, the true winner will have a chance to shine."

"Doris?"

"Doris! No, of course not. I'm a shoo-in to win this year. Everyone says so!"

Of course.

"Besides, poor Doris doesn't stand a chance of winning again." She leaned in and whispered, "Old age gets the best of all of us, you know."

I nodded. "How old is Doris?"

Alice looked toward the ceiling. "Oh, I'd say in her late eighties. She's really beyond being able to *properly* tend to a garden."

I wasn't sure what *properly* tending to a garden referred to in Alice's eyes but felt suddenly grateful for the yellow tape preventing my meager efforts from coming under this club's scrutiny. "Well, I imagine she still enjoys participating anyway," I offered.

With a slight upturn of her lips, Alice countered with, "She'll be, shall we say, relinquishing her membership soon, I would think."

"Relinquishing . . . but you said she has a lifetime . . ." I shuddered involuntarily. "Oh, you mean . . . ?"

She must have noticed because she started trying to mollify my obvious reaction. "Oh, don't take it so seriously, dear," she said, reaching across the table and patting my hand. "That's how it goes. Out with the old and in with the new. Why, even in the garden you have to deadhead the old blooms so the new ones can burst forth and flourish."

I pushed aside my half-eaten sandwich. The reference to deadheads in the garden dug up unwanted imagery of the skull buried under my hawthorns. "Getting back to the event," I said, taking another sip of soda and willing the queasiness in my stomach to settle, "would it be possible for you to include information about Damian's events in your brochure? Also, when you finalize the garden walk map, it would be wonderful if the last stop was as close as possible to the Secret Garden. That's where we're holding the signing and dinner. The extra convenience might just add up to more book buyers for us."

She hedged. "You were originally number thirteen on the walk, so you would have been the last stop. Now with Ms. Crump taking your place, I'm not sure if that would work. I'd have to change the entire map."

My shoulders sagged. "Really? Does she live far from the Secret Garden?" Funny how I had no idea where Vicky lived. I'd never even thought to ask. Maybe because she was always the first to arrive and the last to leave the office. I just couldn't picture her anyplace else.

"No, she lives right down the street from the nursery, actually."

I scrunched my face in confusion. "I don't get it."

Alice took a long deliberate sip of her soda before explaining. "Giving Vicky the last stop on the tour would put her at an unfair advantage in the contest. She's . . . well . . ." She rolled her eyes. "Let's just say that she's an above-average gardener. And everyone knows the last gardens to be judged usually hold a slight edge over the first entrants."

Ah . . . Vicky's gardening talents were a threat to the other contestants, whereas my talents, or lack of talents, made me a safe bet for the coveted last-stop position. "I understand. And who determines the order of the tour?"

Alice guffawed. "Me. After all, I *am* the president of the club."

I stared in disbelief. "And, once you've rearranged the map, whose garden is going to occupy the last stop on this year's tour?"

"Well, I'd already occupied the twelfth spot, so when I place Vicky's little plot somewhere toward the beginning of the lineup, I guess it will just naturally be mine. Don't worry, my house isn't far from the Secret Garden. Besides, I'm sure Damian's book buyers won't mind a little extra exercise."

I was starting to believe that Big Ed was right when he handed this woman the Cruella De Vil card today. She was perhaps the most self-serving person I'd ever met. I could just imagine her plotting to kill cute little Dalmatian puppies to satisfy her obsession for fur, or in this case, plotting and conniving to assure she obtained her most coveted prize, the van Gogh award.

After my unpleasant meeting with Alice, I was more than happy to hunker at my desk and lose myself in the final scene of my cozy mystery. As I flipped the pages, I became so entranced by the author's easy cadence and lively descriptions that I actually felt like I was transported to the bleak moorlands of Cornwall. I easily envisioned rolling hills covered in gorse and heather and jagged rock formations standing strong against the pounding sea. I found myself strolling the brick-paved side streets of the perfectly scripted hamlet and spending my evenings in the pub, right alongside the spunky protagonist, serving up bitter ale and justice to the town's raucous hooligans. By the time I'd turned the last page I was convinced I could easily sell this manuscript to a top publisher. I was ready to make my call.

No sooner had I picked up the phone than Zach came charging into my office. "Have you heard what's going on?"

I replaced the receiver and waited patiently while he excitedly paced back and forth. "I give up. What's going on?" I prompted.

Zach threw his hands up. "Beats me. But the boss lady just took off out of here like a bat out of hell. Something big must be going down."

I sighed. Couldn't Zach ever call anyone by their real name? "You mean Bentley? Why would she leave in such a rush?" I stood and moved toward my window, which overlooked High Street, where I saw a group of people running past the park and turning down Dogwood Lane. Several police cars zoomed by and did the same. "Oh no. What now?"

Zach rubbed his hands together. "I can't be sure, but I'm betting it's not good."

"Well, there's only one way to find out," I said, abandoning my desk and heading for the hall.

Zach stuck to my heels as we made our way outside and joined the crowd moving down the sidewalk. "This can't be good," he repeated, over and over, as we crossed High Street and started down Dogwood. Up ahead, I could see a few Dunston police cars and an ambulance parked haphazardly in front of a three-story brick home. An officer was outside, bellowing orders at the crowd.

Zach and I pushed our way through the gawkers until we found Bentley. She had her arm around an ashen-faced Vicky. "Something's happened to Vicky's friend Fannie Walker," Bentley informed us.

"Fannie Walker?" I'd just seen her a couple of days ago. "Has there been some sort of accident?"

Vicky removed a starched hankie from the pocket of her skirt and dabbed at her nose. My skin prickled with unease. If Vicky—the most controlled and unemotional woman I'd ever known—was this upset, something big was up.

I chewed my lip, waiting as she sniffed and dabbed a couple more times before finally shaking her head and declaring, "No, this was no accident." She squared her shoulders and sniffed more deliberately this time, trying to restrain the spasms of breath that threatened to escalate into uncontrollable sobs. "Fannie was murdered."

I gasped. Zach gasped. Even Bentley gasped. Poor Vicky shriveled before our eyes, shrinking away and wrapping her hands tightly around her chest as if she were trying to hold herself together.

"Murdered?" Zach and I asked in unison. I glanced his way, noticing he'd acquired a slightly madcap look. "You *are* a murder magnet!" he exclaimed, pointing a stubby finger my way.

"This is not the time, Zach!" Bentley admonished.

I turned back to Vicky. "Are you sure she was murdered?" I couldn't believe it. Who would want to murder Fannie Walker? I'd met her. She seemed like a very sweet older woman, a little competitive about the rose thing, but still, what motive could someone possibly have for killing a widow who spent her days sipping tea and tending roses? But even as I pondered the question, a name popped into my mind: Alice Peabody. She'd whacked her competition just like she would a pesky weed.

"Of course I'm sure. I found . . ." Vicky responded with a shudder, her words trailing off in a round of sobs.

I looked at Bentley for help. Our eyes held each other's for a brief second before Vicky dove back into her arms, seeking comfort. Bentley stiffened. She wasn't comfortable nurturing a houseplant, let alone playing the role of consoler to a weeping woman. Or, knowing Bentley, maybe she was worried about her silk blouse. Whatever the reason, I was about to step in and take over when I caught a glimpse of Sean out of the corner of my eye. "I'll be right back," I said, ignoring Bentley's protests and running after Sean.

"Wait! Sean, wait!" I called out. He turned to face me just as a young officer who was attempting to control the pressing crowd shouted at me to get back.

"It's all right," Sean assured him. "Let her through."

I ducked under the tape and jogged over to him. "What's going on?"

"It's Fannie Walker. I'm afraid she's dead. Did you know her?"

"Only in passing. She's in the local garden club. I visited with them just the other day."

Sean narrowed his eyes. "Is that so?"

I nodded. "Vicky says she was murdered."

He drew in his breath and ran a hand through his blond hair. "You know I really can't comment on that. But do me a favor. Take Vicky somewhere away from here and help her get calmed down. I have her initial statement, but I'll want to follow up with some questions later. And don't let her talk to anyone from the press." His eyes scanned the crowd and fell with a scowl on one of my former colleagues from the *Dunston Herald*. I noticed she was busy snapping pictures of us talking. Around her, the gawkers were beginning to push closer to the yellow tape, vying for the opportunity to catch a titillating glimpse of the scene. What was it about a crime scene that piqued people's morbid curiosity? Did we all just have a weird innate desire to face our worst fears in person? Whatever was inspiring these onlookers, I'd lost it long ago. I'd seen enough death to last a lifetime.

"You'd better hurry and get Vicky out of here," Sean repeated. "If it gets out that she's the one who discovered the body, this crowd will devour her. Not to mention that story-hungry reporter over there."

He was right. Besides, I didn't want her around when the coroner came through with the body. "I'll take her back to the office and wait with her until you get there."

He nodded and took off toward the backyard. I ducked back under the tape and started making my way to Vicky, only to be cornered by the reporter. "Hi, Jan." I eyed her wearily. We used to be pretty good friends back when I worked at the paper, but I'd talked to her only a few times since I lost my job, and each of those times was to ask a favor. As she whipped out her notepad and began pelting me with questions, I assumed today was the day she planned to collect on those favors.

"Is it true that Ms. Walker was found murdered in her own backyard?" she asked, pen poised in the air.

"Really, Jan, you should be asking the police these questions."

She ignored me and continued, "Can you tell me how she was murdered?"

"No."

She glanced up from her pad and eyed me suspiciously. "What do you mean, *no?*"

I shrugged, wondering what it was she wanted from me.

She furrowed her brows. "You don't know the answers or you won't tell me?"

I took a step backward. "I don't know what you mean."

"Well, didn't you find Fannie's body?"

"What? No!"

Jan scrunched her nose. "Really? I'm sorry, Lila. I just assumed—"

"Assumed what?"

"Well, you're usually the one who finds the murdered bodies. Everyone says so."

I blinked twice and leveled my gaze on her. "Everyone says so?"

She stared at me blankly. I didn't bother to ask for further clarification; I knew what she was getting at. My reputation as a murder magnet obviously preceded me. Glancing over her shoulder to where Vicky was still huddled next to Bentley and Zach, I excused myself. "I need to be going, Jan. Sorry I don't have any answers for you."

By the time we got Vicky back to the office and settled in the waiting room with some hot tea, Sean showed up. He breezed by me with nothing more than a curt nod and went directly to Vicky. "I just have a few more questions for you, Ms. Crump. Is there somewhere private that we could talk?"

In the meantime, the whole group had assembled around our office manager, offering comfort and gently trying to pry information out of her. Vicky remained steadfast, however, reiterating that the police had told her not to discuss the details with anyone. But now that Sean was actually there, she seemed almost afraid to relive those details. A slight tremble overtook her as she looked toward me for reassurance.

I placed a hand on her shoulder. "Why don't you use my office? I could come with you if you want."

She let out her breath and I could feel her shoulder muscles relax under my hand. "I would appreciate that."

"Good idea," Flora jumped in, then added, "and after Detective Griffiths finishes his questions, you should go straight home and get some rest. I'll be happy to cover any calls that come in this afternoon."

"And I'd be glad to drive you home," Franklin spoke up. "I'll be heading out in about an hour to meet with Damian anyway. I'll drop you by your house on the way."

Vicky nodded and forced a smile.

"All settled then," Bentley interjected. "Now for the rest of us, I'm calling an emergency DAC meeting. Everyone to the conference room."

I sighed. Bentley had recently taken to abbreviating everything to an acronym, as if she was too busy to use entire phrases. I hadn't heard DAC before, but it wasn't too difficult to figure out it stood for damage assessment and control. Leave it to Bentley to turn some poor person's unfortunate demise into a new task list.

Bentley continued, "We'll need to determine how this recent turn of events will affect our agenda for the rest of the week. Not to mention our image," she added, shooting a black look my way. Then she turned her scowl on Jude and Zach, who were huddled in the corner, heads bent in a private conversation. "Snap to it, boys!" she ordered.

The group dispersed, Bentley's entourage scurrying down the hall ahead of us. Just as they reached the door to the conference room, Zach turned toward me with a playful look. He raised his hand in a mock-gun gesture, mouthing the words "murder magnet."

Chapter 8

"I KNOW WHO DID THIS." THE FIRST WORDS out of Vicky's mouth caused both Sean and me to do a double take. Gone were all traces of her earlier distress and back was Vicky's usual self-possession. She was sitting on the edge of her chair with the straight-back discipline of a proper English lady about to receive high tea.

I noted the determined tone in her voice and treaded carefully. "What makes you say that?"

Sean also leaned in. "Yes, who do you have in mind, Ms. Crump?"

Vicky's head ping-ponged incredulously between the two of us. "Grant Walker, that's who. Fannie was terrified of him. Just the other day, he threatened her."

I recognized the name of the hotheaded man I'd seen in Ruthie Watson's office the previous Saturday. I bit back the urge to fire off several questions. Instead, I settled into my chair and let Sean take over the interview. His interview.

My mind flashed back to the first time I met Sean. It was right after I'd found a local homeless man dead on the sofa in the agency's reception area. Back then, I was impressed with Sean's professionalism as well as the gentle way he handled me during a time of distress. I was still impressed. His easy, courteous manner was just the thing to channel Vicky's single-mindedness and get needed answers.

I watched as he took out his notepad and pen, his bright blue eyes darting between Vicky and the paper as he probed for information. Sean was obviously a good cop, dedicated to his career. I admired that, but lately I wondered if he would be as devoted to our marriage. Or was there room for only one love in his life—his job.

"It was awful," she said. "To see Fannie's lifeless body slumped over her roses like that. I can't even count the times I helped her in her garden, tending those very same flowers. Now . . ." Her voice caught in her throat, a slight stumble in her fortified emotions. "Now I'll probably never visit Fannie's garden again." Sean started to reach for a box of tissues on the edge of my desk, but Vicky waved it away.

"Why did you go over to Mrs. Walker's home in the first place?" he inquired.

"I'd called her to let her know I was going to be in the garden walk this year. She was so excited for me. We got to talking about roses and she invited me over on my lunch hour to see her most prized rose. One she'd cultivated herself."

"After you . . . uh . . . found her, did you move anything? Touch anything?" he asked gently.

Vicky drew in her breath and squared her shoulders. "Of course not! I've read enough mysteries to know better than to disturb the scene. I didn't even touch the spade that he used to . . . to kill her."

I winced. *Bludgeoned with a garden spade? How horrible!*

"And you say she was being threatened by Grant Walker."

"Yes, that no-good stepson of hers. I'm telling you, he's got anger control issues."

I could vouch for that. I'd seen the guy's temper. It was ugly.

"What would be his motive?" Sean asked.

"Greed. Isn't that always the reason? Grant's father was Dr. Robert Walker, a well-respected physician in the area. A wonderful man, really. He passed just last year. Fannie was devastated." Vicky shifted in the chair, crossing her ankles and readjusting her skirt before continuing, "You see, both Fannie and Dr. Walker lost their first spouse, so it was a second marriage for both of them. A second chance at love, Fannie always said. And she did adore him. They were very happy together."

"But her stepson didn't approve?" Sean interjected.

Vicky shook her head. "Grant was in his early teens, I believe, when Fannie came along. She adored him, but he never accepted Fannie. He treated her terribly. He's an only child and I'm afraid that his mother, Robert's first wife, indulged him. He's been angry with Fannie ever since Robert's will was read. You see, Robert divided the estate between Fannie and Grant, leaving Fannie the house and a share of his investments. Part of those investments include some land in the hills outside the Valley. Fannie and Robert were going to build their dream home up there. She was so excited with the prospect."

Suddenly, the argument I'd overheard at Sherlock Holmes Realty made sense. Grant was trying to sell the land and Fannie was holding out. Now that I knew the whole story, I could certainly understand why. She must have felt a sentimental attachment to the land where she and her husband had staked their dreams.

"But Grant wants to sell," Vicky went on. "He's been hounding Fannie to sign it over, but she won't budge. Grant's furious, of course."

Sean was scribbling away on his notepad. "And, he threatened Fannie."

Vicky's expression turned dark. "Yes, he told her that he'd get her to sign over the property one way or the other."

Sean quirked his head. "That could mean anything. Perhaps he was taking legal action."

"That's doubtful," Vicky corrected him. "You'd have to know Grant. He has a fierce temper and reacts on impulse. Taking the time to pursue proper legal routes wouldn't even occur to him. He's impetuous."

I couldn't stay silent any longer. "She's right. I saw his temper at the real estate office just the other day." I relayed my experience at Sherlock Holmes Realty. "But there's another possible suspect you're not considering—Alice Peabody."

"Who's Alice Peabody?" Sean asked.

"She's the president of the garden club," I explained. "And she's ruthless. I'm under the impression that she'd do about anything to win this year's van Gogh award."

Vicky's head bobbed in agreement. "Yes, you're right about Alice; she's very competitive. However, I don't think she's capable of murder." She turned to Sean with confidence. "No, Grant Walker is your man, Detective."

"You may be right but . . ." Visions of Grant's anger morphed into the image of Alice when we'd met today.

"But what?" Sean pressed me.

I looked up, realizing my mind had wandered into the field of possibilities. "I met Alice for lunch today. She was running late and when she finally got there, she was disheveled and her slacks were covered with dirt stains." As soon as the words were out of my mouth, I knew how silly they sounded. I shrunk back in my seat and glanced toward Sean. To his credit, he remained poker-faced, although I thought maybe I detected the semblance of a smirk tugging at the corner of his mouth. "It's hard to explain. Just a feeling I have, I guess."

"Just dirt stains or did you notice blood on her pants as well?"

I could feel my cheeks redden as I shook my head. "No, I didn't see any blood. Just dirt."

Sean cleared his throat and stood. "Well, I think I've got everything I need for now. Ms. Crump, you should take your coworkers up on their suggestions and head home for the day. You've experienced quite the shock." Then turning to me, he asked, "Walk me out?"

I stood and followed him back down the hall. As soon as we reached the back door, he turned to me and in a quiet voice, asked, "How about some dinner tonight? It won't be Voltaire's but we could go somewhere else. Make an evening of it."

He was offering me an olive branch, and I was tempted to take it because after finding out about two murders in one day, nothing would be better than to feel the warm safety of Sean's arms around me. Still, a tingle of apprehension lingered within me. After all that had transpired between us the last couple of days, I needed some alone time to sort through things. Not to mention that I was behind on my own work. "Not tonight, Sean. It's been a long day and I'm not really feeling up to going out."

He snatched up my hand. "Let's stay in, then. I

could get some takeout from Wild Ginger and bring it by your place."

I pulled away, my ambivalence quickly turning to annoyance. Why did he always expect me to be available at the drop of a pin? Never mind that he was always too busy to make plans, or worse yet, just didn't bother to show up for the plans we had. "I'm sorry, but I really am exhausted, and I still have some work to do tonight."

His blue eyes sparked. "With that York guy?"

Suddenly, what was simply annoyance a few seconds ago was churning into anger. I opened my mouth to snap back, but was unable to come up with a suitable retort. Instead, I spun on my heel, letting his question hang in the air as I walked away. I knew it wasn't the wisest thing to do. By keeping silent, I was letting him think that I *did* have plans with Damian York. But really, did he think he was the only one with a career? If he weren't so egocentric, and took time to really listen to me, he'd realize that all I planned to do was go home, take a hot bath, and soak away my stress with a glass of wine and a few proposal chapters.

I didn't get the chance to do any of those things, though. I fully intended to head straight home, but as I maneuvered my Vespa through the streets of Inspiration Valley, my mind wandered. In the course of one day, I'd discovered two people had been robbed prematurely of their lives. First, the poor girl buried in my yard and now Fannie Walker. The more I dwelled on the whole situation, the farther I veered from my usual route home. Next thing I knew, I was on the road to Mama's house. I parked in the drive behind her pickup.

She was waiting for me on her front porch, rocking in one of the cane chairs. Next to her was a small table set with a bottle of Jim Beam and two shot glasses. I also spied a covered plastic container, which I hoped contained some of her chocolate banana bread. I'd come to learn that Mama's banana bread could calm even the most frazzled nerves.

She waved me over as soon as I removed my helmet. "Come on over and sit with me a spell."

I made my way onto her porch, ducking under a few wind chimes and around several large planters of flowers. Mama's porch was perhaps even more cluttered than her house, if that's believable. She had every type of porch knick-knack possible: an assortment of colorful bird-houses, a wooden wagon wheel, an old painted milk can, and at least a dozen wind chimes in all sorts of shapes and sizes. When a breeze came through, which wasn't often this time of year, it sounded like front-row seats at the symphony.

I nodded toward the glasses. "Hello, Mama. Were you expecting someone?"

She gestured toward the open chair and

reached over to pour me some Jim Beam. "Just you, hon."

I should have expected that.

"Rough day?" she asked, popping the lid to the container to reveal several neatly stacked slices of banana bread. I gladly helped myself.

"Only if you count two murders as a bad day." I bit into the bread, closed my eyes, and let the sweetness roll around my mouth for a second.

When I opened my eyes again, I saw Mama's head cocked to the side. "You mean new books you're gonna agent, honey?"

I realized how flippant my response had sounded; no wonder she didn't take it seriously. Was I getting jaded to murder, as the Murder Magnet that I'd been dubbed? Or was I just too numb from the shock of it all to react properly?

I pressed my lips together, shook my head. "Sorry, Mama. I mean for real."

Unable to say more for the moment, I took another bite of bread. I swear, my Mama's bread was magical. I took a sip of whiskey, hoping it possessed some magic as well. It did. Surprisingly enough, its flavorful bite seemed to blend with the savory sweetness of the banana bread, and I felt some of the stress in my neck and shoulders begin to melt. Of course, Mama would say that Jim Beam pairs well with any food. Just one more reason, in her book, that it was the superior beverage of choice.

I turned to Mama again and saw the shock on her face. "Two?" she croaked.

I nodded. "The body in my yard belongs to a young woman. It's been there for about thirty years. The police found evidence she was murdered."

"My lawd!" Mama muttered under her breath. She grasped at her stomach with one hand and snatched up her glass with the other. "A young woman? That's horrible."

"I know, Mama. It breaks my heart, too. And to think she's been there all this time and no one knew."

"But . . . you said two," she muttered before draining the rest of her drink.

"Fannie Walker."

"Fan . . . ?" Her face went white as she shook her head in disbelief. "That can't be. Why, I just saw her a few days ago. And you said they were both . . . murdered?"

"Yes, Mama, it's true." I leaned over and took the empty glass from her trembling hand, refilled it, and set it on the table in case she'd need another in a few minutes. "I'm sorry, Mama."

"This can't be," she whispered. "The other day when I laid out the cards for her, I kept askin' about the roses. That's what she wanted me to . . . but . . ." She clenched her fists. "Those damn roses! No wonder the cards weren't speakin' to me. I was askin' the wrong questions."

"How could you have known?"

"It's my job. What I do," she said, biting her lip. She picked up the glass I'd filled and clutched it like a life ring and asked, "How did it happen? Who—"

I held up my hand. "Mama, I don't know. Sean's people are working on it."

"Oh lawdy," she mumbled again, tears filling her eyes.

Mama stood and moved to the porch railing. I went right along with her, wrapping my arm around her shoulders as she stared into the woods that surrounded her house. The sun was beginning to slide lower on the horizon, the clacking rhythm of cicadas fading away just in time for the initial calling of the tree frogs and the sharp trills of crickets. Funny how everything in the world can go awry, but without fail, every evening settles in with the same prenocturnal din. I could see why my mother loved living in this peaceful setting. There was something calming about watching the day's end from the rustic comfort of her front porch.

Mama gave a little shudder, her eyes drifting over the evening's landscape. "Fannie'd started comin' regular to me after her first husband died, all depressed, you know, and I told her someone special was gonna come courtin', and she'd just laugh." Mama smiled lightly, recalling the happiness she'd brought Fannie in those sessions.

I knew many people came to Mama for something deeper than a spiritual reading and sweeter than even her banana bread.

"And then, right as a summer rain, Dr. Walker and his boy came along, just like I'd said, and they were so happy. She'd still come by but with smiles and we'd pass the time talkin' 'bout, well, just life, you know. And, oh, how she loved that boy of his, although I don't know how she had patience for the little hooligan. Nothin' but trouble, he was." Mama took a deep swallow of her whiskey, still looking out at the darkening sky. "When Doc Walker passed, well, she was at peace with it in a way. Like she knew they'd had somethin' real special and it had been a privilege, not something you could hold on to forever. Just like she'd accepted his gettin' calls in the middle of the night and having to run off to tend to patients, miss special occasions, even. Some things are so special you take it in whatever doses you can get, and be happy for it."

My arm slipped from her shoulder and I couldn't help releasing a heavy sigh. Sean was like that. So special, so right for me, yet so devoted to his career as well . . .

I realized Mama had turned her head to me, a knowing look in her eyes. "What is it, honey? Somethin' with that man of yours?"

I nodded. Mama did seem to have a way about her, a knowing way. "Sean's a good man and he loves Trey. I'm just having trouble seeing how things are going to work."

She turned to face me squarely. "Why's that, sug?"

I shrugged. "Lately, he's been consumed by his job. It always comes first. Before me."

"You know, hon, being a cop's wife would take a healthy dose of understandin' and respect. Why, you and me, we can't even begin to imagine what he sees on a daily basis. All those things you read about in your murder mysteries, all safe and comfy at your desk, helping authors figure clues and catch the bad guys and whatever . . . well, he's *facing* them in real life. And, no one's sugarcoatin' it with smart words and fancy descriptions for him. And it doesn't always end all tidy and neat, either."

Mama placed her glass on the railing and rubbed her hands up and down my arms. "You won't ever be able to separate a good man like him from his work. Just like Fannie couldn't stop her doctor hubby from doing his doctorin' whenever it was needed. It just isn't possible and you shouldn't want to. It's what makes him who he is." She placed her hands on either side of my face, forcing me to look directly into her eyes. "I understand your frustration, sug, but if you're going to be angry and resentful about what he does, things just won't work between you two.

You'll have to decide if you're cut out to be a cop's wife, that's all."

She was right. It really was *that* simple. Here I'd been manipulating Sean, trying to mold him into something I wanted, a man who fit one of Flora's romance authors' heroes, a man who falls at my feet, anxious to please me at my every whim and need. When really I just needed to figure out if I could accept him for the man he is . . . a good man, a loyal man. The man who loved and accepted me unconditionally. "You know what, Mama?"

"What?"

"You *are* amazing."

Chapter 9

I HELD THE PHONE AWAY FROM MY EAR AS a loud shriek came over the line. To say that the author was glad to hear from me was an understatement. "I have just a couple of suggested changes before we start submitting," I interjected with a few giggles of my own between her joyful babblings. I'd chosen to start my Tuesday on a happy note and called the author of the English cozy mystery to make an offer of representation.

"No problem! I can make changes," she gushed. "What's a few changes after I've rewritten it at least a hundred times over the past three years?"

I couldn't help but smile into the phone. Making calls such as this was one of the things I enjoyed most about my job. Most authors I'd encountered had spent years trying to find a publisher for their book, and finding an agent was just one step closer to achieving their dream. "Well, all those rewrites have definitely paid off. I enjoyed reading your story. In fact, I already have a couple of publishers in mind." This author's descriptions of the soft purple of heathers, the rolling fog-shrouded landscape and rocky seaside of her English countryside created such vivid images I nearly felt I'd been transported there. I knew I could find a publisher who would feel the same.

After another round of sniggering, I began explaining our agency's contract for representation and a few other things to expect as we began the process of getting her book sold to a publisher. "I'm looking forward to working with you," I said, wrapping up the call. "And I can't wait for the day when your books finally get into the hands of readers."

Little shrieks of happiness were still emitting from the line as I hung up the receiver. "A happy author, I take it." My eyes snapped upward. Vicky was standing in my doorway, straight as a soldier, chin held high as if she was trying to put on a brave front.

"Yes. Remember the English cozy query you put on my desk a couple of weeks ago? I've just made an offer of representation."

"That's wonderful," she replied flatly. Despite her valiant front, the telltale signs of grief were evident in her blotchy skin and red-rimmed eyes.

"You should have taken today off, Vicky."

"I'd rather keep busy," she stated, walking to my desk and offering a stack of papers. "Here are a few queries I thought you might be interested in reviewing."

I took the papers and glanced through them with a quick nod before placing them in the center of my desk. "Thanks. I'll look at these first thing." Then, noticing that she was still hovering, I asked, "Are you sure you're okay, Vicky?"

"I am." She smoothed nonexistent wrinkles on her skirt and glanced toward one of my chairs. I motioned for her to take a seat and then waited patiently while she fussed some more, straightening the hem of her skirt until it cut in an exact horizontal line across her knees.

"Vicky?" I prodded.

She exhaled, her shoulders shifting down a notch. "I'm sorry. My mind is preoccupied this morning."

"Understandably so." I folded my hands across the top of my desk and waited.

"I meant what I told Detective Griffiths yesterday. I'm convinced that Grant Walker killed Fannie."

"It's possible. From what I saw of him at the real estate office, he has quite the temper."

Vicky bobbed her head. "Exactly. I'm sure he went to confront Fannie about the property, lost his temper, and killed her."

"If that's the case, Sean will figure out a way to prove it. Don't worry, he's a good cop. He'll get to the bottom of this." And of my backyard mystery, I hoped. I hadn't mentioned it to anyone, but in my mind, I'd started thinking of the young woman in my yard as Helen, after the character Helen Burns in *Jane Eyre*, who also died tragically at a young age. At least by calling her

Helen, I could quit thinking of her as "the skeleton" or "the buried body" or . . . the reference I hated the most, "Jane Doe."

Vicky sighed. "That's the problem. I am worried. That's why I was wondering if you wouldn't mind looking into things."

"What do you mean? What things?"

"Things that might have led to Fannie's murder. Nothing against Detective Griffiths; I'm sure he's industrious, but I'd feel better if I knew we had all our bases covered. And, as a civilian, you might have a better chance of ferreting out the truth about Fannie's murder."

I checked my expression before it gave me away. On one hand, I felt angry that Vicky would ask such a thing of me. Not only would Sean not appreciate me poking around his case—and we were already on shaky ground—but doing so might land me in a dangerous spot. It's happened before that my curiosity's gotten the better of me. Then again, I found Vicky's request compelling. Not to mention that I was intrigued by the case, and just a wee bit flattered that she obviously thought I was capable of helping to bring justice to Fannie.

She must have taken my silence as a no, because she suddenly stood, adjusted her sweater, and stared down at me with a pained expression. "I'm sorry. I know I don't have the right to ask such a thing of you."

"No." I stopped her. "Sit back down, please. I just have to take a moment to think about this. For instance, what makes you think I could find out anything that might help the police investigation?" I asked after she'd resettled in the chair.

"Because you have before on several occasions. You seem to have a penchant for that sort of thing."

I frowned. I really was developing a reputation in town. For what, I wasn't quite sure. The idea of having a "penchant for solving crimes" certainly sounded better than Murder Magnet, but still . . . "Vicky, I would love to help you, but I'm not sure how I would even get started. I don't even know Grant Walker. Besides, we're just over a week away from a major event here. I couldn't possibly pull time away from work."

"I understand completely. I'm not asking for anything big. Just a little poking around." She pinched her thumb and forefinger together to emphasize her point. "It wouldn't take much of your time at all. As for getting started, I've already arranged the perfect opportunity for you to speak to Grant."

I blinked a few times. "You have?"

She deliberately crossed her legs and clasped her hands on her lap. "Yes. Earlier today, Franklin mentioned to me that he was taking Damian to view the Walkers' land. It's Damian's first choice for building his new showcase home. Franklin and Damian are meeting Grant there around three o'clock tomorrow afternoon and I suggested you accompany them. Ruthie can't be there until three thirty, so that might give you a little time for personal talk. All I want is for you to ask a few questions." She paused for a few seconds, allowing me to process what she was saying. "And don't worry, Franklin's already on board with the idea. He's explained to Damian that you'll be coming along to offer another opinion on the property."

I shook my head. Boy, was I ever easy. Biting the inside of my cheek, I suppressed the smile tugging at my lips. Truth was, as irritated as I was for having been baited so easily, I had to admire the efficiency with which Vicky reeled me in—hook, line, and sinker. She'd known all along that I wouldn't be able to resist a little sleuthing. Besides, after thinking the situation through, I realized she had a point. As busy as Sean had been lately—the big drug case, my case, and now Fannie's murder—he was stretched thin. Besides, what would it hurt to just ask a few questions?

I tipped my head back and exhaled. "Okay, okay," I relented and reached for my calendar. "Three o'clock tomorrow? I'll be there."

I was awarded with a rare show of affection as Vicky bolted from her chair and reached across my desk to squeeze my hand. "Thank you, Lila. Thank you. There's just one more thing," she added, staring down at me with a concerned look on her face. "It's Eliot."

"Eliot?"

"Fannie's cat. I'm worried about him. With Fannie gone, no one is at the house to take care of him."

"Certainly Grant has thought of that."

Vicky snorted. "Grant? He hates Eliot. Why, he'd let the poor thing starve just out of spite."

The terrible thought of a cat wandering that old house, scared, hungry, and all alone was a lot to bear. I could see why Vicky was upset. "What can we do?"

Vicky stuck her chin out stubbornly. "There's only one thing to do. We need to rescue Eliot. Fannie gave me a key to her house long ago. I took care of Eliot and her houseplants whenever she and Robert traveled and—"

I held up my hand. "Hang on. We can't just go over there and take Eliot. There has to be some rule about that."

Vicky straightened her shoulders and fixed a determined gaze on me. "If you won't go with me, then I'll go alone. One way or another, I'm going to get Eliot before Grant Walker neglects him to death, or worse yet, disposes of the poor creature the same way he did Fannie." My mind's eye flashed to a horrible image of a sweet little kitty being offed with the steel edge of a garden spade. I shuddered. "Okay, okay. But let's be sensible about this." I couldn't believe I'd actually just said that to Vicky. She was usually the epitome of sensible. "I'll call Sean this afternoon and see if he'll arrange for us to get the cat after work. Just promise me you won't go over to that house alone. What if you're right and Grant *is* the killer? Would you really want to face him down in that giant house alone?"

Vicky lowered her chin. "What do you mean, *if I'm right?* Of course I'm right. Grant Walker is a murderer and I'm counting on you to prove it. As for Eliot, I'll wait for you to call Detective Griffiths."

Before she left my office, I promised I'd get back to her later that afternoon with an answer about Eliot. I still felt a bit duped about the Grant Walker thing, but after considering it further, I decided it might actually work out. I could let the afternoon do double duty, since Franklin and I needed to work with Damian on the upcoming events anyway. Plus, Damian certainly wasn't unpleasant to be around. Grant Walker, although decidedly unpleasant at Ruthie's office, might have a different attitude when talking to Damian about selling his property. And who knew what I just might discover in the process? In the meantime, however, I wanted to focus on my new pile of queries. I bribed myself with the promise of a midmorning cup of coffee if I could make decent progress on my stack.

I began leafing through the pile, feeling a familiar rush of anticipation. The possibility of finding a new story was a thrill I never grew tired of experiencing. Nevertheless, the first few queries fell flat before the title *Murder and Marriage* caught my eye. Probably because I seemed to have nothing but marriage—and unfortunately, murder—on my mind these days.

I snapped up the query for a closer inspection. The title needed some work, but I didn't let the lackluster name of the book deter me from reading more. In my experience, titles were no indication of an author's capabilities. Take Jane Austen's *Pride and Prejudice*. Most people didn't realize that it was submitted to her publisher under the title *First Impressions*. For being such a talented author, Austen seemed ambivalent toward titling her works, as are many of the authors who seek my representation. At first, I didn't understand this ambivalence. To me, a title was a glimpse into the soul of the book and should be chosen with as much care as one would choose their own child's name. Now that I'm a more seasoned agent, I just overlook the title and jump right into the query. This one was a treasure.

Dear Ms. Wilkins,
Thirty-two-year-old Emma White's much-anticipated wedding is only a couple of weeks away when preparations suddenly

go awry. Her invitations are lost in the mail, her flaky seamstress hems the wedding gown too short, and the groom-to-be is acting strangely. But things soon go from bad to worse when the cake designer ends up facedown in three tiers of fondant perfection and Emma's maid of honor is the main suspect. Will Emma be able to sift through all the ingredients for murder in time to find the cake maker's real killer, or will her best friend have to trade her bridesmaid dress for stripes and shackles?

Murder and Marriage is a 75,000-word completed humorous mystery that won first place in the Bay Town Mystery Contest. I've worked in advertising for over twenty years and have won multiple awards for my work in print ads. I look forward to sharing my full manuscript with you.

Sincerely,

Lynn Werner

"Yes!" I said out loud. The author's light, witty voice worked perfectly for the type of story line she was proposing. I set the query next to my computer. Later, I'd email and request a synopsis and a partial read. If the first few chapters proved to be as tightly written as her query, I might have a new author.

Rubbing the kinks in my shoulders, I decided I'd earned a little reward. The rest of the queries could wait awhile. I was in dire need of a caffeine fix. Besides, I wanted to touch base with Makayla to see how the plans for decorating were coming along.

I'd just started down the back steps when I ran into Flora. I retreated to the landing to allow her to maneuver the narrow stairway. "Hello, Flora," I chimed brightly.

She met my greeting with a dark look. "Hello." Her voice lacked its usual cheerfulness and she was huffing, out of breath from her ascent up the stairs.

"I'm just going to grab a quick cup of coffee. Can I bring you up something?"

"No thank you. And what do you have on your agenda today?"

"Just trying to get ahead on paperwork. The rest of my week seems to be filling up with appointments." I was already having misgivings about agreeing to the Grant Walker thing. Driving out to the property and inspecting it with him on a ruse really wasn't a good use of my time and rather, well, sneaky. As eager as I was to help Vicky, my schedule was already jam-packed for the next week and a half leading up to the dinner and signing, and just how much good would I be able to do for her anyway? Not to mention Vicky's expectations that I would surely prove her right (when I might not) meant extra stress. And, heaven knows, I already had enough stress.

Flora's chin jutted out. "I see. And I suppose one of those appointments is with Peggy Cobb." Her features were growing tight.

I squinted. "Peggy Cobb?" Suddenly the name rang a bell. With all the events of the last couple of days, I'd forgotten that I'd mentioned my home's previous owner to Flora. "No, I haven't had time to track her down. Why? Did you want me to tell her something?" I remembered that Flora had mentioned knowing the Cobbs.

"Oh no. Why would I?" Flora said, tugging her polyester chartreuse blouse away from her body and wiggling a bit under what I thought was a stifling fabric choice for our mid-June heat and humidity. "I just wondered what you were up to," Flora continued, pulling a hankie from her purse and dabbing her décolletage.

I wasn't sure how to respond. I wasn't "up to" anything. But I no sooner opened my mouth to ask what she meant than she pushed past me and headed into the building.

How strange, I thought, continuing down the steps toward Espresso Yourself. Flora was usually the most cheerful person in the office, but considering yesterday's tragic events, it did make sense. Flora liked to believe the world was as magical as the fairylands created by her children's book authors, so it only stood to reason that tragic events like Fannie's murder upset her more than most people. I made a mental note to try to do something extra nice to cheer her up later.

The first thing I did as I entered Makayla's shop was inhale. The slightly burnt smell of coffee grounds mixed with the sweet scent of chocolate laced with spicy cinnamon enticed my senses and drew me to the counter like an eager pup to a bone.

Before I even uttered a word, Makayla turned and started steaming milk. "I wondered if I'd see you today."

"You know I can't make it through a single morning without my usual sweet jolt of caffeine."

Makayla's lovely laugh rang through the empty shop. "Actually, I'm glad to see someone. It's been incredibly slow."

"Probably the heat. It's unusually warm today, don't you think?" I glanced toward the back of the room. "Is Trey around?"

"Afraid not. I sent him out to pick up some supplies," Makayla said, topping off my caramel latte with a healthy dose of whipped cream. She also plated a two-bite streusel muffin and shoved it my way. "On the house. You look like you need a little extra sweetness this morning. I heard what happened to Fannie. It's so awful."

"I didn't really know her, but still . . ." I let my words hang while I gripped my mug and took my first sip of deep, warm, sweetly laced richness—nectar gifted straight from the hands of Makayla, the caramel latte goddess. I exhaled with satisfaction. "By the way, is there a time we can get together and go over your decorating plans?"

"Why not now?" Makayla chimed in her melodic voice. "There's no one here, so this is perfect. Just let me make myself a little something."

I watched as she turned and filled a mug with steaming water and removed a tea bag from one of the glass display jars that lined the shelves behind the counter. She motioned for me to head to one of the tables while she disappeared in the back. A second later, she emerged with a large binder and a copy of Damian's book under her arm. She plopped them on the table in front of me and went back to grab her tea.

As she joined me, I detected a pleasant fruity scent coming from her mug. "Arctic raspberry," she explained. "A new organic herbal blend I'm trying. I think my tea-loving customers are going to like it. Rich raspberry with a cool nip of spearmint and a little something else." She raised an eyebrow suggestively.

I gripped my latte a little harder, hoping she wasn't going to expect me to forgo my usual carb-loaded creaminess for something that sounded ultrahealthy. "What do we have here?" I asked, pointing at the binder.

"Just a few things Jay and I have brainstormed for Damian's signing next . . ." She paused, blinking a few times. "Oh my, do you realize we only have about ten more days to pull all this together?" Then noticing what must have looked like a panicked expression on my face, she quickly sucked in her breath and put on a brave front. "We can handle this—don't worry." Flipping open the binder, she soldiered on. "Most of the ideas are straight from Damian's book, which I love, by the way. I'm sure it's going to be a bestseller."

"Bentley certainly hopes so. She's got a lot wrapped up in Damian. Not to mention the costs of such an extravagant event."

Makayla tapped the binder. "Luckily, most of his ideas have to do with transforming the ordinary into extraordinary, so decorations won't drag down the budget."

"She'll be glad of that." I rotated the binder and opened the cover.

"Speaking of bestsellers," Makayla interjected, her voice almost a whisper, "any news about my book yet?" A couple of months ago, Makayla let me read her own book, *The Barista Diaries*—a charming collection of seven interwoven short stories narrated by a young barista and set entirely in a coffee shop. I'd loved the book and offered to represent it right away. Unfortunately, I hadn't been able to find the right publisher yet. I shook my head, hating to dash her hopes yet again. "I'm sorry. No response yet."

She put on a brave smile. "No worries. I just couldn't help asking," she added, scooting her chair around the table so she was next to me and cocking her head to one side as we flipped through the pages of her binder. She'd assembled a scrapbook of ideas she'd acquired, some from decorating magazines, but most straight from the pages of *Perfect Outdoor Spaces*. "These are wonderful!" I commented, taking in her clippings and notes.

She beamed and started pointing out her ideas. "Addison says there's only enough seating for around seventy under the pergola, so I thought we could bring in some long tables like these." She pointed to some rustic-looking wooden tables.

I leaned forward. "Are those doors?"

"Yes. Isn't it clever? Damian actually uses this idea in his book. There's a dilapidated farmhouse being torn down just outside of town. I've already talked to the owner. He's going to eventually take them to the architectural salvage yard in Dunston, but he'll let us use as many of the old doors as we want for the dinner. Jay's already started making bases for them. Franklin's thrilled with the idea."

I was impressed. "I love it, too!"

She became more enthusiastic as she went on. "We'll keep the table coverings simple. I'm thinking linen runners—that way we can keep as much of the distressed wood exposed as possible. We'll do the same with the round tables under the pergola. Since the dinner will take place in early evening, we'll string lights like these." She flipped through *Perfect Outdoor Spaces* until she located a picture with little white party globes intertwined through overhanging branches. "These will be perfect, don't you think?"

I bobbed my head ardently.

"Good. I found some of the lights at the party store in Dunston. I told Franklin to rent at least two dozen strands."

"Wow!"

She giggled. "It'll be beautiful, just like we're dining directly under the Milky Way. And what do you think of these centerpieces?" I glanced at a picture of tinted mason jars filled with white candles. "Franklin found a couple cases of these types of jars at that new resale shop, Beyond and Back. He said Damian prefers to repurpose as many items as possible, so I think these will be perfect. Especially if I wind grape vines around the bases."

"Perfect!" I echoed. And I meant it. It was surprising how well Makayla and I clicked. I couldn't have come up with ideas any better than the ones she was showing me.

She tapped her finger to her chin. "I'm just thinking the tables will need a little something more, but I haven't quite figured it out yet. Damian's book touts the idea of using nature in tablescapes. It's easy in the fall, when there are gourds and mini pumpkins aplenty, but I'm not sure what to use now. I want something more than just flowers."

I agreed, but couldn't figure out what it would be. I thought of those soft-toned heathers of that mystery book I'd just accepted; each locale offered a unique color and tone to any book—or event. "Whatever it is, it should be regional. If he wants the food to be local, I'm sure he'll want the decorations to fit the same theme. Speaking of food, later this week I'm meeting again with Paul Cohen, the catering manager at How Green Was My Valley, to finalize menu choices. Sometime in the next couple of days, you should contact him to discuss plates and flatware. You'll probably want to choose something that melds with the rest of your decorating scheme."

"Definitely. I'll do that first thing tomorrow." She snapped the binder shut and settled back in her chair, taking another a sip of tea. "Now tell me how things are going with you and Sean."

I stared down and swirled the dregs left over in the bottom of my cup. "Well, we're both busy."

Makayla's green eyes clouded. "He hasn't popped the question, has he?"

"Not yet. I don't seem to be high on his priority list these days."

She shook her head. "He stopped in yesterday afternoon, you know?"

"Really?"

"Yes, late afternoon."

"Oh, that must have been after he finished upstairs. He was questioning Vicky about discovering . . . well, you know." Makayla nodded and stared at her tea. I eyed her curiously. "And?"

She looked up, her face drawn with concern. "This isn't my business, Lila, and I definitely don't want to get mixed up in all this, but there's something you should know."

My heart thudded in my ears as I waited for her to continue. What could she possibly have to tell me that seemed so serious? "Go on, spill."

She let out a long sigh. "Sean and Trey exchanged a few words."

My brow shot up. "Meaning?"

She ran her finger along the brim of her teacup, searching for an explanation. "Meaning they had quite the argument. Seems Sean has it in his mind that you're seeing someone else."

"Oh no."

Makayla nodded. "Yes, and Trey overheard him asking me about it. He lit into him. Got right in his face. Told Sean you're not that type. He was really angry, Lila."

A horrible guilt settled over me. Of course Trey would jump to my defense. He'd seen, firsthand from his own father, how infidelity hurt families and destroyed lives. He valued loyalty in his own relationships and was fiercely loyal to my mother and me. I'd seen evidence of that loyalty last year when he came to my rescue, saving me from a ruthless murderer.

Numbly, my gaze wandered away from Makayla to the front window of her shop. Outside, I saw people scurrying on the walk. A bank of dark thunderclouds had moved in, threatening rain. The arrival of the dark skies seemed to mirror the sudden change in my own mood. This was mostly my fault. I'd known Sean felt insecure about Damian and I'd used those insecurities to try to manipulate him. I'd played a dangerous game with Sean. I'd hurt him and even worse, I'd hurt his relationship with Trey.

"Lila?"

I snapped back and started explaining. "Saturday night, Sean cancelled our date at Voltaire's because he was tied up at work. That's been happening a lot lately, but I was especially frustrated that night because I thought . . ."

"You thought it was *the* night."

I nodded. "I ignored him most of Sunday, then yesterday he caught up with me. He wanted to reschedule, but I told him I was too busy. I wasn't really. I was just being spiteful, that's all."

"That's understandable. You've been waiting a long time for his proposal, Lila."

"Still, I told him I was busy with planning Damian's event. I said some stuff that probably led him to believe that I was personally interested in Damian."

Her green eyes widened. "And are you?"

I shook my head. "No. Oh, I admit, he's good-looking. I couldn't help but notice that." I chuckled, then sobered again when I noticed her sharp look. "Honestly, Makayla. I don't feel that way about anyone except Sean."

"Well, let me tell you, girlfriend, you need to be getting things cleared up with Sean before it's too late. You've got that poor fellow all worked up in a tizzy. Nothing good's going to come out of this game you're playing."

I hung my head in shame. Here I was, supposedly the older, wiser one and yet Makayla was straightening me out. "You're right. I'll talk to him today."

We both turned as the shop's doorbells jingled. A middle-aged man wearing cutoffs and a short-sleeve T-shirt with paint stains blew in with the wind, a mix of the humid summer's breath and angry ozone assaulting our noses. "Whew, sure is blowin' up a storm out there," he commented. "Weatherman says it'll be short-lived, though. Thought I'd come in to get some coffee and ride it out before gettin' back to work."

Makayla jumped up and moved toward the counter. "I, for one, love a good hard rain. It always seems to cool things down and make everything seem new and fresh again," she said to the man. Only I knew what she was really getting at: My friend was trying to tell me that every relationship has its cloudy days. I knew, however, that I was mostly to blame for this stormy patch in my relationship with Sean. I'd have to set things straight soon, before it was too late.

Chapter 10

LATER THAT TUESDAY, AT FIVE THIRTY sharp, Vicky and I pulled in front of Fannie's house. Already the place had an empty feeling. The overgrown lawn was bending under the stress of the heat, neglected flowers drooped sadly, and lifeless windows stared out toward the street like grief-stricken eyes begging for Fannie to come back.

Vicky looked at the house and sighed. "Thanks for asking Detective Griffiths to meet us. I guess I do feel better knowing he'll be here."

"Me, too," I agreed, turning my eyes from the gloomy house and focusing instead on the myriad of cat items that filled the backseat of Vicky's Prius. "Did you get this stuff at All Creatures, Feathered and Furry?" The quaint pet shop had opened a couple of months ago just a few blocks down from the agency. What was once a dilapidated mechanic's garage was fully renovated and housed over two thousand square feet of every pet item imaginable. The new owners had even put an adorable paw-print awning over the front entrance and stamped the floors with cat and dog paw prints. I didn't own a pet, but I'd ducked in a few times on my lunch hour to play with the adorable puppies that frolicked in the back room.

Vicky's eyes followed mine to the backseat. "Yes, I shopped there on my lunch break. Do you think I got enough? I want Eliot to feel comfortable in his new home."

I eyed the three-story cat house that doubled as a scratching post, what must have been a fifty-pound bag of kitty kibble, and enough cat toys to stock Cats "R" Us, if such a store actually existed. "I think you've got it covered," I assured her.

Just then, Sean's dark blue Ford Explorer pulled in front of us. We exited Vicky's car and joined him on the curb, exchanging a few pleasantries before tentatively following his lead up the walk. "How are you doing today, Ms. Crump?" he asked as he keyed into the front door. So far, he'd been playing it pretty cool with me.

"Better. Thank you, Detective," she replied, shooting me a quizzical look. Apparently, the tension between Sean and me was noticeable.

"Eliot!" Vicky called as soon as we'd made our way inside. From where we stood in the foyer, I had a full view of the formal living room and admired its partially exposed beams, large sash windows, and a magnificent paneled fireplace. It was nicely decorated with heavy, upholstered, button-tufted furniture that seemed to suit the home's style. Fannie's house was a turn-of-thecentury colonial, with clean simple lines and walls painted in soft colors that decorators would describe with fancy names like daffodil yellow, porcelain blue, and muted taupe.

"Eliot! Here kitty, kitty," Sean echoed. When no response was heard, we moved down the hall and through a modern kitchen to a well-appointed formal dining room and a comfortable family room. This must have been Doc Walker's favorite room; it was decorated with a masculine flair and lined with over-stuffed bookshelves. Sets of bound books, in mahogany leather and gold lettering, their spines cracked with age, beckoned to me, when I heard something. If my ears were hearing correctly, it was also Eliot's favorite spot in the house. I turned about, trying to pinpoint a faint rustling noise. Finally, a very robust, orange cat popped out from behind a navy blue leather recliner.

"Well, hello there," I cooed. He was wide-eyed and twitchy-whiskered, probably scared to death after being alone for a couple of days. I bent and held out my hand and he immediately rubbed against it. "What a fine fellow," I said, stroking his soft ginger-colored fur and admiring a bushy tail that reminded me of a feather duster. I scratched along his fat cheeks, noticing that the plush creamy tufts of fur under his chin coordinated perfectly with his cream-colored socks and stripes.

"Isn't he a handsome guy?" Vicky said, tucking her skirt around her folded legs as she joined me on the floor. Eliot alternately rubbed against us, obviously enjoying the attention. "Fannie named him for the poet George Eliot. Who was really a woman, you know?"

I nodded, remembering that George Eliot was the pseudonym for Mary Ann Evans. "I love her work."

Vicky sighed. "So did Fannie. Her favorite, of course, was her piece titled 'Roses.'" She picked up Eliot, pulling him firmly against her chest and began uttering lines from the poem, "'You love the roses—so do I. I wish / The sky would rain down roses . . .'" Her voice broke. "I miss her, too, Eliot," I heard her whisper to the cat.

Sean cleared his throat. "We should be going," he said, his eyes landing on mine for a second, but quickly moving away. Vicky stood, with a content Eliot in her arms, and started to follow Sean. I lingered for a second, taking one last look at the family room. Everything looked as if Fannie had left a few minutes ago: a throw blanket bunched on the end of the sofa, a cold cup of tea with a lipstick stain on the rim on the end table along with the television remote and a vase of browning flowers. Across the room, next to the fireplace, was a small card table set up with a jigsaw puzzle, the edge completed and one corner pieced together. A collection of framed photos on the fireplace mantel caught my eye and I crossed the room to inspect them closer.

"Lila," Sean prodded. I looked over my shoulder to see him and Vicky waiting for me on the other side of the room.

"Just a sec," I replied, squinting at the photos. Most of them were of young children, some smiling and waving to the camera, others with more sullen expressions. "Who are all these kids?" I asked Vicky.

"Those were Fannie's kids," she informed me.

I glanced back at the photos, noting that many were of different ethnic backgrounds. "Her kids?"

Vicky chuckled. "Well, that's what she called them. Fannie never actually had children of her own. Instead she devoted her life to helping kids stuck in the foster care system find their forever families."

"She was a social worker?"

"That's right," she affirmed. "And those are just a few of the kids she's helped over the years."

"Incredible." I scanned the photos one more time. Somehow, seeing these photos put a face to something I'd thought about only abstractly. How rewarding—and heartbreaking—Fannie's job must have been.

"Let's go, Lila," Sean called again from across the room.

"Okay," I mumbled, picking up one of the frames for a closer look. A picture of a pigtailed girl with freckles and plump, pinch-worthy cheeks caught my attention. It was something about the eyes. I looked closer, noting her corduroy jumper and Peter Pan collar blouse meant the photo was taken sometime in the mid to late '70s. Still, those eyes . . .

"We need to go now," Sean repeated, impatience creeping into his tone.

Then it dawned on me. I was looking at a young version of Flora Merriweather! Stunned, I fumbled as I replaced the frame, knocking over several others. I quickly righted them before turning to follow Sean and Vicky back through the house.

I decided not to mention anything to Vicky or Sean. The photo could mean anything, after all. Still, was it possible that Flora had once been one of Fannie's kids? If so, no wonder she'd been acting so unlike her normal self. But why didn't she mention anything about it after Fannie's murder?

"Do you think you can get Eliot home okay on your own?" I asked Vicky once we were back outside.

"Of course. We'll be just fine, won't we, Eliot?" she said, snuggling him again before loading him into a plastic cat carrier and securing it in the passenger side of her car. She then scurried around and hopped in herself, seemingly eager to get the cat back to her apartment, or maybe just anxious to get away from the tension that still hovered between Sean and me.

I waved as she pulled away from the curb and then turned back to Sean. "My Vespa's still at the agency. Give me a lift?" Ever since learning from Makayla about Sean and Trey's argument, I'd been eager to set things straight. Now would be as good a time as any.

He nodded, his expression softening a bit as he motioned toward his SUV. Once inside, he turned the key, releasing a blast of cold air and deafening music into the vehicle. "Sorry," he said, adjusting the volume of both before turning toward me. "I swear someone sneaks in here when it's parked and turns up all the knobs. The radio never sounds that loud when I'm driving around."

I giggled, glad for a little break in the unease between us. "I know what you mean. Must be mischievous fairies or something."

"How about we pick up your Vespa and then I follow you home, we drop it off, then we go grab a bite to eat?"

My lips eased into a smile. I felt lighter than I had for days. "I'd like that."

We rode the short distance back to Novel Idea in silence. I wanted to bring up the subject of Damian York, but I thought it better to hold off until we were actually at the restaurant. Safety in numbers, as they say.

After getting my Vespa at work, I drove back to my place, Sean following closely behind in his Explorer. While driving, I rehearsed a dozen different ways to bring up the touchy subject of Damian. By the time I reached my street, however, I decided honesty was the best approach. I'd simply reassure Sean that there was nothing between Damian and me, and hope for the best.

Only, those hopes were dashed when I pulled up to my house and found Damian's sleek rental parked at my curb. I pulled in behind it, cut the engine to my scooter, and tentatively scanned the yard.

"Whose vehicle is this?" Sean asked the minute he climbed out of his own vehicle.

I stammered for a response, but his question was answered when Damian walked around the side of my house, looking exceptionally handsome in dark jeans and a simple button-down white shirt. Next to me, Sean tensed, his muscles balling up as if he was going to spring forward at any moment.

"There you are, Lila!" Damian said, joining us on the curb. "I hope you don't mind my stopping by, but I got to thinking about all that you and Franklin are doing for my book launch and I wanted to do something to repay you." He tapped the clipboard in his hand. "Thought I'd sketch out some easy landscaping ideas for you. After seeing your place the other night, I thought you might appreciate some help."

Sean's head snapped between Damian and me. "The other night?"

I cringed at Damian's unfortunate choice of wording. "Damian, this is my boyfriend, Sean Griffiths. Sean, Damian York."

They shook hands, sizing each other up. The little muscle in Sean's jaw started twitching. Not a good sign. "Didn't you notice the crime scene tape, buddy?"

Damian's eyes slid toward the tape as he casually shrugged. "I only walked the edges and was careful not to disturb anything."

A growl-like noise rumbled inside Sean's throat.

"Hey, thanks for looking at my yard, Damian," I said, grabbing Sean's arm and steering him toward the Explorer. "I'd be happy to see your ideas later. Right now Sean and I have plans."

"That's okay, Lila," Sean bit out. "You two go ahead. Discuss landscaping plans over dinner, why don't you?" He shook off my hold and spun on his heel. "I'm heading back to the precinct. I've got work to do."

"Sean, wait!" I called after him, but he kept going. Without looking back, he hopped into his Explorer and roared away.

Red-faced, I turned to Damian, trying to form an explanation for Sean's irrational behavior. Surprisingly enough, there was no need. Damian, seemingly unfazed by Sean's outburst and quick departure, launched into a spiel about sun and wind patterns and the advantage of indigenous plantings. He started walking the perimeter of the cordoned area as I took one last look at the now-empty street where Sean had blazed away. I sighed, then caught up with Damian, and we worked our way to the back of the house, where he paused to make a few planting suggestions. "As far as this area goes, I would start with a strong focal point, like maybe that maple there in the corner." He pointed to the far end of the yard. "You could place a water feature, perhaps a small fountain, in front and surround it with a seasonal bed. Add a small table and chair and you'd have a great little outdoor reading nook."

Damian's suggestion brought a warm image to mind of me sitting with a book in hand and enjoying sounds of babbling water and buzzing bumblebees, finally pulling my heart away from the image of that empty street. I followed his gaze to the very spot where, just a few months ago, I'd started planting a few primroses before a trowel-wielding murderer threatened to deadhead me like a spent bloom. Perhaps converting the spot to something positive, like a mini reading retreat, would help erase those awful memories. "That would be perfect!"

"That's what I'm all about—*Perfect Outdoor Spaces*." He chuckled, then stopped and exhaled loudly. "That's where the body was found, isn't it?" He pointed toward the foundation of my home, where my hawthorn hedge had once concealed the remains of a forgotten young girl for over thirty years. A feeling of sadness settled between us.

"Yes, I'm afraid so."

"So tragic. Do the police have any idea who she might be?"

I shook my head. "I don't think so." Truth was, if Sean hadn't taken off like a wounded pup, I might have gotten a chance to ask him what progress had been made. Certainly since the status of the case had been updated to murder, they were investigating suspects. "My boyfriend's on the case," I explained. "But I haven't had a chance to ask him about it. The only thing I know is that she's been there for around thirty years." Which reminded me that I still wanted to track down Peggy Cobb.

Damian's shoulders sagged. "And all that time, no one knew."

"Oh, someone knew, all right," I corrected, a sense of injustice rising in me. "Her murderer."

Chapter 11

I ARRIVED LATE TO THE OFFICE WEDNESDAY morning, wishing more than anything that I'd had time to pop into Espresso Yourself for my usual morning fix. After Damian finally left the evening before, I'd tried to call Sean, but was unable to reach him. I slept fitfully, tossing and turning through the night, only to fall into a sound sleep just before my alarm sounded. Now my brain felt as fuzzy as a midsummer peach.

Perhaps that's why I hesitated in the reception area, blinking a few extra times, trying to decide if what I was seeing was real or simply a mirage induced by sleep deficiency. "There's no way Bentley is going to let you keep him here," I said, looking blurry-eyed at the sweet little bundle of orange fur curled on the reception room chair.

Vicky practically snorted from behind her desk. "I've already set her straight on the matter. And for your information, Ms. Burlington-Duke is quite enamored with our new agency mascot."

"Mascot? Really?" It was difficult to see Bentley as a cat lover, considering she couldn't even remember to water a houseplant let alone care for a pet. Then again, no doubt all duties involved in such care would fall to the ever-efficient Vicky anyway. Actually I loved the idea of the cute furry feline as a mascot for the agency. I bent over and ran my fingers between Eliot's ears. There was something about books and cats that just seemed to go together in my mind. He stood and stretched, lifting his bushy tail high into the air and letting out a soft purr.

"Besides," Vicky continued, "how could I leave Eliot alone after the loss he's suffered?"

I nodded, remembering the semi-ruse I'd agreed on for Vicky: the three o'clock meeting with Damian and Franklin at Grant Walker's place. There was also something else I wanted to do. "I'll be leaving around eleven today, Vicky. I have an errand to run before my three o'clock with Franklin and Damian." The night before, I'd popped in on one of my older neighbors, Mrs. Bailey, who'd lived on Walden Woods Circle since the early 1970s, and learned that Peggy Cobb was living in a residential home for seniors in Dunston. I wanted to stop by and pay Peggy a visit to see if she'd remembered any young women in the neighborhood years ago.

My mind flipped through my mental to-do list as I entered my office and settled in for work. I'd just turned on my computer when a soft knock sounded on my door. I looked up to find Franklin standing in my doorway. He appeared quite dapper in a lightweight blue and white striped seersucker suit, red dotted tie, and crisply ironed pinpoint shirt. What really caught my eye, though, was the Espresso Yourself cup in his hand. "I was just downstairs discussing decorating plans with Makayla. She sent this up. She was surprised you hadn't stopped by yet, but thought you might need a little caramel fortitude to get you through the morning."

I practically dove at the cup. "Bless her," I mumbled before taking the first warm delicious sip.

"She is a wonderful girl, isn't she?" Franklin commented, brushing at a few stray orange hairs that were clinging to his lapel. He must have already met the newest member of our literary team. "She and Jay have come up with a delightful decorating scheme for the signing and dinner. Damian is going to be so pleased. Speaking of which, will you need a ride this afternoon out to the Walker place?"

From what I'd gathered, the Walker land was located a few miles out of town. Normally, I would need a ride, although since I was hoping to meet with Peggy Cobb before the appointment, I planned to borrow Trey's car. "Actually, I think I'll check with Trey and see if I can use his car. I have quite a few errands to run this afternoon," I told Franklin. "I'll get directions from Vicky and meet you there."

"Fine," he said. Then holding his tie in place, he bent forward and with a gleam in his eye, whispered, "Vicky told me about your sleuthing plans. I'll be looking forward to being a part of the detecting team this afternoon." He straightened and spoke in a normal tone. "Well, I'll let you get on with your morning. See you at three o'clock."

I stared after him, wondering how much Vicky had told him. I hated the idea of her spreading unfounded rumors about Grant Walker. Sure, the guy was a jerk, but whether or not he was a murderer hadn't been proven yet. And I was barely comfortable with this clandestine interview/interrogation as it was, let alone with having someone else anxious to watch me "in action"! Plus Sean was upset enough with me without Vicky making me head of a team for her unauthorized detecting purposes.

I took another swallow of caramel heaven to soothe my apprehension, then dialed Espresso Yourself. I thanked Makayla for the coffee before asking to speak to Trey. After sweetening the deal with the promise of topping off his gas tank, he agreed to loan me his "ride," as he called it. "Just promise to have it back by five. I've got plans with a couple of the guys tonight. And take it easy on the clutch."

I readily promised and made arrangements to pick up the keys in a couple of hours. I filled the rest of the morning with answering emails and reading proposals, none of which caught my eye this time. Before I knew it, I was walking out of Espresso Yourself with another caramel latte and

Trey's car keys, getting ready to head for Dunston.

"Oh, Lila!" came a voice from behind, just as I was juggling my shoulder bag and coffee, trying to turn the lock on the Honda. I turned to see Alice Peabody fast approaching.

I sighed and faced her head-on. "Mrs. Peabody," I greeted, mustering the most pleasant tone I could manage. She looked more presentable than she had the other day at Catcher in the Rye. Today, her silver hair was swept up in a neat twist and secured with a jeweled comb and her cheeks were tinted with bright pink circles of rouge.

"I was just stopping by to see if Damian was at the agency."

I glanced at the steps leading to the agency door. "No, I'm afraid he's not. Why? Is there a message you want me to give him?"

She patted her hair. "Why, no. I was just hoping to meet him and perhaps discuss the criteria for judging the garden walk entrants."

I narrowed my eyes. "Speaking of which, what will you do now that Fannie has . . . has . . ."

"Passed," she completed for me. I swear I noticed a little upturn of her lips as she said the word. "Horrible, isn't it?" she continued, shaking her head and making a clucking sound with her tongue. "Poor Fannie. So unfortunate." Then switching gears faster than an uphill cyclist, she donned a bright smile. "Don't worry, though. As soon as I heard the news, I was able to get right over to the printers and eliminate her garden from the map. Luckily, I caught the printer just in the nick of time. Can you imagine how much it would cost to reprint all those brochures?"

Unable to think of any sort of suitable reply, I simply nodded and bid her a terse good-bye. As I headed down the road toward Dunston, I couldn't help but wonder just how much luck was involved with Alice's timing—or was it a premeditated manipulation of the worst kind? The woman rubbed me the wrong way. I was apt to think she was much more than just an over-zealous garden club organizer. In my mind, Alice Peabody was a cutthroat competitor who would stop at nothing to win this year's van Gogh award, including squashing the competition like a pesky garden bug.

The residential group home where Peggy supposedly lived was located in a neighborhood just a couple of blocks from the Dunston Police Department. As I passed the station, I couldn't help but scan the parking lot to see if Sean's vehicle was there. I briefly considered giving him a call to see if he had time for a quick lunch, but decided that I'd better let him cool down for a spell. He'd seemed pretty steamed after finding Damian at my house. Of course he'd jumped to the wrong conclusion, but that was mostly my doing. I'd foolishly planted seeds of doubt in

Sean's head. It wasn't his fault they'd grown into an ugly green monster.

I located the home, a sprawling ranch-style house surrounded by colorful gardens, with a discreet sign out front that read: *Dunston Manor: Adult Care Home.* After parking at the curb, I took a path lined with well-tended flower beds to the home's entrance. A well-dressed middle-aged woman answered the door. "Can I help you?"

"Hi. I'm Lila Wilkins. I'm here to see Mrs. Peggy Cobb."

The woman hedged. "Are you family?"

"No, I purchased my home from her a while back and wanted to ask a few questions."

After a quick up and down, the woman opened the door and waved me in. I followed her through a charming entry area and into a cozy living room. "Make yourself comfortable. I'll find Ms. Martin, our director, and tell her you're here."

While she went to fetch Ms. Martin, I took the opportunity to check out the place. It was a lovely older home that had been nicely renovated to accommodate the physical needs of its senior residents while still maintaining a homey feel. I admired the décor, with freshly painted walls in cheerful hues of yellow, rich drapery framing large sunny windows, and upholstered furniture in coordinating blue and yellow floral patterns. To me, the whole room felt like an inviting garden. If a time ever came that I wouldn't be able to manage completely on my own, I would hope to be able to live in a place just like this one.

A group of jovial seniors walked in, one of them carrying a deck of cards. "Good evening, young lady," a pink-cheeked woman greeted, her sharp blue eyes inspecting me with a discerning gaze. "Would you be interested in joining us in a game of five-card draw?"

"Oh, I'd love to, but I'm waiting for Ms. Martin."

"Aw, that's too bad," one of the gentlemen chimed in as they settled around a small card table. He was mostly bald and sported shiny wire-rimmed glasses. "We always appreciate fresh blood."

That garnished a round of chuckles from the group. Another man, this one much shorter and with a full head of hair, jumped into the spirit of things. "You're just looking for another pocket to pick, Frank." Then looking at me, he added with a wink, "Frank's won the last five games. He's about cleaned me out."

I watched as they all anted up a couple of quarters. The pink-cheeked woman started shuffling the deck, her nubby-knuckled hands working the deck like a pro. I watched in amazement as she did a one-handed cut and spread the deck faceup on the table. Then, with one finger, and a sly glance my way, she deftly flipped the deck and gathered it again before passing the cards at whirlwind speed. I became so engrossed in watching their game I didn't even hear the director approach.

"Excuse me, Ms. Wilkins?" I looked up to see a woman wearing a pinstripe pantsuit with a badge clipped around her neck. "Hi, I'm Janet Martin. I understand you'd like to visit Mrs. Cobb."

I stood and reached out to take her hand and took a closer look at her badge. It showed a long list of initialed credentials behind her name. "That's right," I replied. "I just have a couple of quick questions for her about her old house on Walden Woods Circle."

"Are you with the police?"

"The police?" I shook my head. "No, I bought the house from her and her husband a while back." Apparently the police had already questioned Mrs. Cobb. Strange that Sean hadn't mentioned it. Of course, we hadn't really talked much in the past couple of days and even if we had, I wasn't privy, as he liked to remind me, to all the details of his cases.

Janet nodded. "I see. Well, I'd be glad to take you back to see Mrs. Cobb, but I should warn you that she's not having a very good day. Some days are good, some not."

Frank spoke up from across the room. "Peggy just gets a little confused, that's all." He laid out his hand with a smug look. "Gotcha," he announced, raking in the pile of change. The others threw down their cards and groaned.

"Frank's right," Janet agreed. "Peggy may or may not be able to answer your questions."

"I understand."

"Good. She's due to have lunch in about ten minutes, so if you could keep it short, I would appreciate it."

I followed Janet down a long hallway with polished wood floors and tasteful art on the walls. As we neared the back of the house, my nose was treated to the tantalizing smell of spicy meat wafting from the kitchen area. My stomach grumbled in response.

We were halfway down the hall when I heard a whirring sound. Janet inhaled sharply and grasped the wall for support. "Watch out!" she warned just as a man in a power scooter came whizzing toward us. "Buck Cartwright, you slow down right this instant!"

"Can't," he yelled over his shoulder. "Late for a card game."

"I'm so sorry," Janet apologized, recomposing herself after our near collision. "That was our resident speedster. If I could fine him for every time I caught him speeding, I'd make a fortune." She waved toward an open door. "Here's Peggy's room."

We found Mrs. Cobb in her room, sitting in a worn recliner with a navy blue blanket tucked tightly around her legs, working a pair of knitting needles. She was a tiny woman with short white wispy hair and lively eyes, which she fixed on me. "Do I know you?"

"I'm Lila Wilkins," I started, settling into a pretty patterned chair next to her. Her room was simple, with only a bed, a couple of chairs, and a coffee table. Despite the lack of space, it was nicely decorated in a pleasing palate of beige and mauve. "I live in your old cottage on Walden Woods Circle."

Mrs. Cobb worked her jaw back and forth a few times before actually speaking. "Walden Woods Circle, you say?"

I nodded. "Yes, your old house. Do you remember it?"

Her eyes took on a dreamy look as her fingers worked the needles. "Walden Woods Circle? I used to live there?"

I wasn't sure what she was making, but it was a lot wider at the top than the bottom and seemed to curl in on itself. "That's right. You lived there with your husband, Doug."

Her eyes grew wide. "Doug?" She glanced toward Janet then back to me, her lower lip trembling slightly. "He's passed away."

Janet moved to place a hand on Peggy's shoulder and shot me a weary look. I wished I had chosen my words more carefully. "I'm sorry about your husband, Mrs. Cobb. Do you remember the cottage you lived in? It's yellow with periwinkle shutters and has an English garden out front." *Well, it used to, anyway.* "You must have enjoyed gardening," I added, trying to steer the conversation toward something more pleasant.

Her eyes moved past me and gazed out the window on the far wall. I turned to see what had captured her attention and saw she was admiring a border planting in the backyard. My eyes lingered a second, taking in the striking combination of yellow coreopsis, gray dusty miller, and blue lily of the Nile.

Janet interjected, "Peggy loves to walk through our gardens, don't you, Peggy?"

Peggy nodded and peeled her eyes from the window view and focused on me once again. A slight smile formed on her lips.

Encouraged, I started my questioning. "My son and I live in your old cottage now and we're so happy there. I can tell that you took good care of it. Do you have any children, Mrs. Cobb?"

Her smile vanished as quickly as it came. Clamping her lips tightly, she shook her head and shifted in her seat until her shoulder was turned toward me.

Janet patted her back. "It's okay, Peggy. We'll let you get back to your knitting. Someone will be by to take you to lunch in a few minutes."

At the mention of lunch, Peggy's expression

lightened a little, but she still refused to look my way, turning her focus instead back to her knitting. She began quietly humming a tune I didn't recognize, her needles making light clicking sounds as she worked.

I thanked her and stood, following Janet toward the door. We paused for a second and looked back. "Like I said, this isn't a good day for Mrs. Cobb," Janet told me in a low voice. "The police came by asking questions yesterday and it upset her terribly. We had to give her extra meds just to get her settled into bed last night."

"Does she get many visitors?"

"Rarely. Some of her old neighbors used to come by, but their visits have been few and far between. I suppose it's not easy for them. Oftentimes she's confused and becomes easily agitated with them."

My heart went out to her, this poor woman with few visitors. "Doesn't she have family around?"

Janet shook her head. "Her husband passed last year and she lost her only sibling, a sister, a few months back. She doesn't have any children."

"Oh, that's so sad."

Suddenly Mrs. Cobb spoke out, a spark of energy alighting in her eyes. "My children? They left me. I don't know where they are."

I walked back to her. "What do you mean, Mrs. Cobb? What children?"

"I'm afraid she's confused," Janet said from across the room. "You don't have any children, Mrs. Cobb. Remember?"

The old woman reached toward me, her wrinkled hands trembling outward until they landed on my arm. "Where are my children?" she asked, her eyes pleading with me for just a heartbeat before breaking away to focus on a young man entering the room. He was wearing jeans and a polo. I guessed him to be a little younger than Trey. A volunteer badge swung from a cord around his neck.

"Time for lunch, Mrs. Cobb," he declared, his voice upbeat and the smile on his face genuine. "May I walk you to the dining room?"

Immediately Peggy set aside her knitting and started working her way out of the recliner. The young man sprang into action, gently lifting her and looping her arm in his. "It's one of your favorites today, beef and noodles," he said as they shuffled toward the door.

"How long has she been this way?" I asked as soon as we were down the hall and out of earshot.

She shrugged. "A year or so, maybe. I've only worked here for six months."

"Are you sure she doesn't have children? She seemed to think she did."

"I'm afraid Peggy is prone to confusion. Most days she's fine, just a little forgetful, but the

174

police visit yesterday really upset her. She's been a little distracted ever since."

"That's too bad," I said, although a trickle of doubt entered my mind. She didn't seem confused when she asked about her children. In fact, she seemed determined that I find where they were. Or maybe I already had. Did the skeleton in my yard belong to one of Mrs. Cobb's children? While I wanted to find the identity of the young woman in my yard, I hoped it didn't turn out to be one of Peggy's children.

Chapter 12

I DOUBLE CHECKED MY DIRECTIONS several times before I hit on the right road leading to the Walker place. I was running about ten minutes late when I finally located the *Sherlock Holmes Realty* sign marking the acreage.

Franklin, Damian, and Grant were already waiting for me. "You made it," Franklin said, greeting me at my car door. Stepping onto the grass, I surveyed the area. I could see why the acreage had been so appealing to the Walkers. Located on a high ridge, just outside the Valley, the wooded land offered pristine vistas, privacy, and the convenience of not being too far from all of Inspiration Valley's amenities. "It's beautiful up here!"

"Yes, it is," Damian said, approaching with his usual charming smile. "Thank you so much for taking time out of your schedule to join us, Lila." Grant, looking a little less charming, was standing off to the side, kicking his boots in the dirt.

"Lila," Franklin began, "this is Grant Walker. Grant, Lila Wilkins, another one of the agents from Novel Idea. She's helping me take care of Damian this week. I hope you don't mind that she's joined us. Damian values her opinion as much as mine."

Damian nodded enthusiastically. "Am I right in thinking this would be a perfect locale to build my design home?" He pointed to the road. "Easy access for construction workers and my film crew. I'm thinking the setting is just right, too—slightly primitive with a beautiful view and almost twenty acres to showcase my gardens."

"I think your fans will love watching you transform this plot of land into a showcase home," Franklin added, making a sweeping gesture with his hand. "And there's more than enough room to create a dozen or more garden themes out here."

Grant's dark eyes were practically dancing with dollar signs. "It can be yours, Mr. York. All you have to do is make a good offer."

"Let's wait on Ms. Watson to get here with the paperwork before we start discussing numbers," Damian replied, a hint of his business savvy coming through. "But, this is promising. Very promising," he said as he started to pace off the land, spewing his plans for construction. As he and Franklin walked the acreage and talked garden design, I stayed behind with Grant, waiting on Ruthie's arrival.

"I was so sorry to hear about your recent loss," I said, hoping to start a conversation about Fannie.

Grant shoved his hands into the pockets of his torn jeans and shrugged. "Yeah, well . . . we weren't all that close." He glanced over his shoulder to where Franklin and Damian were looking at a cluster of wild olive trees, probably trying to decide how to tame the woody growth, which had invaded a large portion of the back of the property.

"Still, it's tragic the way she died. So senseless," I offered, trying to keep him interested. "Have the police made any progress yet?"

He narrowed his eyes. "How would I know?"

I took a step backward. "I just thought you might be keeping up on the case, since she was your stepmother."

He crossed his arms in front of his chest. "The stupid cops haven't got a clue who did in the old lady."

I cringed at his choice of words, then corrected myself. It wouldn't be wise to put him on the defense. "Who do *you* think did it?"

Grant tipped back his head and let out a raucous laugh.

"What's so funny?" Franklin interrupted as he and Damian rejoined us.

"This gal"—he jerked a thumb in my direction—"she just asked me who I thought might have killed my stepmother."

"You think that's funny?" I asked incredulously.

He laughed again, only not as heartily this time. "Only the fact that you would ask. The cops, heck, most of the people in town, seem to think I knocked her off."

I struggled to maintain my composure. Next to

me, Franklin and Damian remained speechless. I hated the fact that Damian was witnessing this little tirade. "Actually, I would think there are a lot of possibilities."

Grant leveled his gaze on me. "Oh yeah? Like what?"

I shrugged. "For starters, it could have been an intruder. Or someone that held a grudge against your stepmother." I switched gears. "By the way, thanks for letting us retrieve Eliot from the house. He's found a good home with one of my coworkers."

"No problem. I hate that ugly fur ball."

I stiffened, but ignored his comment. "While we were in your stepmother's home, I couldn't help but notice all the photos of children."

Grant rolled his eyes. "Those were her kids. At least that's what she always called those rug rats from her work."

"Rug rats?" Damian asked.

Grant looked his way. "Don't get me wrong, man. I feel for those kids, I really do. Caught up in bad situations, being shuffled from home to home. Gotta be tough. But my stepmother got too caught up in their lives." I noticed his fists clenching at his sides. "Heck, she put more time into those kids than she ever did me. And they didn't even live in our home."

"I'm sure that type of work would be consuming," I interjected, trying to soothe his rising anger. "It would take a special type of devotion to deal with broken families on a daily basis."

He kicked at the dirt some more. I felt a twinge of sadness for this young man. I remember Mama saying Grant was in his early teens when Fannie and Doc married. That's a turbulent time for most adolescent boys, even in the best of situations. Losing his doting mother at that age and living with what sounded like workaholic parents—a father who was busy with his medical practice and a mother more devoted to her foster kids than her own stepchild. No wonder he had such a tough exterior; he probably needed it to cover the vulnerability he felt inside.

I continued, my voice softer this time. "I'm sure she did the best she could, Grant."

"That's right," Franklin added. "Working with those kids must have been difficult. I know I wouldn't want that type of responsibility."

I nodded in agreement. "Social workers have to make difficult decisions. Is it possible that she made an enemy along the way? Maybe a drug-addicted mother who had her children taken from her?"

Grant considered the idea for a second, obviously mulling over another option that could lead to a murder suspect. Then he shrugged. "Beats me. I do know before my dad died, he got some nasty letters from one of his patients. I told the cops about it. They didn't seem too interested in what I had to say, though. They're hell-bent on pinning this thing on me."

Damian cleared his throat. "Sounds like Ruthie's here."

In the distance, I could hear the crunching gravel of Ruthie's approaching car. I knew I didn't have much more time for questions. "Which patient?" I prodded.

"I don't know. Some guy whose wife died. He claims my dad misdiagnosed something. He went as far in one of his letters to say he wished my dad could feel his pain."

"That's awful," I lamented. Of course, I knew that grief could often bring out the worst in people. The question was, did this man's grief drive him to the breaking point? Was it possible that poor Fannie was murdered out of revenge for a mistake made by her dead husband? It didn't make much sense, especially since Dr. Walker couldn't feel the loss of Fannie a year after he'd already died. But revenge didn't often make sense to anyone but the avenger.

"Yoo-hoo!" We both looked over to see Ruthie stepping out of her sedan and coming our way on tippy-toes to keep her heels from sticking in the ground. She must not have had time to change; she was still wearing her trademark skirt and blazer and two-inch pumps.

"Sorry I'm late," she called out, making her way to us with her arms outstretched like a tightrope walker holding a pole as she attempted to balance her heels on the uneven ground. "My last showing ran late," she finished breathlessly, finally reaching us. "Lila! I'm surprised to see you here."

"Uh, well . . . Franklin invited me to come along and offer a second opinion on the property."

"And?" She regarded me eagerly. "What do you think?"

"Yes, what *do* you think?" Damian echoed.

"I think it's a perfect spot for what you're looking to do, Damian," I replied honestly.

Ruthie let out her breath. "Good. And you'll be glad to know, Grant, that I spoke with the attorneys and everything is in order. Since Fannie had no children, her property rights transfer directly to you."

Grant clapped his hands together. "Fantastic!" He turned toward Damian and smiled. "Looks like the property is yours if you want it for my price, Mr. York."

I excused myself while the three of them started discussing details. Franklin walked me back to Trey's car. "Thanks for playing along with our little game, Franklin," I whispered. "I'm sorry if Damian found any of the discussion upsetting."

Franklin got that little gleam in his eye again. "Glad I could help. And don't worry, Lila. I told Damian all about you being our agency's own version of Nancy Drew. He didn't mind a bit that you wanted to come out and pump Grant Walker for clues."

I smiled, but my heart sank to think yet another person held out what looked like false hopes that I could solve this crime. My gaze slid to Grant, who was deep in discussion with Ruthie and Damian. "I know Vicky's convinced that Grant killed his stepmother," I said, "but for what it's worth, I don't think he did it."

Franklin's face tightened. "It's hard to say, Lila. He does seem like a very angry young man. Maybe you'd better save judgment until you have more facts."

With all the dismal distractions recently, it was nice to focus on something positive. So, first thing Thursday morning at work, I busied myself checking off the smaller items on my long list of tasks. First, I called a sluggish editor and pushed for an answer to a proposal she'd sat on for a couple of months. I knew the book and the author were a perfect fit for this particular publishing house; the editor just needed a little extra convincing. By the end of the call, I think I'd persuaded her to take a chance on the rookie writer.

Next I worked on some presubmission edits from a promising author who had a great project idea, well-developed characters, and an exciting plot, but just needed a little help strengthening the story's hook. In my experience, editors were all about that little "snappy-something" that tantalized readers and caught book buyers' attention. In essence, a good hook sells books. For this particular mystery, the main character, who had a penchant for solving mysteries, worked as a fashion designer for doggy apparel. Coming up with a hook seemed simple to me: Add more cute puppy tidbits and pitch the series as something like *The Trendy Tails Mysteries*.

I was so absorbed in my work, the morning flew by. I was surprised when I looked at my watch and saw it was already time to leave for my two o'clock meeting with Paul Cohen, the catering director at How Green Was My Valley. When I arrived at the market, I was delighted to find Paul had arranged for me to sample menu ideas for Damian's upcoming dinner event. Having worked straight through lunch, my stomach was rumbling in protest. I had to control myself to keep from diving into the tantalizing samples he'd placed before me.

"Try this one," he suggested, lifting a tiny plate of appetizers my way. We were sitting across from each other at a small table set up outside the store's catering kitchen. Paul, a short, bald, bespectacled man with a passion for food and the girth to prove it, was the success behind How Green Was My Valley's catering department. The market, which touted itself as the area's premier source for natural, organic, and local products, had launched their catering division less than a year ago. With Paul's expertise, they'd gone from offering boxed lunches and deli trays for business functions to developing an extensive menu suitable for any event. And, by the looks of things, he'd hit just the right mixture of fresh and local fare that was sure to please Damian's readers.

"What I want to achieve with this menu, and what I think is important to Damian—I do love that man's food philosophy," he added with sincere admiration, "is a sense of conscious, artful cuisine. All locally provided, of course, and of the utmost quality."

I nodded, grabbing a fork and stabbing at my caprese salad. I savored my first taste. The tomatoes had that earthy, sun-ripened taste that reminded me of Grandma's heirloom garden. Their acidity paired perfectly with the creamy sweetness of the mozzarella *fresca* and spicy, crisp basil leaves.

"That cheese is made locally at Itsa Gouda, by the way. That's the new goat farm that opened up at the old co-op on Red Fox Mountain. Isn't it delish?"

I smiled the best I could with a full mouth, and moaned my approval.

"Here's what I'm thinking," he started, passing another plate my way. "We start with passing appetizers, such as these, at the signing. I'll secure a couple of extra waitresses for the job. At the dinner, we'll offer the caprese salad first and then move to two choices for the main course." He lifted lids on two hot plates and pointed to scrumptious-looking meals. The smell that wafted from the platters caused my mouth to water. He went on, "A hickory nut–encrusted pork shoulder, which is braised in white wine, wrapped in bacon, and plated with fresh shallot jam; and for vegetarians, grilled zucchini and eggplant Parmesan. For side dishes we could offer either white asparagus with a brown butter vinaigrette, or cheese polenta with carrots."

I kept sampling and smiling. Everything was superb.

"And, here's something for a little refreshing cleanse. Try this heavenly rhubarb fruit salad." He handed me a little glass bowl brimming with colorful bits of fruit.

I took a spoonful, my tongue practically dancing with delight. "Oh my goodness. I've never tasted fruit salad like this before. It's wonderful!"

His chest puffed out. "Isn't it? I've combined green grapes, cantaloupe, strawberries, and of course, rhubarb. It's the Grand Marnier and honey that give it just the right touch of sweetness. You like?"

I took another spoonful. "Yes, I like. It's all wonderful, Paul. I couldn't be happier with your ideas and I'm sure Damian will be thrilled."

Paul sat back, a smug smile forming. "Be sure to tell him it's strictly farm-to-fork cuisine. All local and fresh. He talks a lot on his show about the importance of buying local."

"You're a fan?"

He reddened. "Absolutely. I've followed his television program for years. Even before it became as popular as it is today. I knew him from when he lived around here, you know."

"Really? You're the first person that I've run into who remembers Damian from his younger days."

"Well, that's understandable. He was nothing like he is today. I went to school with him over in Dunston. He had a difficult childhood. His father abandoned the family when Damian was in junior high. The mother struggled, trying to take care of the kids and keep food on the table." Paul shook his head. "It was difficult for Damian, I remember. He was withdrawn. A real loner. That's why people probably don't remember him. He was one of those kids that just blended into the background."

"What finally happened to the family?"

Paul shook his head. "I don't know the whole story. Something happened to the mother. No one really talked about it much and I was just a kid, so I really didn't understand what had happened at the time. Looking back on it now, I wonder if she didn't commit suicide."

"That's horrible."

Paul sighed. "Anyway, sometime during the summer before our freshman year of high school, Damian just disappeared. I always assumed he went to live with family somewhere."

"I had no idea."

"Well, you can understand, then, why I'm so interested in his career. It's a feel-good type of story. A kid, with so many strikes against him, rising above it all and finding success."

I nodded, my mind working overtime. "That is an inspiring story." One that would make for a great memoir. I wondered if Franklin knew about Damian's personal history. Nothing made a hotter bestseller than a memoir of a known celebrity, the rags-to-riches variety especially. I'd have to make sure and ask him about it later. I finalized the menu and setup details with Paul, reminding him that Makayla would be in later to select dinnerware and coordinate the setup time with him.

As I was making my way back through the store, I spied Brian, Flora's husband. He was in the produce department, filling a bag with fresh peaches. "Brian! I haven't seen you for a long time," I greeted. "How have you been?"

He turned and nodded curtly before turning back to the peaches. "Fine, thanks."

I was taken aback by his terseness. At well over six feet tall, with the build of a linebacker, Brian was, as Flora always said, "nothing but a big ol' teddy bear." Laid-back and quick to smile, Brian knew no stranger. He was usually the epitome of friendliness. "Is something wrong, Brian?"

"No, I'm just busy," he replied with a clenched jaw as he placed his selection into a cloth tote bag and strolled away without a backward glance. *Now what was that about?* As I stared after him, it hit me that something big must be going on with Flora. After seeing the picture of her at Fannie's house, I'd been meaning to ask if she was once a foster child, but hadn't had a chance. But it would make sense that such a personal connection with Fannie could be behind Flora's sudden change in demeanor. Losing someone instrumental in your life would upset even the happiest person. But now Brian's disconcerting attitude made me wonder if there was something else going on. Then I recalled the way Flora huffed and puffed after climbing the outside steps to the agency the day before; the excessive sweating and her pale skin.

I jogged after him, catching him just before he reached the checkout lane. "Is it Flora?" I inquired, panic seeping into my voice. "Is she ill or some-thing? I've noticed she's been acting strangely lately."

Brian wheeled and glared down at me, his usually bright eyes flashing with darkness. "I know it's hard for you to do, Lila. But for once, just mind your own damn business."

I flinched and felt heat rising in my cheeks as if they'd been slapped. I opened my mouth to respond, but Brian's vehement tone had struck me dumb. Instead, I glanced around nervously, wondering who else had witnessed his outburst. Luckily, the other customers in line seemed not to notice our heated exchange.

In the meantime, Brian starting unloading his items on the conveyer belt, turning his back to me. Obviously, the subject was closed, so I simply left, feeling confused and helpless. What was going on with Flora and Brian? We'd always been friends. In fact, Sean and I often met up with them after work at the James Joyce Pub for dinner, drinks, and always a ton of laughs. What could possibly be so horrible that they couldn't share it with me?

I decided to forgo the rest of the afternoon at work and just head home. My mind reeled with questions about my friend as I maneuvered my Vespa back toward the center of town. Did Fannie's photo mean that Flora herself had once been a foster child? If so, why all the secrecy? Thousands of children were touched in some way by the foster care system. There must be more to it.

Come to think of it, Flora had always been a champion of children, whether it was assuring that the children's books our agency represented were of the most outstanding quality, doting on her nephews and nieces, or knitting hats for patients of the children's cancer center. I always just assumed it was her nature to love children, but it dawned on me that I'd seen a different, more protective side of Flora before.

When I'd first started with the agency, before we knew a local man was to become a well-noted posthumous author, we thought of him as the town vagrant. Practically homeless, he spent his days wandering from bench to bench, loitering in parks and receiving handouts from local business owners. One of his frequented spots was the Wonderland Playground, where he'd sit and watch the children for hours on end.

I remember Flora was upset about this man's presence at the playground. She'd even called the police on him several times. At the time, I thought she was overreacting, inappropriately judging him by his appearances, a standard that proved impetuous after the real reason for his vagrantlike tendencies was revealed. Only now that I was looking back on it, maybe Flora wasn't over-reacting, but simply *reacting* to something from her past. Perhaps something had transpired during her childhood that caused her to spend her adulthood trying to compensate for her own losses.

Friday morning, I once again skipped my usual stop at Espresso Yourself and took the steps leading to the agency two at a time. I'd spent most of the night awake, before finally coming to the conclusion that I needed to address my concerns to Flora directly. Despite Brian's warning to mind my own business, I decided that Flora's well-being *was* my business. I was her friend, after all. And if something was bothering her, I wanted to help. I intended to go directly to her office and clean up the bad air between us.

Only, once inside the reception area, I stopped short at the sight of Alice Peabody standing in front of Vicky's desk, arms flailing and shoulders gyrating as she berated our office manager. "How dare you tell the police that I had something to do with Fannie's murder! I bet you did that just so you could knock me out of the competition."

Vicky stood straight-backed, jutted her chin out, and placed her hands on her hips. "I would never do such a thing. I'm not the type of person who would damage someone's reputation for the sake of a competition." Eliot's whiskers twitched as he curiously watched the scene from the waiting area's chair.

Alice shook her fist in Vicky's face. "Don't you stand there and lie to me, Vicky Crump. You pretend to be all prim and proper, but I know how competitive you can be. Don't forget it was that competitiveness that got you kicked off the garden club board in the first place."

Eliot uncurled and jumped down from the chair,

moving across the room with a hunched back and a low growl in his throat. I couldn't be sure, but I thought I heard Vicky growl, too, as she took a step closer to Alice. "No, Alice. The reason I got kicked off the board is because you *claimed* you saw me sabotage Doris Mosby's prize Belinda rose plant, but there's no—"

"Whoa!" I interjected, stepping between the two of them before they came to blows. "What's going on here?"

Vicky pointed her finger. "I went to fill Eliot's water bowl and when I came back I found Alice standing here in the reception area. She immediately started accusing me of telling the police that she killed Fannie."

"Well, you must have," Alice reiterated. "Some officer came by my place late yesterday afternoon to interview me. He said a reliable source suggested that I might have motive to want Fannie dead. Who else would say such a thing?"

Slowly Vicky turned her head from her adversary and looked my way, narrowing her eyes at me. "Who else indeed," she muttered. Then turning back to Alice, she added, "Ms. Wilkins was present the entire time I was interviewed. She can vouch for the fact that I said no such thing, can't you, Lila?"

I bobbed my head, but kept my mouth shut. Mostly because I knew my lower lip was trembling. I was terrified Vicky was going to reveal that I was the one who ratted Alice out to the cops. Heaven knows what the crazed rose gardener might do to me then. Wait for an opportune time and spade me to death? I shivered.

We turned at the sound of footsteps coming down the hall. Bentley and Franklin spilled into the reception area with Damian right behind them. He shot me a quizzical look as Bentley inserted herself into the scene. "What exactly is going on out here?" she demanded, glaring at Vicky and soliciting a hiss from Eliot, his tail bristling as he stood by Vicky's feet.

"I'm sorry for the interruption, Ms. Burlington-Duke," Vicky said, scooping up the feline and stroking his fur until a low purring sound started. "Just a little misunderstanding. Everything is under control now."

Alice, who seemed to have quickly forgotten the previous hubbub, turned her focus to Damian, who hovered quietly behind Bentley and Franklin. Her scowl turned upward to a sappy sweet smile. "Is this the famous Damian York?" she inquired. With her hand outstretched, she brushed past Bentley and Franklin. "I'm Alice Peabody, president of the Dirty Dozen. It's such a pleasure, Mr. York."

The sudden change in Alice's demeanor gave me mental whiplash. I watched in amazement as she shook Damian's hand and poured on the charm. "On behalf of the garden club, let me thank you for agreeing to judge this year's van Gogh contest. We feel so fortunate to have someone of your expertise and reputation judge our modest competition."

Damian took her hand and flashed a little charm. "My pleasure, Ms. Peabody. And I'm sure your roses will be a treat to see."

Vicky and I exchanged a wide-eyed look. Alice's emotional flip-flop had left us both a bit breathless.

I glanced over to where Alice had cornered Damian, the poor guy's back against the wall as she stood in front of him, hand over her chest and batting her lashes like a silent film star. I swear she was about to swoon. "I'm especially looking forward to your expert opinion of my humble garden. I have worked so hard this year to cultivate award-worthy roses."

A pained expression crossed Damian's face, but he recovered well. "I'm sure your garden will be a pleasure to see," he managed, diplomatically.

Alice gasped with delight and shook his hand again, pumping it over and over while she gushed on about all the work she put into her garden: fertilizing this, pruning that, and even mentioning some strange solution she concocted with mouthwash and vinegar to thwart powdery mildew. "Oh," she continued, "we'll have to get together soon and discuss the regulations for judging this year's van Gogh contest. May I call you and set up a time?"

Damian politely withdrew his hand and shoved it into his pocket.

Franklin stepped forward. "Just call the office, Mrs. Peabody, and I'll be happy to schedule a time for you and Damian to meet."

Unabashed, Alice gushed a little more before finally turning to leave. "Well then, I must bid you all adieu. I'm off to tend to my roses." She moved to the exit, turning to wiggle her fingers and flash yet another sappy sweet smile toward Damian. "As you know, a gardener's job is never done."

"Well!" Bentley exclaimed. "I have no idea what that was all about." She held up her hand. "Nor do I want to know. Let's just all get back to work, shall we." She clapped her hands together. "Chop-chop, people. Damian's big event is only one week away." Then turning to me she added, "Come to my office right away. I have something to discuss with you."

My heart did a little somersault. Whenever Bentley said she had something to discuss, it meant she'd been scheming. Nine times out of ten, when her schemes included me, it meant I was in for something unpleasant.

Before taking off to follow Bentley, I turned quickly to Vicky. She'd just returned Eliot to his perch and was settling behind her desk. "Thanks for not throwing me under the bus. I hate to think what Alice might have done to me if she'd known I was the one that sicced the police on her."

Vicky raised her brow and straightened a stack of papers. "Of course, Lila. Besides, we already know who the real killer is, don't we?" she said with a pointed look. Then her ironclad façade cracked a little. "Although, I have to admit, I was caught off guard by Alice's erratic behavior."

I patted her hand. "Don't let it ruin your whole day, Vicky. By the way, have you seen Flora this morning?"

"She was in earlier, but left, saying she had some sort of appointment."

I sighed. "I was hoping to catch her first thing. Did she say when she'd be back?"

Vicky shook her head and started to reply, but stopped short when Bentley bellowed down the hall. "Lila! In my office!"

I scurried to comply, finding her seated behind her desk, impatiently tapping her silver-plated fountain pen. "Glad to see you're finally ready to join us, Lila." She pointed the pen toward an extra chair someone had dragged in from the conference room. Franklin and Damian were already occupying her two guest chairs. "Take a seat. This won't take much time. I just wanted to inform you that today is your lucky day."

I cringed. This was going to be worse than I'd initially thought.

She continued, "I just got off the phone with

Detective Griffiths and he's assured me that all restrictions on your yard have been lifted. The crime scene tape will come down this morning."

"Oh really?" I replied apprehensively. Normally that would be good news, but with Bentley, good news meant good for her, not necessarily me.

"I also spoke with Damian's producer this morning and we've decided a great way to promote his upcoming event was to have a mini yard makeover."

"A yard makeover?" Oh no. I knew where this was heading.

"Just something small," Damian interjected. "Perhaps the outdoor reading nook we discussed the other day."

Bentley nodded fervently. "Perfect. A reading nook for a literary agent. Of course, you'll mention Novel Idea by name."

"Of course," Damian agreed. "And there'll be a lot of mentions regarding next weekend's signing on my national broadcast. Doing a makeover of a garden in the area of the book signing will surely bolster exposure. Plus the local news is going to recommend their viewers watch the national broadcast because of the community-interest angle, so it'll attract a lot of attention at all levels."

Franklin, who'd been a quiet observer so far, finally jumped into the conversation. "I think it's a wonderful way to draw local and, who knows, maybe national, too, book buyers to our event, don't you, Lila?"

"Plus," Damian added, "you'll get a little free landscaping out of the deal. My producers will cover all expenses. You just have to be up and ready to go first thing tomorrow morning."

"First thing . . . when?"

"Tomorrow. My film crew will be by at the crack of dawn."

"Great," I replied, forcing a smile.

"There's more good news," Franklin added. "Damian's offer on the Walker land has been accepted. He'll break ground on his new showcase home later this summer."

Damian nodded enthusiastically. "And while overseeing the construction, I plan to pen my next book: *Nature-Inspired Décor for Every Room*."

A tiny squeal emitted from Bentley. "Sure to be a bestseller! What do you say we all head downstairs to Espresso Yourself and celebrate with coffee? My treat."

Sounded good to me. With the way things were going, I'd need a hit of caffeine to get through my day. I shouldered my purse and followed the group out the back door.

After an extralong coffee break and listening to Bentley's numerous reiterations of her most lucrative deal-closing stories, I was sufficiently fueled to spend the rest of the afternoon getting work done. The first thing I did was begin suggesting revisions for the cozy English mystery I'd just signed. The author had yet to title the work, so I started brainstorming some possibilities. Considering the protagonist was a pub owner, I thought maybe the title should reflect something to do with an English tavern. I pulled out a legal pad and began scribbling: *Death on Tap, Brews and Clues* . . . no, that wasn't the feel I was going for. Moaning under my breath, I scratched those out and let my pen hover over the paper while I contemplated more. My mind wandered to one of my favorite authors, Martha Grimes, who wrote the series featuring the protagonist Richard Jury. Each of those books was centered on English-style pubs and, if I remembered correctly, was titled after famous pubs from around the world, not just in England. It had been years since I read the series, but I still remembered titles like *The Dirty Duck, The Old Silent*, and of course, *The Horse You Came In On*. I'd actually been to the pub Grimes named that book after. It was on Thames Street in Baltimore, and as I recalled, it seemed nothing like the pub described in Grimes's English mystery. Nonetheless, it was a great title.

Maybe . . . just maybe . . . I put down my pen and took to my keyboard, searching for the author's synopsis. Scanning it, I found the name of her pub, the Tumble Inn. I smiled. I knew just the title: *Tumble Inn and Die: An English Pub Mystery*. We could even market it with something like "Callie Flannigan, spirited pub owner and amateur sleuth, serves up shots and stirs in murder . . ." Blah, blah, blah. I leaned back in my chair and exhaled, clasping my hands behind my head. Helping an author polish a book proposal was like putting icing on a cake—turning something already good into something perfectly scrumptious, ready to be devoured by hungry readers. I chuckled to myself. Even as a kid, I'd duck out of the kitchen when Mama was going to all the work of measuring, pouring, and stirring up a cake, just to return later to slather on the frosting and add little touches of candied ornaments. Guess I was a polisher, even back then.

By quitting time, I'd typed up almost five pages of editing suggestions for the author. Not that the book was far off the mark, but I wanted to present the most marketable version to editors. I had no doubt that if the author followed my advice, she'd find herself with a contract from one of the top five publishing houses. Then in one of Bentley's next glowing stories of her agency's recent accomplishments my new author would be right up there with the other gold stars.

I decided to celebrate my work accomplishments with takeout from Wild Ginger, the local Chinese restaurant. I'd also been meaning to talk to Trey about his argument with Sean and was hoping that a little of his favorite Asian dish, beef and broccoli, might set the right tone for that conversation. Trey always did discuss things better with a full stomach.

When I pulled in front of the house a while later, I was surprised to find my mother's truck parked in the drive. "Mama?" I called out, juggling the door, my bag, and the take-out order. "Trey!"

"In the kitchen, Mom."

By the way the house smelled, I should have guessed where they were. I followed the sweet scent of warm banana bread through the family room and into the kitchen, finding them bent over a large mixing bowl, adding ingredients. There were already several loaves of bread cooling on my counter. "What's this?" I asked, smiling at the sight before me. Mama and Trey were so much alike: both tall and sinewy—built for action. Trey also possessed a healthy dose of my mother's uncanny intuition, something I learned last spring when he came to my rescue just in the nick of time to save me from a treacherous death at the hands of a coldhearted murderer. Now, it looked like he shared Mama's baking abilities, also.

"Just teachin' my grandson the family secret," Mama said, her face beaming with pride.

"I've already made a dozen loaves," Trey added. "Nana's going to freeze them for the church bazaar at the end of the month."

"Hope you'll save a couple loaves for me." I

plopped the take-out bags onto the table. "Anyone have time for a little break? I brought Chinese. I didn't know you were going to be here, Mama, but you know how much there usually is. I can never eat it all by myself."

Trey dropped the stirring spoon and headed straight for the bags. "Beef and broccoli?"

"Of course. And sesame chicken," I replied, grabbing three forks and a few cold sodas from the fridge.

"Don't mind if I do," Mama said, pulling up her own chair. "I was fixin' on just stayin' here tonight, if that's okay."

"Sure, Mama. You and Trey planning on baking banana bread all night or something?"

She glanced his way, then back at me. "We might," she hedged.

Trey looked up from his container of beef and broccoli and squinted at us. Sensing something was up, he grabbed his soda and stood. "Mind if I eat in front of the television?" he asked me.

I answered by tipping my head toward the family room, never quite taking my eyes off Mama. *What in the world is going on now?*

"Sorry, sug," she started as soon as Trey was out of the room. "I just have the need to be close to y'all right now. Couldn't explain it even if I wanted to." She glanced around and leaned forward. "I didn't want to say anything in front of the child, but I just have this feelin'."

"A feeling of what?"

"Dread. A deep-down feelin' of dread. Like some sort of bad thing is comin' for our family."

Suddenly sesame chicken didn't sound so good. I put down my fork and sat back in my chair with a thud. No matter how odd, or even downright weird they seemed, my mother's bad feelings usually held merit. Oh, sometimes I think she liked playing the part of drama queen, talking up her feelings as if she were an all-knowing sage or some sort of prophet, but nine times out of ten, they did precede something bad. Like the time when I was a teen and she got one of her "feelings" right before the big dance. Well, I hadn't even made it to the first song before I got in a fight with my best friend, spilled punch down my dress, and caught my date in a dark corner with Della Mae Thompson. Oh, then there was my wedding day. She rushed in at the last minute and instead of doing that motherly thing of helping me with my veil or giving me a special family heirloom, she held out a tarot card. "I've got a bad feelin' about this marriage," she'd said. I'd thought at the time that it was the worst thing any mother could do: spoil her own daughter's wedding day with her dramatics. But oh, if only I had listened.

"You know what, Mama," I finally said. "You can stay as long as you like."

• • •

A fierce pounding from the front of the house woke me at the crack of dawn Saturday morning. I sat straight up in bed. "Oh no. Of all the mornings to oversleep!"

"Well, if that don't beat all!" I heard my mother call out from the front of the house. "Looks like you've got company, sug."

I ran down the hall and passed Trey and Mama, who were already dressed and had coffee cups in their hands, and skidded to a stop at the front window. I cracked the curtains and peered through. "It's Damian! I forgot to tell you they're filming a segment for his program here this morning." Guess with all the talk of dread and doom the night before, I'd forgotten to mention the yard makeover.

"Here? Why our house?" Trey asked, running a hand through his hair.

I rolled my eyes. "One of Bentley's brilliant ideas."

The doorbell rang. I jumped and scurried for my bedroom. "Can you stall them, Mama?" I asked from down the hall. "I just need to fix up a bit."

I heard her answering the door as I hopped in for a quick shower, avoiding my hair, because I certainly didn't have time for blow-drying. After toweling off, I tore through my closet for something to wear. Damian hadn't been very specific about what part I would play in the filming of my yard project. Hopefully, I wouldn't be interviewed on camera, or worse yet, be expected to participate in the actual work. Not that I minded hard work, but I cringed at the thought of my clumsy gardening skills being forever archived on film.

After a few more passes through my racks, I settled on a pair of dark wash cropped jeans and a tan madras plaid shirt. I thought the hues of brown set off my coffee-colored eyes, which would be a bonus if I did have to be on camera. As for the rest of me, things weren't going to be so easy. My hair looked like a massive fur ball, but no matter how much I brushed, it seemed to get worse. Finally, I slicked it back into a ponytail, slathered on some lipstick, and called it good.

About thirty minutes later, I found Mama in the kitchen, flipping pancakes like crazy. Trey, Damian, and a couple of other guys were at the table, hunched over tall stacks of steaming flapjacks. The syrup bottle was being passed around at breakneck speed.

"There she is," Mama said, handing me my own plate. "Now eat up. You'll need a full stomach to take on today."

After several minutes of grateful munching and smacking sounds, a chorus of thank-yous rang out from the film crew guys as they carried their empty plates to the sink and excused themselves to get things started outside. After they'd left, my mother turned to Damian and snatched up his empty plate. "Let me just fill that back up for you," she cooed. "A man like you needs a good breakfast."

Damian flashed his smile. "Oh, I really couldn't eat another bite. But your pancakes are simply amazing, Althea."

"Oh, *psshh,*" she said with obvious delight. My eyes darted over to Trey, who met my gaze with a slightly raised brow. I could scarcely believe it. Mama was smitten by Damian's good looks.

"Though it's fittin' you'd say that," she continued. "Folks around here do call me the Amazing Althea."

I quickly swallowed my mouthful of pancakes and opened my mouth to intervene, but she was too fast.

"I do readin's, you know?"

"Mama, I don't think—"

Damian put down his fork. "Readings? Are you an editor?"

Trey spoke up, a hint of pride evident in his tone. "No, my grandmother reads people. Like in psychic readings."

I closed my eyes and winced as Mama elaborated. "That's right. And I'd be tickled pink to lay out cards for you. Free of charge, of course," she added.

Damian ran his hand over his chin. "Cards?"

Encouraged by his curiosity, Mama turned from the sink, reached into her apron pocket, and withdrew her ever-handy tarot cards. She pulled out a chair and spread the deck in front of him. "Tarot cards. They're my specialty."

Damian's eyes grew round. "Well, I don't know."

I placed my plate of half-eaten pancakes on the counter with a thud. "I'm afraid Damian doesn't have time for that now, Mama. Maybe later."

Pushing back from the table, a relieved Damian agreed, said good-bye to Trey, and thanked my mother for her hospitality. "But I'd love to take you up on your generous offer another time," he added, nodding toward the tarot deck and bringing another girlish smile to my mother's face.

As soon as we were outside, I began to apologize. "Sorry about that. My mother means well, she just doesn't realize that not everyone's a believer."

The little lines around Damian's eyes crinkled. "Actually, I think your mother is very charming."

I had to chuckle a little. I'd never actually heard anyone call my mother charming. I'd add that to the long list of adjectives I'd heard over the years when people discussed my mother. Words like "straight-talking," "flamboyant," even "ornery," and of course—"amazing." Always amazing.

We were making our way to the corner of the

yard where Damian's crew was gathered with what looked like enough film equipment to shoot a major movie when suddenly nerves kicked in and I wished I hadn't eaten any pancakes at all.

Damian cast a sad look toward my foundation, where the row of hawthorns once lived. "Are the police any closer to discovering the identity of the young woman who was found here?"

"I'm afraid not, but I've been doing a little checking of my own."

He raised a brow. "Is that right?"

"We're ready for you, Damian," one of the guys called impatiently.

Damian held up his hand, "Be right there, guys." He chuckled. "Franklin was telling me that you have a bit of Nancy Drew in you."

"Oh, please don't listen to everything people say about me. Most of it isn't true."

"Most of it?" he asked with a wink, then we both chuckled again.

"By the way," I continued, "a friend of yours is catering the dinner next week: Paul Cohen. Do you remember him? He says he knew you way back when."

He blinked a few times. "No, that name doesn't sound familiar." He turned to check the crew's position and turned back with an enthusiastic expression. "What do you say we get to work on your outdoor reading nook?"

I met his enthusiasm with my own lukewarm

response. "Sounds wonderful," I said, but inside I was really wondering just how wonderful it would be. First, the idea of being on television, a national broadcast even, made me about half sick with nerves. I was a behind-the-scenes type of gal: the agent who helped form bestselling authors, the mom who nurtured and raised the successful college student, the daughter who endorsed the antics of the Amazing Althea. Well, most of the time, anyway. Point being, now that I thought about it, I'd successfully avoided the limelight my whole life, and being featured on national television wasn't my cup of tea. Nor was having professionals redo my yard, turning it into something Damian's fans would love. But, would *I* love it? I'd always dreamed of converting my gardens into something that resembled the soft, fuzzy hues that I admired in the paintings of the famous Impressionists. What if these so-called professionals gave me something more like . . . well, like splatter art? Or a starkly sterile Zen garden, like an india ink drawing? What then?

"Lila?" Damian called out, pulling me from my gloomy reverie.

"Coming," I replied, sighing deeply and cursing Bentley under my breath.

Chapter 13

BY THE TIME I REACHED THE OFFICE Monday morning, the heat had already gripped the day in a viselike hold, squeezing the colorful energy out of my world. Everywhere I looked, things seemed droopy. Flowers bowed under the scorching sun and blades of grass were tinged brown around the edges and bent with stress. Even Eliot's normally bushy tail seemed deflated. "Good boy," I said, grazing my fingertips along his curled spine. He was coiled into a tight, fuzzy ball on his usual chair in our reception area.

Vicky appeared, balancing a full bowl of water. She placed it on the floor next to her desk on a rubber mat she'd brought in for Eliot's food and water. "How did the filming go?" she asked.

"Really well," I admitted, still stroking Eliot's fur. Truth was, I was feeling a bit guilty about my previous attitude toward the makeover. The whole thing went much better than I ever anticipated. After a couple of short interview takes, my participation in the whole affair was limited to the sidelines, where I watched the crew transform the drab, barren corner of my yard into a lush outdoor living area. One that I actually liked! Plus, the filming, which took all of Saturday and didn't wrap up until late Sunday afternoon, turned out to be a fascinating venture. "They're rushing it through editing and hope to air by midweek on our local channel. Damian is also doing a teaser for the national broadcast on tonight's evening news." Eliot let out a low meow as I accidently rubbed in the wrong direction. I quickly pulled away my hand. "Sorry fellow." I turned back to Vicky. "My yard project looks great, but I hope the new plantings don't go into shock with this heat."

"Tell me about it. I spent the whole weekend watering my garden. I sure hope this weather doesn't carry through the week. Heat like this will discourage people from coming to the garden walk on Saturday."

I sighed. "And Damian's signing." I started toward my office, then stopped. "Oh, I was hoping to talk a few things over with Flora before this morning's status meeting. Is she in yet?"

Vicky nodded and pointed down the hall as she began firing up her computer. She'd probably have ten queries ready for my appraisal before I even got settled in my office.

I rapped lightly on Flora's door. "Come in!" She glanced up as I entered and quickly capped her fountain pen and shuffled the paper she was reading to the bottom of one of her piles. "Oh, it's you, Lila." I noted the downward turn in her voice. "I'm a little busy now."

I walked across the room and stood directly in

front of her desk. "Certainly not too busy for a friend."

She eyed me warily.

"We are still friends, aren't we, Flora?"

My directness seemed to frustrate her. Her eyes darted around the room, avoiding my gaze. "Of course we are," she replied with a shortened breath. She extracted her hankie and began dabbing her forehead with ink-stained fingers.

"Then tell me what's been bothering you. Are you ill? Because if so, I want to be here for you."

She let out a long, exaggerated sigh. "No, I'm not ill."

Her upholstered chair let out a little puff of air as I plopped into it, determined to stay until I got to the bottom of things. Folding my hands in my lap, I let my eyes wander around her office while she nervously shuffled more paperwork. I noticed her bookshelves seemed to be crowded with more books than ever. Flora represented both children's book authors and romance authors and was one of the agency's most consistent agents. She usually signed several top-selling authors a year. "Have you come across any new, promising authors recently?" I asked, trying to break the awkwardness and initiate some sort of conversation.

Except Flora's expression only seemed to grow tighter as she nodded and pretended to be occupied with her paperwork.

"You'll have to talk to me eventually, Flora.

We'll need to discuss this weekend's event and what you've come up with for a cake."

She looked up, her eyes widening. I noticed a slight tremor in her hand as she extracted a piece of paper from atop her whitewashed desk. "Of course. I did mean to discuss this with you. After talking to Nell at Sixpence Bakery, we came up with something slightly different than a cake."

"Different?" I leaned forward and took the sheet of paper. It was an order form for about three dozen baked pies.

"I do hope you don't mind. It's just that after considering the overall theme of the dinner, we decided that the venue called for something more down-to-earth than a tiered cake. Besides, I don't know if you noticed, but several of the photo layouts in *Perfect Outdoor Spaces* feature pies. Flaky crusts, perfectly brown lattice bursting with sweet berries or . . ." Her eyes took on a dreamy look. It was the happiest I'd seen her in a while. "Or mile-high meringue." She pointed down at the list. "Lemon meringue is my favorite. I ordered extra."

I stared at the list, dumbstruck, until a tiny whimper caused me to look up. Flora covered her mouth with trembling fingers, tears threatening the edges of her eyes. "You hate the idea."

"What? No, Flora. I think it's wonderful." I let out a nervous little laugh. "Actually, it's the best

214

thing since apple pie," I said, trying to lighten the air.

But she kept crying. I leaned across the desk, taking both her hands in mine. It was time to get to the bottom of things. "I was at Fannie's house the other day," I started. "And I saw a framed picture of you as a little girl. It was mixed in with a bunch of other pictures of kids. Kids Vicky explained were Fannie's clients from the days when she worked as a social worker placing kids in foster homes."

Flora nodded, pulling one hand away to snatch her handkerchief from the desktop and hold it to her face.

I continued, "I ran into Brian at the market a couple days ago. He was adamant that I mind my own business about all this, Flora, but I'm not going to do that. Something's bothering you and I want to help."

She dabbed under her eyes and nodded. "You're right. It'll be a relief to unburden myself."

I leaned back, gripped my knee, dread settling in the pit of my stomach. What did she mean by "unburden" herself? Was Flora somehow involved with Fannie's death? Certainly someone as gentle and loving as Flora could never strike another person, let alone bludgeon them with a garden spade. I shook my head. No, it just wasn't possible. But perhaps . . . "Flora, do you know something about Fannie's death?" I finally asked.

She stopped dabbing and moved her hand to her heart. "Why heavens, no! Why would you ask something like that?"

I exhaled with relief and shrugged. Still, what could possibly be eating at Flora?

She opened her desk drawer, removing a tin of mints. She opened it and passed it my way. "Mint?"

"No, Flora. Now quit stalling and tell me what's going on," I pleaded.

She dropped the mints back in her drawer. She kept her gaze on her desk as she started to explain. "It's the young woman buried in your yard. I think her death is all my fault."

My breath caught. Her words hit me like a bombshell. "What do you mean?"

Her face puckered and she broke into another round of crying, choking out an explanation between sobs. "It's the Cobbs . . . I was placed with them for a while . . . right there in your little cottage. It's such a sweet and happy place now . . . but back then . . . back then it was awful . . . Doug Cobb was nothing more than a mean drunk . . . I finally ran away."

"Oh, Flora. Did he . . . did he hurt you?"

She swiped at her tears. "Not in the way you're thinking. But he would lose his temper. Especially when he was drinking, which was often. He'd push me around. He even struck me a few times. And I think Peggy was scared of him, too."

I shook my head in disbelief. "You ran away? Where'd you go?"

"I stayed with friends here and there. But when that didn't work out, I was out on the streets."

My hand flew to my throat. "That's horrible. I'm so sorry, Flora. I never knew."

"No, of course not. It's not something I talk about. It's painful to think back to those years and how alone I felt. If it weren't for Brian . . . that's why I always think of him as my hero. Because he saved me from what could have been a lost life." She paused and collected herself, wiping under her eyes and blowing her nose, before continuing. "You see, I stumbled into a soup kitchen one day. He just happened to be there, volunteering. He wasn't much older than me, maybe nineteen." Her eyes took on a faraway look and I noticed that a quiet peacefulness came over her. "He approached me after the meal and asked some questions. I can't explain it, but we seemed to instantly connect. He always brought me a book he'd finished reading and encouraged me to read it. We started seeing each other more often and sometimes just talking for hours, at first about books, then eventually, about everything. He was so kind and encouraging. I fell in love with reading . . . and with Brian. Can you imagine, a girl like me with a handsome young man from a well-to-do family? I felt like a fairy-tale princess."

My own eyes were misting over. "That's one of

the most beautiful love stories I've ever heard." I clasped my hand over hers again. "But, I don't understand why you feel you may have had something to do with the young woman's death. Did you know her?"

Her gaze moved downward. "No, but don't you see? If only I would have told someone about Doug Cobb's temper. Warned someone at the foster care agency not to place another child in their home . . ." She let out a shaky breath. "Maybe her death could have been prevented. Instead, I just ran away."

"You were only a child, Flora. None of this is your fault. None of it," I emphasized. "But you do have an obligation to take what you know to the police. You have the key to helping them identify the young woman. To possibly bringing peace to her family."

Flora lifted her shoulders and adjusted her blouse. "You're absolutely right. I'll give them a call soon."

I stood, reached into my bag, and took out my cell. "How about now?" I said, punching in Sean's number. "I'll call Sean. He's working the case. Besides, it would be so much easier to explain this to someone you know, right? And get it behind you?"

She hesitated, then nodded, taking a couple more deep breaths as I connected with Sean and explained the situation. He was already in the

Valley taking care of some other business, so he said he'd stop by soon and take Flora's statement.

After disconnecting with Sean, I walked around Flora's desk, leaned down, and gave her a quick hug. "I know this is hard for you, but you're doing the right thing by coming forward with what you know."

She sighed, a small smile forming on her lips. "Thank you, Lila. I do feel much better."

I left Flora's office, mindful of the time. If I got busy, I could just make it through a few emails, duck downstairs, grab a coffee at Espresso Yourself, and have a little time left over to visit with Makayla before Bentley's ten o'clock status meeting. My boss liked to start the week off by reviewing our current projects and passing out tasks. With Damian's signing at the end of the week, her to-do list was sure to be a doozy. A caramel latte and Makayla's happy face were just what I needed to put myself in the right frame of mind.

I breezed into my office, threw my purse in my desk drawer, and pushed the button to boot up my computer. That's when I noticed the envelope on the corner of my desk with my name scratched in black ink across the front. For some reason, the hairs on the back of my arms prickled. I slowly reached over and picked up the envelope, staring at the angry handwriting for a few seconds before finally slitting the seal. I opened the threefold sheet of typing paper, a knot of fear forming in my belly as I read the words: *Mind your own business or you'll end up like Fannie.*

My free hand jerked to my mouth, stifling the scream that threatened to form. Taking a few deep breaths, I forced myself to stay calm and think rationally. Someone had been in my office this morning, and no one gets by Vicky unnoticed.

Clutching the letter, I made my way down the hall and back to Vicky's desk. As I approached, she looked up from the stack of brochures she was sorting. "What is it, Lila? You look as white as a ghost."

I held out the letter for her. "Who's been in this office this morning?"

She took the letter, glanced at it, and immediately dropped it onto the desk as if the paper were caustic to the touch. "This is a death threat, Lila. You should know better than to handle it this way." She reached for the phone receiver. "What if you've ruined the opportunity for the police to lift prints? I'm calling them right now."

"No need. Sean is already on his way. He should be here in just a few minutes. I asked you who was in here this morning." Already my mind churned as I realized all the agents would already be in the office, plus, if any . . . I glanced down at the brochures on her desk and tapped the pile with my forefinger. "How did these get here?"

She hung up the phone and stared blankly at the brochures.

I repeated my question. "When did these arrive?"

"Just twenty minutes ago. That insufferable woman brought them over."

"Alice Peabody?"

"Yes. Why?"

"Did she go anyplace else in the office?"

"No . . . oh, wait." She looked at me, realization shining in her shrewd eyes. "She was carrying a large box of brochures when she came in and left the door ajar behind her. Eliot shot out." Vicky's back stiffened defensively. "I had to go after him. But I was only gone a few minutes."

"Long enough for her to slip into my office and leave this?"

Vicky fidgeted in her seat and began straightening the pile of brochures. "It's possible, I guess."

I was at a loss for words. Was Alice Peabody crazy enough to come into this agency and leave a threatening letter on my desk? It seemed awfully nervy. Perhaps that was her or some- one's intent—to show that they could invade my personal fortress. Reach me anywhere. To emphasize that there was no place where I was safe. Well, they'd done a fine job of it! I needed to speak to Bentley right away. Maybe she could install some sort of security system. Of course, what would that really do? If the killer could get into my office, he or she could find me anywhere.

"Sit down, Lila," Vicky ordered. "You're not looking well."

I moved to the guest chair, lifted Eliot onto my lap, and settled in to wait for Sean. Still, my mind was reeling with horrible thoughts. The killer had to be someone familiar. Someone the other agents trusted enough to be inside the agency. Someone who could walk right in here and not seem suspicious.

Vicky picked up the receiver and punched another number. This time, she was dialing Bentley's office, informing her of what had transpired. A few seconds later, I heard her door fly open and the sound of heels clacking down the hallway. Franklin and Damian were right on her heels.

"What's going on out here?" Bentley asked.

Damian moved to my side. "Lila? What's wrong? You look sick. Are you okay?"

Vicky spoke up. "She found a threatening letter on her desk and I'm afraid she's in shock. Detective Griffiths is on his way." She excused herself and went to fetch a glass of water for me. Meanwhile everyone else gathered around, fussing and asking questions about the letter, still lying open on Vicky's desk. Before I knew it, all the agents except Flora had gathered in the reception area, the air buzzing with a mixture of excitement and apprehension.

"So, the killer was probably here. Right in our own office?" Zach asked, his eyes bugging out. "Wow, Lila. You really are a—"

"That's enough, Zach!" Vicky scolded. "Can't you see how upsetting this is to Lila? There's no need to exacerbate the situation."

Just then, Sean walked in. "What's going on here?" He glanced down at me, a worried expression on his face.

"I can tell you what's *not* going on here. Work!" Bentley declared, her sharp eyes roaming the group. "Thank goodness someone in authority is here. The excitement is over and Detective Griffiths is here to take care of the situation. So, back to work, everyone! Status meeting at ten sharp." She leveled her gaze on Sean. "Your business will be done here by ten o'clock, right?"

Sean shrugged but didn't offer any promises. "What situation is she talking about?" he asked after the crowd dispersed. "I thought I was coming over here to talk to Flora about . . . something," he hesitated, eyeing Vicky, who was hovering at her desk just a few feet away.

"You were, but in the meantime I found a threat letter in my office." I pointed to Vicky's desk. "It's over there."

He crossed to the desk and, without touching the paper, leaned over and read the note. Then, handling the edges only, he placed it into a plastic bag he'd removed from his suit pocket. When he finally turned back to me, his face was dark with concern. "This means someone involved in the murder was right here in this office."

My mouth suddenly felt dry. "I know," I whispered, rubbing my temples. "I was in Flora's office for about twenty minutes first thing this morning. Anyone could have put it in there during that time."

"Excuse me," a voice interrupted from behind. Sean and I looked up to see Franklin. "There's something you should know. Grant Walker also came by this morning looking for Damian. He had a copy of the original deed for his land, which Damian wanted to view before signing the offer. Apparently Ruthie is in Dunston all day with a client, so she asked him if he could deliver a copy directly to Damian or to me so I could pass it along to him."

"What?" Vicky asked from her desk. "What time was this?"

Franklin turned toward her with an apologetic look. "It was early this morning, well before eight o'clock. You weren't in yet, Ms. Crump."

"How long was he here?" Sean asked.

Franklin wrung his hands. "Not long at all. And, never alone, I might add. I met him here in the front office. He handed me the paperwork and left."

"Still, he could have snuck back in when you weren't looking, Franklin, knowing no one else was in the office yet." Vicky's voice was tinged with accusation. "And I wouldn't put it past him to write a letter like that."

I looked toward Sean and shook my head. "I know there are several strikes against him, and his presence at the same time a threat letter shows up does look suspicious, but I still don't get those type of vibes from him."

Sean's brow furled. "Vibes? Lila, killers don't necessarily give off vibes. This isn't one of your books where the characters' negative attributes are carefully sketched by crafty authors. In real life, normal people do bad things. Very bad things."

I felt myself sink deeper into the chair. His words echoed in my mind: "bad things. Very bad things." He was right. I needed to keep an open mind. Anyone could have killed Fannie. Although my bet was still on Alice Peabody. I relayed the details of Alice's morning visit to Sean. "She was dropping off a box of brochures and the cat snuck through the open door. Vicky went after him and it took her a few minutes to track him down."

"He'd climbed into that overgrown evergreen at the base of the steps," Vicky explained. "I had to coax him out."

I continued with my theory. "So, Alice was alone in the office for enough time to slip into my office and leave that nasty letter."

Vicky folded her arms. "I still think Grant's more the threat-letter type."

"Okay. I'll look into both possibilities," Sean said, patting his suit pocket. "In the meantime I'll have the techs see if they can lift any prints off the paper."

"That might not be possible, Detective." Vicky spoke up with a smug expression. "Lila handled the letter before bringing it to my attention. I, of course, reminded her of the importance of preserving the integrity of whatever prints may have been left behind by the perpetrator, but I'm afraid I was probably too late."

Sean nodded her way. "Thank you, Ms. Crump."

I sighed heavily and shot her a sneering look before motioning for Sean to follow me down the hall. I stopped in front of Flora's office and turned to him. "When I was out at the Walker farm—" I started, but Sean held up his hand, stopping me midsentence.

"Hold on." He eyed me closely. "The Walker farm? You didn't tell me that. Were you asking Grant questions about Fannie's murder?"

I cringed inwardly, hoping I wasn't about to start up either his disapproval of my sleuthing or, worse yet, his jealous streak, again. "Franklin's been helping Damian look for land in the area to build his showcase home."

Sean scowled at the mention of Damian's name. I noticed the muscles in his forearms noticeably tensing. "Go on."

"Franklin asked me to give a second opinion on

the property," I continued. "So, I went up there; it's just a few miles out of town."

"I don't get it. Why does a literary agent need to help his client pick out property? And why does yet another literary agent's second opinion add any weight?" Sean asked.

"It's more complicated than that. Damian is an important client. He's a celebrity. Having him sign with our agency is a big coup for Bentley. She wants us to pamper him, keep him on board. That means little perks sort of like . . ." Sean furrowed his brow and muttered something under his breath while I searched for the right words to explain. "Sort of like when a big company rents out box seats at a major arena so they can woo their clients." Sean let out a long sigh of relief, making me wonder exactly what type of perks he might have thought I meant.

"Whatever," my indignant glare finally prompted from him. "So, you went out to look at Damian's property and I'm sure he valued your opinion." His voice dripped with sarcasm.

Refusing to rise to the bait, I simply shrugged.

He continued, "I suppose, knowing Grant is our top suspect, you took it upon yourself to ask a few questions about Fannie's murder." There was no mistaking the look on his face. Sean was ticked.

I glanced at the floor. "He did happen to mention his father had received a threatening letter . . ."

Sean sighed impatiently. "We know all about it. It's from a former patient who's recently lost his spouse. He felt like Dr. Walker's negligence caused his wife's death. But, I checked into it. The man's in his late eighties. He wasn't physically capable of killing Fannie. He's just some poor lonely soul, grief-stricken by his wife's death and lashing out in the only way he knew how: by writing a mean letter."

"How sad," I offered. Only Sean didn't seem sad. He just seemed angry. Angry that I'd once again butted in where I didn't belong. And for good reason, obviously. Now I was the one receiving threatening letters. I decided to turn the topic back to matters at hand. "I had Flora call you because she has some information that will identify Helen . . . I mean, the Jane Doe." Sean would laugh if he'd known I'd gone ahead and given the young woman in my yard a name. "But take it easy on her, okay. She's been through more than you can imagine."

With that said, I left him at Flora's door and retreated back to my office. After about fifteen minutes of trying to read email, I realized my efforts were fruitless. My eyes kept wandering to the very spot where the threat letter, delivered right here, on my desk, arrived just this morning. A shiver blanketed me as I thought of a killer being in my very office. What was next, my home?

I jerked upright, startled at the sound of someone entering my office. and breathed a sigh of relief when I realized it was just Sean. "Flora told me everything," he said. "Thanks for talking her into coming forward with this information."

"You'll be able to figure out who the young woman is, then?"

"Hopefully."

"What do you mean, hopefully? All you have to do is check the records of foster children the Cobbs took in, right?"

He shifted from foot to foot. "It sounds easier than it is. We'll have to get a court order to have the files unsealed. It could take a while."

"How long?"

He sighed. "Depends. For one thing, it's not as simple as having Mrs. Cobb sign a release for her own records; she's not of sound mind. We'll probably have to jump through a few hoops. I'll type up the warrant and affidavit this afternoon and get it to a judge."

"Maybe it won't take too long, then."

"Well, once I have the warrant signed, I'll have to find the person in charge of records at social services. Hopefully, they'll hand the paperwork over without needing to confer with their supervisor, but . . ." He shrugged. "All I'm saying is that these things take some time. It's not always like you see on television, where they get a warrant immediately. Especially if there's not a threat of danger. This is a decades-old murder. Other things take precedence."

Yes, like my very recent threat letter. Still, how much longer was it going to take to identify the young woman in my yard? "So, it could be a few days," I reiterated, my heart sinking. How much longer would Helen . . . no, her real name wasn't Helen, I thought, my heartache turning to frus-ration. Her *real* name was buried somewhere in those files. And, her *real* family was some-where out there waiting and wondering, perhaps even still grieving after all these years. And what about Mrs. Cobb? She'd practically begged me to find out what happened to her children.

"Lila," Sean said, crossing the room. "You're upset. And rightly so. You've just received a threat against your life. All this worry over the Jane Doe in your yard is just the way your mind is coping with your fear. You're trying to distract yourself."

"You're right, Sean. I am upset." I could feel my emotions rising, bubbling up to the surface like a pot about to overboil. Anger, frustration, fear— all threatening to cascade in tears or strike out with . . . what? Fists? The silly image of me slug-ging away at someone (who?) or something (what?) made me shake my head, take a breath. I did need to get control, see the facts, and lay it all out to the only person who understood me. "I'm upset that someone delivered that evil message to me right here in my own office." I jabbed my finger against the surface of my desk. "And I'm upset that people around me keep getting murdered. Do you realize that the people of Inspiration Valley have dubbed me the Murder Magnet? Like it's my fault that someone was murdered and buried under my hawthorn bushes. Then there's Fannie's murder. Vicky's so sure it was Grant Walker who killed her, but—"

"That's my territory, Lila. You need to stay out of Fannie's murder." He patted his pocket. "You've obviously been asking questions around town. Something you've done has someone thinking you're involved. Isn't this threat letter enough of a wake-up call for you?"

I clamped my mouth shut. So much for me wanting to lay out the facts and get control; those very actions had caused me to be the next potential victim, magnetizing murder to myself! He was right. And he definitely wouldn't be happy if he knew I'd gone to the Walker farm yesterday for the sole purpose of questioning Grant. I knew this sleuthing mission Vicky had sent me on wasn't a good idea, but I'd gone anyway. And although I didn't want to admit it, only a couple of people had motive and opportunity to leave that letter. Grant, because I'd been asking him questions about his stepmother's murder, and Alice Peabody, because by now she probably realized I was the one who'd sicced the police on her. Of course lots of others had access to my desk: Flora, who, until a bit earlier, wanted nothing more than for me to quit snooping around. My mind flashed back to when I'd entered her office earlier. That was a black pen I saw her nervously cap. And the paper she shuffled to the bottom of her pile? Another threat note waiting to be delivered? *Stop it, Lila!* I was doing it again, digging myself into a hole, seeing suspects now even among people I trusted. I'd set myself up for this whole threat-letter thing and had no one else to blame.

Sean softly touched my arm, drawing me away from my thoughts. "Let me take you home. Maybe you can pack your bags and head over to your mother's for a couple of days. Let things cool down."

I wanted nothing more than to hole up some-where and let Sean take charge and deal with all the murders and suspects and doubts. I hesitated, glancing over my pile of to-dos for the event, another pile of letters from authors, my computer screen blinking with incoming emails . . .

Before I could respond, Sean said, "Everything will wait for you. It isn't like—"

"It isn't like what? I can't just pick up and leave! And it won't wait!" Those emotional bubbles burst through and I snapped at him. *Like his job is important and mine isn't?* "There's too much to do before this signing and dinner event, and everyone else is already overloaded; there's no way I can just go home." I waved my hand toward a stack of papers on my desk. "I have a status meeting this morning, plus all these queries to go through, brochures to deliver, and . . ."

He grabbed me by the shoulders and steadied me. "Okay, okay. I understand." He let out a breath. "Listen, I'm just worried about you, okay? Why don't you come over to my place for a couple of days? Both you and Trey. Just until things blow over."

I inhaled and held my breath for a few seconds, willing my mind to stop reeling out of control. His offer was tempting, but could I really afford that type of distraction right before such a big event? Exhaling, I put on a brave smile. "It's okay, really. My mother's been staying at the house with Trey and me, so it's not like we're alone."

He shook his head, worry evident in his expression. "Still, I'm going to see about having a patrol car in your neighborhood tonight." He leaned in and wrapped me in his arms. "I've got to get back to the office. Just promise me you'll be careful," he pleaded.

I nodded and promised. Yet deep down, I knew if the letter was delivered right here, in my workplace, the killer could get to me anywhere. No, my best hope was that Sean would find the murderer soon. Until then, I wouldn't be able to find any peace.

Chapter 14

EVEN WITH MAMA SLEEPING IN THE FRONT room, and the knowledge that a police officer was patrolling our neighborhood, I still didn't sleep soundly. Sometime between a vivid nightmare involving a humanlike rosebush and the sound of my alarm clock, I gave up on sleep and simply lay in bed staring at the ceiling. The thing about the quiet moments before the day breaks, is that you're completely alone with your thoughts. That morning, forced to face my feelings surrounding the events of the last week, I decided I needed to get on with business as usual. I knew my brain would work overtime on something and I couldn't afford to allow it to work on suspects—all that had garnered so far was a death-threat letter. No, I needed to keep my mind busy on something else. And with Damian's signing and dinner just a few days away, I had plenty at hand to do just that.

So, later that morning, armed with an extra tall latte to spur me on after a restless night of sleep, I worked my way south on High Street, delivering brochures. At the corner of High and Dogwood, I stopped at Sixpence Bakery. There I nibbled on a scone and chatted a bit with Nell about the pies she was making for this weekend's dinner. Afterward, I moved on to Sherlock Holmes

Realty, where I left a large stack of brochures for Ruthie's clients. Ruthie wasn't there, but I left the brochures with her secretary.

Next, I stopped in All Creatures, Feathered and Furry Pet Shop and formally introduced myself to the new shop's owner, Matt Reynolds. He was a giant of a man, with a grizzly beard and a shoulder spread that rivaled any NFL linebacker, but when he handled the animals, he was as gentle as a lamb. He took me back to the puppy area to show off his newest arrival. "This is Olive," he said, handing me the tiny ball of fur. "She's a Cavalier King Charles spaniel, purebred," he explained. "She won't get much bigger than this." He spread his hands about a foot apart.

I looked down at the pup nuzzled against my chest. "She's so cute!" I raved, cradling her like a baby. She was a fluff ball of cream and brown fur, with big furry brown ears that were practically bigger than her whole body. And her eyes—giant, solemn brown eyes that I could get lost in forever. My earlier anxieties had already been subdued to a degree by my busy morning, but now they melted away completely with this sweet baby in my arms. A lick to my nose and I giggled with delight. What a charmer! They said having a pet can lower a person's blood pressure and I surely believed it now.

Reluctantly, I gave her one last nuzzle and handed her back to Matt. She was so completely adorable, I could hardly stand to leave her, but my bag was still bulging with undelivered brochures. I pulled out a stack and explained to Matt about the weekend's events.

"I've seen this advertised," he commented. "The wife and I are planning to go. We're new to the area, so we thought it would be a great way to meet people. Plus, my wife's a huge fan of Damian York." He grinned and glanced at the floor. "I think she has a crush on him."

I laughed. I'd heard similar stories all over town. Seems Damian had charmed the entire female demographic of Inspiration Valley. "Well, she's not alone. I think most of the Valley has a crush." On the way back to the front of the store, I detoured through the cat section and picked up a catnip mouse for Eliot. Since I didn't have a pet of my own, I was glad Vicky had chosen to share Eliot. I was growing quite attached to the fellow.

I caught back up to Matt at the checkout counter. While he rang up my order, I thought of another question. "Did you know Fannie Walker? She probably shopped here for cat supplies."

He nodded. "Yes. Eliot, right?"

"Wow, you remember the names of your shoppers' pets?"

He handed me my bag and smiled. "I'm embarrassed to admit that sometimes I remember their pets' names before theirs." He paused, his eyebrows furrowing. "Speaking of Eliot, what's happened to him since . . . since—"

"Since Fannie died?" I finished for him.

He looked down and nodded. "Yes, a terrible thing about that."

I nodded. "But Eliot's fine—he's found a home in our own agency as our mascot, in fact." He smiled at that, but Fannie's death still hung in the air between us for a moment. I tapped the brochure. "She was a wonderful gardener, you know. So active in the Valley's garden club."

A smile crossed his face. "I know, she spoke often about her involvement with some group that calls itself the Dirty Dozen." He chuckled at the mention of the name, then sobered again. "That woman did love gardening." His expression lightened as he made a mental connection. "Come to think of it, I bought this store from some other lady who belonged to that garden club. Alice Peabody."

My antenna shot up. "Really?"

"Yes." He waved his hand in the air, his face full of pride. "All she talked about was roses. I don't think she was much of an animal lover. She seemed to deplore her neighbor's dog. A Jack Russell terrier. You know how they are?"

I shook my head.

"Diggers," he explained. "Seems the little fellow got into Ms. Peabody's garden and dug up one of her plants. Boy, was she ever mad."

"I bet," I muttered, hoping she didn't go after the innocent pup with a spade.

"Do you remember what this place was before?" he continued. I opened my mouth to reply, but he answered his own question. "A mechanic's garage, that's what. It was quite the job to turn it into what it is today."

I nodded impatiently. "And Alice Peabody owned it?" I prompted.

"Her husband owned the place, but after he passed, she had a difficult time keeping it up. She finally decided to sell." He shook his head. "She wasn't an easy lady to deal with, that's for sure."

"Really? Why's that?"

"A hard businesswoman. Real cutthroat."

Or heavy-handed. I started to think, my mind jumping into wordplay—a habit I'd picked up from reading so many cozy mysteries. *Heavy-handed with a spade.*

I took my bag and turned to leave. "You're not the only one who's said that about Alice Peabody," I assured him. I started making my way toward the door. "She has a reputation for being murderously competitive," I added, unable to resist a little innuendo.

I left Matt's shop and worked my way around the Nine Muses fountain, pausing for just a second to dip my hand in the cool pool gathered at the feet of the beautiful muses. Their serene expressions tempted me to stay longer, but I couldn't spare the time. Instead, I dug a lucky penny out of my bag, made a quick wish, and pensively watched it sink to the bottom of the fountain alongside hundreds of other talismans. A flicker of doubt entered my mind. How could it possibly be that all those wishes came true? Would my wish for Sean and me . . . ? I shook it off, reminding myself that I'd pledged to spend the day focused on work.

I moved on, crossing to the opposite side of High Street. Next on my route was the Constant Reader, one of my favorite shops in town. And since the bookshop was connected inside by a large archway to the James Joyce Pub, I'd timed my visit at the end of my route, planning to grab a sandwich to take back to the office. As I approached the store, I noticed a large crowd gathered by the door, admiring a small billboard advertising Damian's signing. "He's adorable," one young lady gushed. Another broke into a spurt of giggles, while yet another mockingly fanned herself. "Adorable? Hot's more like it."

I smiled and approached with a handful of brochures. "Here's some pamphlets about this weekend's event, girls. Damian York would love to have you at his book launch," I added, garnishing another round of chortling. Perhaps I should tell Bentley to order extra copies of the book. Considering the size of Damian's apparent fan base, we might need more books than we originally thought.

I dispensed the brochures to the eager young women and turned to enter the shop, stopping short when I noticed the *Will Return* sign on the door. I glanced up and down the street, wondering where Jay was; the note indicated that he'd return at noon and it was already a quarter past the hour. Then, as if on cue, I saw him hustling down the walk, a small plastic bag clutched protectively to his chest. "Glad I caught you!" I said when he reached me.

"Sorry, Lila. I just stepped out to run a quick errand, but it took longer than I expected." He unlocked the door and stepped inside. As he turned the door sign back to *Open*, I caught a glimpse of the bag he was carrying. There was no mistaking the small telltale blue and white bag from the local jewelry shop.

"Been doing a little shopping, Jay?" I was racking my mind, trying to think of when Makayla's birthday was, then it dawned on me. "Jay! Is that what I think it is?"

Color rose to his cheeks as his face broke into a wide grin. "You're sworn to secrecy." He laughed. "But, yes, it's what you're thinking. I'm going to ask Makayla to marry me."

Both my hands flew to my cheeks. "Jay! That's wonderful news," I gushed. "Can I see it?"

He motioned for me to follow to one of the

store's cozy nooks, where he opened the bag and brought out a velvet box. Turning to me, he popped the lid, revealing the most beautiful solitaire diamond ring I'd ever seen. "Oh, Jay," was all I could manage. The ring was gorgeous; Makayla was going to love it.

No one deserved happiness as much as my friends Jay and Makayla. Still, as I stared down at the sparkling gem, a little envy nipped at the joy in my heart. "Makayla's a lucky lady," I brought myself to say, my eyes growing moist with tears of happiness tinged with a little bit of sadness.

"No, I'm the lucky one. Makayla"—his face lit up as he spoke—"well . . . she's like the happy ending to my story." He shook his head, color rising to his cheeks. "That was corny, wasn't it?"

I couldn't help but laugh a little. "Yes. Corny, but sweet."

He stared down at the ring, a shadow of doubt crossing his face. "Now, let's just hope she says yes."

"Are you crazy? Of course she's going to say yes. When are you going to pop the question?" I gulped down the feeling of desperation that swelled inside me. I'd been waiting for my own magic moment, the day that Sean would propose to me. The way things were going between us, I might never see that moment.

Jay fumbled with the box, wrapping it back inside the bag. "I'm trying to think of the perfect way to ask her. I want her to always remember my proposal."

I reached out and touched his arm. "I'm so happy for both of you."

Back at Novel Idea, I walked through the reception room, snatched up Eliot, and headed straight for my office. "I just need to borrow him for a little while," I said over my shoulder.

"I completely understand," Vicky replied, not missing a beat on her keyboard.

I shut my office door and placed the comforting creature on my desk, stroking his fur until he settled into a position. For the next couple of hours, I addressed the onslaught of emails I'd received the last few days plus a new pile of queries that had shown up on my desk. I always tried my best to respond to authors in a timely manner; I knew how much of their souls they'd poured into their work and how anxious they were to hear my response. Sometimes, though, my other agent responsibilities got in the way of my daily work. Events like Damian's book launch consumed a lot of my reading time. Now that it was just a few days away, the rest of my week was sure to be hectic, so I intended to clear my desk by the end of the day. That way, I could spend the next few days focused on the event. It was exciting and important to Novel Idea, and therefore to my career, as well. But as I heard the soft purr of Eliot, snoozing contentedly on my desk, I knew what I really wanted at this moment was to get through this week and all its work-related events so that I could finally breathe enough to have a good sit-down with Sean. I owed him an explanation, if not an apology of sorts. That's all we needed, a little time together. Sean's caseload lately had been overwhelming for him, too. I'd only added to it with that death-threat letter, plus a skeleton in my backyard. So I'd unintentionally piled on him more reasons we couldn't . . . wait . . . Perhaps I could help him with at least closing the cold case; it would carve out more time for us.

My mind was still stuck on something Mrs. Cobb had said. Now, thanks to Flora, I knew when Mrs. Cobb asked about her children, she was referring to her foster children. If I could only get a name, Helen's real name, perhaps I could trigger Mrs. Cobb's memory and some real answers to what might have happened years ago.

Then it dawned on me. The pictures at Fannie's house. Maybe, if I gathered them and took them to Mrs. Cobb, she might recognize a face. Certainly it might be quicker than waiting for a court order. I snatched up my phone and dialed Sean's cell. He answered on the first ring. "Everything okay?"

"No, I'm sorry. I just happened to think of something. Did you interview Mrs. Cobb personally?"

"Yes, me and another officer, but she was having memory problems when we talked to her. We didn't get much."

"I found the same thing when I met her. But she does have some moments of lucidity."

"What are you getting at exactly?"

"When we were at Fannie's the other day, I saw pictures of foster children. We know at least one of them, Flora, was placed with the Cobbs. Maybe others were taken in by the Cobbs as well. Would it be okay if I took some pictures to her, just to see if it triggers any memories? Maybe something that would help the case?"

"We already did that. She didn't recognize any of the photos. I turned them back to Walker. He's getting ready to clear out the old home; he's getting it ready to sell. He said something about an estate sale first thing next week."

"What?"

"It's his home now, Lila. We scanned the pictures to keep on file and returned the hard copies to Walker. He can do anything he wants with them; the photos are really no use to us. Besides, as soon as we get the social services records, we'll have all the information we need."

"Still, I'd like to try showing Peggy the photos myself. Is that possible? Maybe if someone other than a police officer approached her, she might be more relaxed. You said yourself it might take a while to get the state's records released."

He let out a long sigh. "I can get the photos if you want, but not until later. I have other things more pressing at the moment. But I'll be talking to Walker this afternoon. I'll see if he'll give us permission to borrow the photos again. I don't think he'll put up a fight about it. He's not in the position to be anything but cooperative."

"Well, if he's okay with it, Vicky's got a set of keys I can borrow. I could head over there tonight and pick them up. I'd hate for him to get rid of them before I had a chance to show them to Peggy again."

"You're not going over to the Walker home alone, Lila. It'll have to wait."

"I understand your concern, Sean. But I wouldn't go alone. I'll find someone to go with me."

This time, an even longer sigh sounded over the line. "I'll tell you what. Get someone to go with you and I'll send an officer by the place to meet you. One of the guys lives over in that area; he can stop by on his way home. Will seven work?"

"Yes. Seven would work fine."

"Promise me you'll wait for him to get there."

I promised and hung up the phone. I knew just the person to ask to go with me—Makayla. I needed to drop some brochures with her anyway. Plus, after hearing Jay's news, I'd skipped my plans for picking up a sandwich from the pub and come straight back to the office. Suddenly I felt famished.

I found Makayla in her usual position behind the counter. Today she was wearing a dark purple T-shirt tied off on one hip, cropped jeans, and beaded earrings that swung on her earlobes as she worked. As soon as she saw me, she started steaming milk.

"Here you go," she said a minute later, sliding my caramel latte across the counter and handing me a folded paper bag.

"What's this?" I hadn't ordered anything except my usual latte. Although, admittedly I'd been deliberating over something decadent from her pastry case.

"I'm trying some new bagel flavors. This one is an Asiago bagel with vegetable cream cheese. I mixed the cream cheese myself. I think you'll like it."

"Sounds yummy," I said, but my eyes betrayed me by sliding longingly toward the chocolate chip muffins. My stressful morning had left me with a hankering for something sweet. Years of pacifying my emotions with Mama's sweet bread must have set my bar for comfort food and I wasn't quite sure this cheesy bagel would do the trick. But not wanting to hurt Makayla's feelings, I took the bag with a smile. "And these are for you." I reached into my shoulder bag and extracted a bundle of brochures. "Push one on everyone who comes through the door, will you? We need all the advertising we can get."

"Will do," she chimed in her melodic voice, and began wiping the counter with a rag. I wanted to bring up the topic about my threat letter, but it would probably be too long a discussion and I was pressed for time. Best to save it for later. Besides, I noticed she seemed exceptionally happy this morning and I hated the idea of ruining her good spirits.

"Anything new?" I asked, eyeing her suspiciously and wondering if the glow on her face had something to do with Jay's pending proposal.

A telltale blush crossed her cheeks as she dipped her chin and grinned mischievously. But instead of explaining, she simply shrugged. "No, not really. Same old same, really."

I squinted, not quite believing her, but knowing that she'd tell me in her own time. "Same old same, huh? Well, perhaps you need something to shake things up a bit."

Her brows shot up. "What do you have cooking in that mind of yours, girl?"

I leaned over the counter and whispered conspiratorially, "A little sleuthing. I've got an idea about how I might be able to figure out the identity of the body in my yard." The bells jingled over the door as a couple of customers walked in and headed our way. "I can't give you all the details now, but it's important. And, unless you want to ride on my cargo rack, you'll have to drive. Are you in?"

She nodded. "Of course. When and where?"

I glanced over at the customers to see if I was holding them up, but they were still squinting at the chalkboard menu that hung over the counter. "Can you come by my place around six?"

She giggled and motioned for me to lean in more. Cupping her hands around her mouth, she whispered. "I feel just like Bess Marvin—Nancy Drew's sidekick—along for the adventure and helping Nancy solve crimes."

"Bess? I think you're more adventurous, like her other sidekick, George," I whispered back. "I appreciate the bagel," I added, gripping my bag and heading for the door. I hadn't even made it halfway up the stairway when my cell phone started buzzing. It was my mother.

"Everything okay, Mama?" I asked, pausing on one of the steps and leaning against the railing.

"That's what I'm callin' to find out. I was just sittin' here when the strangest chill came over me."

"Oh?" I had purposely chosen not to tell her about the threat letter I'd received. With every-thing that'd been going on, I was sure the worry would just add to her stress.

"Yes, I was just here at my house, waiting for a client, when a cold feelin' crept right up my spine. In this heat, the only reason I'd catch a chill was if I was comin' down with something, or my senses were trying to tell me somethin'. Bein' that

I feel just fine, this chill of mine must be a warnin' of some sort. Are you sure everything's all right with you?"

I let out a long sigh and squeezed my eyes shut. Could it be that she was sensing the threat I'd received yesterday? Still, telling her about the threat letter would be like opening a big can of worms. Hard to tell what she'd do if she knew I was being directly threatened. "Everything's just fine, Mama."

There was a long pause on the other end, making me think she wasn't quite buying my story. I was never good at pulling the wool over her eyes. "If you say so, darlin'," she finally replied.

Thankfully, the rest of the day progressed without any more drama. I was grateful, since the past two weeks had contained enough drama to last me a lifetime. Of course, I wasn't expecting to walk in the front door of my house that evening and find my mother sitting in the recliner with a shotgun across her lap. "Mama!"

"Hi, sug. How was the rest of your workday?"

"Work was fine. What is that?"

She raised the gun and held it out for my inspection, her face beaming with pride. "This here's Rusty. I always did say that my two best men are Jim Beam and ol' trusty Rusty."

I scoffed. "I've never heard you say any such thing!"

My mother leaned forward. "Well, I'm sayin' it now. Rusty here used to belong to your daddy. He taught me how to use it, too. If any troublemaker comes round here looking to hurt one of mine, he'll find himself plugged full of buckshot."

Uh-oh. Had she found out about the letter? "Have you been talking to one of the other agents I work with?"

She shook her head.

"Sean, maybe?"

She pursed her lips and narrowed her gaze on me. "No, why?"

"Nothing. Just wondering. Why do you feel like you need . . . uh . . . Rusty?"

" 'Cuz of that chill I was tellin' you about. It just won't go away." She tapped the barrel of the gun. "Rusty gives me a little reassurance, you know. Just in case."

I winced. As much as I hated the idea of having a gun in the house, I recognized the look of determination on my mother's face. Nonetheless, I was going to have to sit Mama down when I got home tonight and talk her into taking Rusty back home. But since Makayla was due at any moment, I decided to let it wait until later. "What's Trey up to?" I asked, changing the subject.

She motioned for the kitchen. "Go check for yourself. He's been in there for the last hour, cookin' up a storm."

I went to the kitchen and found him bent over

in front of the open oven door, pulling out what looked like a pan of bubbling cheese. It smelled divine. "What's this?"

He beamed my way. "Supper. I thought I'd fix something for you and Nana. It's homemade mac and cheese. Made with bacon and three types of cheeses. Nana brought a few tomatoes from her garden. Thought I'd slice them up and put them on top with some toasted bread crumbs."

I beamed with pride and resisted the urge to hug him right then and there. Trey hated it when I went all gushy on him, but I couldn't help but take stock of how blessed I was. My son had grown into the most considerate young man a mother could ever hope to have.

"Is there enough for a guest?" I asked, thinking that Makayla would show up any minute.

His face grew somber. "Sean?"

I drew in my breath. Up to now, I hadn't had a chance to discuss this issue with my son in private. Now was as good a time as any. "Makayla, actually. But speaking of Sean, I heard you two had quite the argument the other day."

He placed the casserole on the counter and covered it in aluminum foil. "Yeah, I guess."

"I think we should talk about it, Trey."

"It's fine. It was mostly my fault. I overreacted to something he said and went all crazy on him." He pulled a couple of perfectly ripened tomatoes from a brown sack, rinsed them, and began slicing.

I crossed the kitchen and leaned on the counter next to where he was working. "You felt angry about something he said?"

He stopped slicing and looked directly at me. "I overheard him say something to Makayla about you having another boyfriend. It ticked me off that he'd talk about you that way and I told him so."

I placed my hand on his arm. "Trey, there are only two men in my life. You and Sean. But I'm afraid I might have said something to make Sean think there was someone else. It was wrong of me and I've hurt him. I'm going to try to set things straight before it's too late."

Trey looked at me with wide eyes. "You lied to him about something like that?"

I shook my head. "No, I didn't lie exactly. I just didn't bother to correct a silly assumption he made. I should have. But a part of me liked the idea of him being jealous."

Trey nodded. "Sort of like in romance novels where men are always fighting over some woman."

I sighed. "I guess so."

"Mom, you need to do less reading. Maybe spend more time gaming, like me. I never have these types of problems."

We both laughed. "Hey, your grandmother has a new friend with her tonight," I said, changing the topic.

"You mean Rusty?"

I nodded. "Do you think it's loaded?"

He smirked. "Naw. She brought a box of shells with her, but I snuck it away and hid it out in the garage." His eyes suddenly grew wide. "That's okay, isn't it? I don't mean any disrespect, but I didn't want her to hurt herself, either."

Now I was truly touched by my son's maturity. I reached up and ruffled his hair. "I'm sure glad you're on my side, buddy. I don't know what I'd ever do without you."

Chapter 15

"THIS IS THE HOUSE OF THE WOMAN who was murdered?" Makayla asked. "What are we doing here?"

For the third time in less than two weeks, I was in front of Fannie Walker's house. And it was as creepy-looking this time as before. Maybe even creepier, because the sun was low on the horizon, casting long shadows over the front yard.

I filled Makayla in on my plan for Fannie's photos. "The police already tried showing them to Peggy, but she didn't recognize anyone," I explained. "But I thought maybe if I approached her, instead of the police, maybe she might remember something."

Makayla agreed. "The mind is a tricky thing," she said. "Hard telling what might trigger a memory. Remember in *The Notebook* when James Garner read to the woman in the nursing home?" She rolled her eyes upward and sighed. "Such a romantic movie! Anyway, all of this woman's memories were gone, but his words took her back in time, gave her a chance to relive the love they'd once shared. The same thing could happen to Mrs. Cobb. Maybe one of these faces will transport her back in time."

"That's what I'm hoping. It might be the only

way to identify the young woman." I explained to her about the sealed social services files. "Anyway, Sean is sending an officer to meet us."

"Thank goodness. This place feels creepy to me."

"Me, too." Despite the sweltering heat, I shivered. "Thanks for coming with me. Police presence and all, I'm still glad to have you here."

While we waited, I told Makayla about everything that happened in the last few days, including my threat letter—which the police lab determined contained only my prints—and my suspicions about Alice Peabody. "Of course, Grant Walker had an opportunity to place the letter in my office, too. Apparently, he stopped by to deliver some papers, although, Franklin insists he was never alone. Whereas Alice had plenty of time to sneak into my office and place the threat letter on my desk."

"Seems like you've gone and got yourself in the thick of things again, haven't you? I don't know this Peabody woman but from what you're telling me, she's as crazy as a loon."

I nodded. "It seems pretty far-fetched, though, to think someone would be crazy enough to kill someone over a garden competition. I think the police are focusing their efforts elsewhere. Namely, Grant, the stepson." I glanced at my watch. "I wonder what's keeping the officer. It's after seven already."

As if on cue, a silver sports car pulled up across the street. "Do you suppose that's him?" Makayla asked, wide-eyed.

I stared at the guy as he hopped out and approached our car. He was wearing jeans and a sleeveless T-shirt and had long scraggly hair and heavily inked arms. He looked nothing like the clean-cut cops I was used to seeing. "Of course it is," I assured her, trying to put on a brave front.

Makayla's voice started to wobble. "He doesn't look like a cop. What if that's really the killer?"

She had a point. Truth was, the threat letter had me looking at everyone suspiciously. I drew in a shaky breath. "Sean said the guy lived in this neighborhood and that he'd be dropping by on his way home. He's just not in uniform, that's all." Still, what if she was right? The guy looked more like one of those mug shots you see on crime-stopper shows than a police officer. I shook it off. "Hey, you're supposed to be like George, not Bess," I reminded her. "George was the brave one, if you remember."

Makayla slid her hand over and pushed the automatic lock button. "Things in real life don't always turn out like they do in the books you read, Lila."

The man was just a few feet from the front windshield when he suddenly reached behind his back. Makayla screeched and ducked down under the dash. "Gun! He's got a gun!"

I wanted to duck, but for some reason I was frozen in place. I watched in horror as he withdrew his hand, then exhaled with relief as he pointed nothing more dangerous than his wallet our way. Unfolding the flap, he exposed his badge and held it up to my window for inspection. I hit the unlock button, a little embarrassed by its telltale clicking sound, and hopped out on the curb. "Hello, Officer. I'm Lila and this"—I glanced back to where Makayla was just beginning to clamor out of her side of the car—"this is my friend Makayla." Makayla nodded, still a bit shaken, based on her lack of response.

"Officer Wilson. Chad Wilson," he greeted with a pleasant voice. The lines around his eyes put him in his mid to late thirties. I noticed a thin white scar along the underside of his chin as he spoke. "Sorry if I scared you ladies." He indicated his attire. "I've been on undercover detail. My shift ended a while ago and Detective Griffiths asked me to stop by here on my way home."

"Thank you," I said, starting up the walk, carrying a small cardboard box I'd brought for packing the framed photos. "I'm not sure what all Sean . . . I mean Detective Griffiths told you, but we're just here to pick up some pictures. They're in the back room," I explained, using the keys Vicky had loaned me to unlock the front door. "We'll just run back and get them and then we'll be out of here. It shouldn't take very long at all."

The house had taken on a musty smell since I'd been there last and a fine layer of dust had settled on surfaces, giving the entire place a ghostly feel. We went directly to the family room and began placing the frames carefully in a box, while the officer hung back a bit.

Makayla startled. "Did you hear that?"

I stopped packing and stood motionless, ears pricked. Officer Wilson also paused, then walked closer to the far wall, where a weird rhythmic thumping sound was coming from right outside the family room window. My heartbeat kicked up a notch. "What do you suppose that is?"

The whites of Makayla's eyes grew huge. "It's coming from the backyard. Isn't that where Fannie was killed?"

"Yes," I croaked, my voice an octave higher than normal.

The officer held up his hand and motioned for us to be quiet, then, glancing around, he signaled for us to move behind the sofa. "Stay here and don't move," he ordered, taking off toward the back door in the kitchen, his cell phone in hand. As he moved down the hall, I could hear him whispering into his phone, calling for reinforcements.

Makayla and I patiently huddled behind the sofa for a couple of minutes. "What now?" she asked, her lower lip trembling. I shrugged and started rubbing at a kink that was forming in my lower back when suddenly we heard a commotion in the backyard followed by a man's voice screaming in agony. I scurried out from behind the sofa, and in a half-ducked position scooted across the floor toward the window.

"What are you doing? Are you crazy? That could be the murderer out there. Get back here," Makayla hissed.

"But Officer Wilson might be in trouble," I said, peeking through the window. What I saw was shocking. Alice Peabody, facedown in the grass, legs and arms flailing, while Officer Wilson crouched above her with a knee shoved in her back. He was struggling to keep her hands held while blood trickled from his head and ran down his shoulders and arms. Next to them on the ground was a spade!

I took off for the back door, ignoring Makayla's screams to stop. By the time I'd made it out the door, I could hear sirens approaching. I still raced on, fumbling a bit with a picket gate that served as an entrance to Fannie's rose garden. Finally the lever released and I burst into the yard. "Officer Wilson, are you okay?"

He looked up, a slightly dazed look in his eye. "I thought I told you two to stay inside."

"Two?" I looked behind me to see Makayla clenching a butcher knife, a determined look in her eye. She was turning out to be more George-like than I thought.

"Is *he* okay?" Alice shrieked. "What about me?

I'm the one who's been assaulted. Police brutality, that's what this is. And you'll be hearing from my lawyer!"

"A lawyer's a good idea, lady," Wilson said, dragging her to her feet just as two other officers exploded into the yard, guns drawn.

"Drop the weapon!"

Next to me, Makayla dropped the knife and shot her hands into the air.

"Take it easy, fellows," Wilson said. "This here's your lady. These two were just trying to help." Another couple of officers showed up, and one of them took a quick look at Wilson and called for an ambulance.

Wilson handed Alice over to the uniformed officers, who proceeded to cuff and Mirandize her. "You're under arrest for assaulting a police officer," one of them declared.

Alice's eyebrows pinched together as she tried to jerk away from the officers. "I didn't know that guy was a cop when I hit him. Look at him! He looks like a thug. I thought he might be the killer."

"The killer who murdered Fannie Walker here just a few days ago with a spade?" I inserted. "Just like that one right there?" I pointed down at the garden tool and paused. Would I ever be able to look again at garden tools and not think of violence?

"That's my spade. I brought it from home."

"Sure, lady," Wilson said. "You can explain it all

down at the precinct." He motioned for the officers to take her away. She didn't go easily, screaming indignantly and fighting the whole way.

"Griffiths isn't going to like this," Wilson said after they were out of earshot. He lifted his hand to his head, gingerly feeling around his wound. "At least we better get what you came for. Come on, let's go back inside and get your pictures before the medics come to take me to the hospital."

Officer Wilson was right about one thing. Sean wasn't happy when he heard about everything that went down at Fannie's house. I was back home, reheating some of Trey's mac and cheese, when he called.

"I should never have let you go over there in the first place," he said.

"Officer Wilson was on top of things. Besides, on a positive note, it looks like you've got your killer."

"That still needs to be determined. I just finished interviewing her and she's sticking to her story. Claims she heard Grant was getting ready to put the house up for sale so she went over to Fannie's to dig up a plant. Some sort of hybrid rose that Fannie bred and cultivated herself. It's not something that can be bought at the nursery."

"And you believe that story? Maybe this wasn't

the first time Alice has tried to pilfer that rose. I bet that's exactly what she was doing the other day when Fannie caught her in the act. Alice probably clubbed her to death with the spade to keep her from telling the other garden club ladies. After all, if it was discovered that Alice was a rose thief, she'd certainly lose her position as president of the Dirty Dozen, probably her membership, too, not to mention any eligibility for the van Gogh award. I can tell you that those things are extremely important to Alice. Definitely motive enough to kill."

"You're jumping to a lot of conclusions. I'm going to need a little more evidence before I can make a murder charge stick. We've got a search warrant in the works. Maybe something will turn up at her residence. In the meantime, we're holding her for the assault and attempted robbery."

"I'm sure it's her, Sean. I told you she was competitive. Imagine, killing someone over a rose. Did you ask her about the threat letter?"

"She denied it."

"But you don't believe her, right? You know you've got your killer. There's no doubt in my mind. At least I can rest easy now. I can't wait to tell Mama and Trey." I lowered my voice. "Maybe Mama and her friend Rusty will finally go back to her place."

"Rusty? Who's Rusty?"

"Never mind, forget I mentioned it. Any progress on getting the foster care files opened?"

"Something strange about that. I don't know how to tell you this, but it seems the Cobbs' file can't be located."

My heart sank. *Missing!* Now the key to determining the young woman's true identity rested solely on Peggy Cobb's feeble mind. "I'm going to call the director of the group home first thing tomorrow morning and set up an appointment to see Peggy. I know her memory is iffy, but she may be able to . . ." I heard a noise behind me and saw that Mama had knocked the jar of mayonnaise off the fridge shelf.

"Everything okay, Mama? If you're looking for the casserole, I already made you a plate. It's on the counter. You might want to put it in the microwave for a minute or so." I pointed out her dish before turning back to my call.

"Anyway, I'll let you know how it turns out," I told Sean. "By the way, there's something important that I've been meaning to talk to you about." I glanced over my shoulder and saw that Mama was still hovering. I wanted to bring up the Damian York thing, but not in front of her. I sighed. "In person," I added.

"How about lunch tomorrow at the James Joyce Pub?"

"Tomorrow may not work . . ." I hedged. At this week's status meeting, Bentley had added ten more things to my to-do list. Of course, once she discovered the president of the Dirty Dozen was behind bars, she would call a DAC (damage assessment and control) meeting. Probably first thing in the morning. Plus I was behind on emails, still had several outstanding proposals to read and anxious authors to respond to, not to mention finding time to visit Peggy at the nursing home. "How about Thursday?" Except, what if I didn't get all my to-dos checked off my list? The event was just a few days away. It'd be cutting things too close. "I mean Friday. Let's make it Friday for lunch," I amended, thinking surely everything would be under control by Friday. Actually, if luck was on my side, maybe Peggy would be able to identify one of the photos and Sean could also mark the cold case file off his to-do list. Then we'd be able to get on with our lives.

No answer. After a half minute of silence, I cleared my throat. "Hello? Sean?"

"How about you just call me back when you get your schedule worked out. We'll talk then." He disconnected before I had a chance to reply.

"What was that all about?" my mother asked as soon as I hung up the phone.

"Um, that was Sean. We were talking about Fannie's murder."

She placed the plate in the microwave and slammed the door. "Didn't sound that way to me," she accused, jabbing the start button.

I sighed. First Sean and now Mama. I don't know why everyone was so prickly, but I was too tired to deal with it all. "If you really must know all the details of our discussion, we were talking about the case. Alice Peabody was arrested tonight." I went on to explain the whole ordeal at Fannie's house and how Alice was caught digging up Fannie's roses with a spade. "Seems the rose plant is valuable. The way I see it, Alice snuck into Fannie's yard last week, intending to dig up the plant, but Fannie interrupted her. Maybe threatened to report her. Alice flipped and hit her with the spade."

Mama pulled a fork from the silverware drawer as the microwave buzzer sounded. "Really? That doesn't seem right."

"What do you mean? Of course it seems right. She was caught red-handed."

"Stealin', but not murderin'. I don't think she murdered Fannie." She paused and took a few bites of the casserole. "I forgot to tell you, but Alice came visitin' yesterday."

I gawked at her. "She did?"

"Yes, wanted me to read her fortune. It was important to her to know the outcome of that garden contest all those ladies are so worked up about."

"Why didn't you tell me this before? How did the reading go?"

"Well, funny thing about that. You see, I started

with a palm readin' and then laid out the tarot cards. I've been feelin' bad about missin' so much in Fannie's readin' that I wanted to get things right. Anyways, the first card she drew was a Sword card, indicatin' trickery to gain power." She took a couple more bites, mulling over her story.

I drew in my breath and exhaled slowly, trying to appear patient.

Mama swallowed and went on, "I assumed that it meant someone was gettin' ready to trick her into losin' that prize. But now that I look back on it, it meant she was the tricky one. But, the point bein', I didn't see nothin' worse than trickery. If she was a cold-blooded murderer it would have been in the cards."

Vicky, Sean, and now my mother. Why didn't anyone believe that Alice Peabody was capable of murder? "Isn't it possible that you missed something, Mama?" I regretted my words as soon as they were out. The hurt look on Mama's face made my stomach bunch into knots. I scrambled to soften my words. "I mean, you can't expect to see everything with just a few flips of the cards."

My mother's shoulders crumpled. "It's possible, sug. I've been missing a lot lately."

"Oh, Mama, that's not what I meant and you know it. I'm just saying that—"

She held up her hand, stopping me midsentence.

Slowly rising, she said, "It's okay, hon. Let's just call it a night. We're both 'bout tuckered out."

"Wait, Mama," I pleaded, but she turned away, placing her empty bowl in the sink, grabbing a glass and her favorite man, Jim Beam, from the cupboard, and heading for a nightcap and her makeshift bed on the sofa.

Chapter 16

A THUNDERING BOOM AND THE SOUND OF shattering glass woke me sometime in the early predawn hours. I sat straight up in bed, my heart in my throat. I knew exactly what I'd heard. The sound of a shotgun!

"Mama!" I screamed, running toward the front room and colliding with Trey in the hall. "Get back to your room and lock the door," I ordered.

In the family room, I found my mother still gripping the gun and staring with a dazed look toward what used to be my front window. It was no longer there. "Mama! Are you okay?"

"What?" She thumped the side of her head. "Lawd! My ears are ringin' somethin' awful. I don't remember this gun packin' so much kick. It's just a darn good thing I had a couple spare cartridges in my purse." She glanced around. "Where in blazes did I put that box of ammo anyway?"

I looked from her to the window and then back again. I was speechless.

"Wow, Nana! Why'd you shoot out the window?"

"I thought I told you to stay in your room," I barked at Trey. I heard the sounds of sirens. I turned back to my mother. "What were you shooting at?"

She pointed toward the window. "An intruder. Right there. Coming through the front window. See, my feelin' was right. Somethin' was about to happen."

I stared at the window, shards of glass around the edges like the teeth of a shark's jaw, menacing and evil-looking. The sirens grew louder. Through the fragmented glass, I could see a couple of police cruisers pull to the curb. Uniformed officers jumped out and ran down our walk, their weapons drawn. "Put the gun down, Mama. The police are here."

"How'd they get here so fast?" she asked, placing Rusty on the recliner.

"Must have been in the neighborhood," I responded, not mentioning the threat letter that prompted Sean to place patrolmen in our neighborhood through the night. I went to the door and threw it open before they even reached the front porch. "Everything's okay. My mother saw someone breaking in and—"

"Step aside, ma'am."

The officers pushed past me and filed into the family room. One of the officers immediately picked the shotgun off the recliner, turned it over, pushed some sort of release, and pulled back the pump to see if it was unloaded. "What's happened here?" he asked, keeping hold of the gun.

"There was a man comin' through that window there. It's been so hot, I had it open for some air," Mama explained.

The officer surveyed the window. "A man coming through there?"

"That's what I said," Mama reiterated. "See, I was sleepin' right here on the sofa when I heard some noise. I looked over and saw this man, well, one of his legs anyways, comin' in through the window. So I got Rusty and shot at him."

The officer glanced at Trey. "Are you Rusty?"

My son shook his head. "No, I'm Trey. That's Rusty." He pointed to the gun.

The officer raised a brow but didn't say anything. He motioned for the other officers to look around. "These fellows are going to check things out, ma'am. Why don't you sit down and rest a minute." Then, turning to me, he said, "I'm going to call Griffiths. Let him know what's going on."

I nodded and went to help my mother to the recliner. I covered her with a blanket. Despite the stifling heat, she was shivering. A few minutes later, one of the officers came back in. "We've checked the entire perimeter of the house and didn't find anything," he said. "There's nothing outside the window that indicates anyone's been injured."

"No blood?" the head officer inquired.

"No blood. I couldn't find any footprints, either.

All the other windows and the back door seem to be undisturbed."

The officer in charge furrowed his brow and nodded toward the bottle of Jim Beam and empty shot glass on the end table. "You been drinking tonight, ma'am?"

Mama folded her arms across her chest, her chin jutting outward. "Just my nightly constitutional, that's all."

The officers exchanged a knowing look. "Are you sure you saw an intruder, ma'am? Could you have been mistaken? See, it's unlikely that some of the scatter from the shot wouldn't have hit him. The window's not that far away."

I knew what they were thinking. They thought Mama was some old drunk who went around shooting at shadows. "Look, if my mother says she saw an intruder, she did."

"Stop, sugar." Mama held out one hand while another clasped her forehead. "Maybe they're right. These old eyes have been playin' tricks on me lately. Maybe I was seein' things. Or dreamin', maybe."

"No, Mama, you're not seeing things," I started, wanting to come to her defense.

I was about to bring up the threat letter, just to ease her doubts, and explain to her how there might be some sort of connection, when the officer pulled me aside. "We'll check the local hospitals and see if anyone turns up with a gun wound." We glanced back at Mama. Trey was bent over, patting her arm and whispering something in her ear. "It just seems peculiar that there wasn't any blood. With the stress of you being threatened and all, well . . . Do you think it's possible that she was just seeing things?"

I shook my head. "I haven't told her about the threat I received. And she usually doesn't act so irrationally." Then again, the body in the yard, Fannie's murder . . . all these things were a lot for anyone to handle. I sighed. "Maybe. I really don't know." I rubbed my temples. Why would someone try to break into our home? Again, the threat letter came to mind as a plausible connection, but still the police had Alice in custody. She was the most logical fit for Fannie's murder—the rose, the whole eliminating the competition thing. Or what if I was wrong and it was Grant Walker all this time? Maybe it was his leg Mama saw.

The officer patted my back. "Things like this happen at her age." He nodded again toward the empty shot glass. "Especially when there's whiskey mixed in. You'd best put up the gun before she hurts someone," he finished.

I agreed, and sequestered Rusty to the top shelf of the linen closet for the time being. I'd no sooner tucked the gun safely behind a stack of old blankets than the phone rang. It was Sean. I spent the next ten minutes or so answering his questions and reassuring him that we were fine. Before hanging up, he spoke to the officers, instructing them to remain positioned outside our home for the rest of the night. As soon they returned to their cruiser, I went straight to my mother and wrapped her in my arms.

She trembled against my shoulders. "You think I'm crazy, don't ya? That this old woman is losin' her mind. You think old age is finally catchin' up to me, don't you?"

"You're not old, Mama."

"Not at all," Trey added. "You're the coolest grandma around."

I glanced over at him. "Honey, would you go out to the garage and see if you can find something to secure this window for the night?"

"Sure thing, Mom."

As soon as he took off, Mama wriggled out of my hold and turned an angry face my way. "You say I'm not old, but I heard you talkin' on the phone about it to Sean this evening."

I scrunched my face, thinking back to the conversation I'd had with Sean before we went to bed. "What? Now you *aren't* making any sense."

"I may be losin' it but I'm not deaf. I heard you tell him you were calling a group home tomorrow to set up an appointment."

Then it hit me; she'd overheard bits and pieces of me telling Sean about visiting Peggy at the group home in Dunston. No wonder she was so touchy. And maybe that added stress had been all it took for Mama's subconscious to "see" something to prove she was needed here, to prove to herself and to us all that she could still protect her family. "You shouldn't be eavesdropping, Mama. But since you were, you might as well know the whole story. I'm not going to the old folks' home to see about you. I'm going to visit a woman named Peggy Cobb sometime this week. She used to own this house." I pointed toward the box of photos in the corner. "I'm taking those photos for her to look at because I think one of them might be of the young woman buried in our yard." I drew in a deep breath, waiting for her to digest all this new information.

"Oh," she said, then shook her head. "Still, I've been havin' plenty of trouble with my predictions these days. First, I didn't see Fannie's death comin', and now you're telling me that I didn't see that Alice Peabody is a murderer. Then, I done gone and shot out the window."

I sighed. Should I tell her about the threat letter? Put her mind at ease about her senses? Or would it just cause her more worry? I'd already, even though mistakenly, given her the stress of thinking I was turning her in to a nursing home, for heaven's sake! And I had a blown-out window to show for it. I didn't think either she or I could afford stressing her out anymore by mentioning the threatening letter. I glanced over at the wall clock. Three o'clock. I could decide just how much I wanted to tell her in the morning. For right now, I needed to salvage what sleep I could; the rest of my week was going to be hard enough as it was. "You just made a mistake tonight, that's all. With everything that's been going on around here, we're all on edge. Besides, everyone has that type of trouble now and then."

Trey came in, carrying a hammer and some boards. "I think I can jury-rig something that'll work."

"Thanks, Son." I placed a hand on my mother's shoulder. "Why don't you come share my bed for the rest of the night? It's big enough for the both of us and you won't be comfortable sleeping out here anymore."

She nodded, so I helped her out of the chair and back to my room. Right before settling into bed, I gave her another reassuring hug. "If your predictions are off, it has nothing to do with your age, Mama. I'm sure of it. There's just something more going on than we can explain at this point." More going on than I wanted to tell her, lest she worry herself absolutely sick. And my house ended up with even more damage!

She nodded her head. "In that case, I might feel better knowin' that there was something wrong with my senses. Because, I'm still having that dreadful feelin' of mine and I'm 'fraid of what it might mean."

Despite my sleepless night, the next day I was able to work steadily. Every once in a while, I looked up from my computer screen to pet Eliot, who was contently curled on top of my desk. "You really do make a good mascot," I told him, peering into his mesmerizing green eyes. "I bet you saw what happened to your owner, didn't you, boy? It was that mean old Alice Peabody, wasn't it?" I asked. For some reason, I didn't feel a bit silly for talking to a cat. Although even as I asked the cat about Alice, my mother's words snuck back to my mind. "Trickery and thieving," she'd said. "Not murder." Her pronouncement caused a little niggle of doubt in my mind. All indicators, at least in my mind, pointed to Alice as Fannie's murderer, still I'd come to trust my mother's instincts over the years. And, there was the leg she saw last night. Her imagination? The police officers seemed to think so. Even Sean, when I spoke to him on the phone early this morning, felt that Mama might have been overreacting. Still, deep down, I knew my mother usually wasn't prone to such irrational behavior. Then again, something didn't seem quite right with her senses these days. Or her behavior. Poor Mama. Could it really be that the strain of the past two weeks was getting to be too much for her? After all, bringing a loaded gun into our home wasn't exactly rational behavior, at least not to me. I thought back to my window, flaps of ugly green tarp peeking between crooked boards, and took a long cleansing breath. I needed to remember to call the glass company.

I shook my head and turned my eyes back to my computer screen. So many things to consider, when what I really needed to do was get through the next few days of work and mark this Damian event down as a done deal. So I homed in on my screen and worked on email correspondence straight through lunch. Then I spent over an hour on the phone with the editor who was publishing Jay's sequel to *The Alexandria Society*. The book was due to be released early next year, so we needed to work out some key editing dates and start making marketing and promotion plans. Since Jay was, in essence, writing the sequel under the original author's name, there would no doubt need to be some extra editing. Jay was a talented writer, but writing in someone else's style and tone was a difficult task. Our main objective was to make the transition from the previous author's writing to Jay's writing as seamless as possible for readers.

After finishing the call with the editor, I glanced at my watch. I'd accomplished quite a bit this afternoon and wondered if I couldn't take time to make it over to Dunston to show Peggy the photos. I hated to take more time from work, but I knew Grant would want all his stepmother's possessions back before the estate sale.

I reached over and absently stroked Eliot's fur, thinking through my schedule. I could head over to Dunston right after work, but I'd need to borrow someone's car. I'd ask Mama, but then I'd have to tell her where I was going. I didn't want to bring up the subject of the group home again and add any more upset to her day. After last night, she needed to rest and put thoughts of aging and death out of her mind for a while. I, on the other hand, wanted more than anything to forge forward and put the mystery of the murdered young woman behind me and Sean as well.

I tapped my fingers on the desk. Eliot took it as playtime and tackled my hand. I scooped him up, cradling him against my chest. I scratched his sweet spot, the knotty fur right behind his ears, thinking that I knew just the person to ask for a ride. It was near quitting time anyway. I moved my hand under the cat's belly and held him at arm's length, peering into his face. "Come on, boy, let's go ask Flora if she'd like to accompany me today, shall we?" I said to the cat, his whiskers twitching in response.

As soon as I opened my door, Eliot abandoned me, wriggling until I let him drop to the floor. He immediately ran for the reception area, probably for his food bowl. I shrugged and turned toward Flora's office, but I'd just raised my hand to knock when Bentley came charging down the hall with Damian on her heels. "Everyone come to my office immediately," she bellowed. "The segment is about to show!"

Doors opened and the agents poured into the hallway, all abuzz with excitement. Once we were settled inside Bentley's office, Jude patted me on the shoulder. "Can't wait to see your film debut, kiddo." We'd all gathered at one end of her office, facing a flat-screen television mounted in the corner. She picked the remote off her desk and flipped on the television. A few channels later and we were tuned in and ready to watch.

"I just previewed the segment this afternoon," Damian stated. "I think you'll be happy with the results, Lila."

"And the publicity it'll bring," added Bentley. "Jude and Zach, what are our most recent sales reports?"

"Tickets are practically flying out the door," Zach said, popping his knuckles. "Sales really picked up today after the news report about Alice Peabody yesterday evening. Seems the president of the garden club being accused of murder has boosted our sales."

Bentley nodded all-knowingly. "Like I always say, there's no such thing as bad publicity."

"That's right," Jude agreed. "I have no doubt that after this program airs, we'll completely sell out."

Flora's eyes darted about. "A sold-out crowd,

you say? Perhaps I should have ordered more pies."

Franklin slapped his knee and let out a hearty laugh. "Not enough pie? Well, that's a great problem to have. Just last week, I had my doubts that we'd ever be able to pull this whole thing together in such a short time. And look what we've done. It just goes to show, this group can do just about anything we set our minds to. I want you all to know I appreciate everything you've done to help organize this event. I just couldn't have done all this without you." His eyes landed on me. "Especially you, Lila. Thank you."

"I agree," Damian chimed in. "I made the right decision when I signed on with this agency. You guys are the best."

A chorus of cheers sounded around the room.

"Shhhh!" Bentley interjected. "It's starting."

We all turned our focus to the television screen, where the local news anchor appeared, sitting behind a desk and speaking to the camera.

"We're bringing you a special segment tonight from Damian York's popular television program. This segment, which can be viewed in its entirety later this week on Damian's nationally syndicated show, was filmed right here in Inspiration Valley, where local literary agent Lila Wilkins is getting a yard makeover. Sheila?"

The picture flipped to a young female reporter holding a mic as she stood in front of my house. I recognized her from my interview the other day.

"This is Sheila Bradford and I'm standing in front of the home of Lila Wilkins, from our local literary agency, Novel Idea."

From across the room, Bentley murmured her approval at the mention of her agency.

"Novel Idea is launching the literary career of local celebrity Damian York with a signing and dinner this weekend. The theme will be rustic dining design, featuring farm-fresh cuisine from How Green Was My Valley, and the opportunity to meet Damian himself. To kick off the festivities, Damian has offered his design talents to Ms. Wilkins, whose yard had been recently destroyed by an unfortunate turn of events."

I sunk down in the chair as my yard appeared on screen. They might as well have been shooting a scene on the moon, that's how barren and desolate it appeared. Then, just like that, there I was, on television!

Another round of cheers rang out. "You look absolutely beautiful," Flora said.

"You do look good," Franklin agreed.

"She always does," Jude piped up with a wink to me.

"And, lucky for us, the reporter didn't mention anything about the dead woman found in your yard," Zach threw out. Leave it to Zach to bring that up at a time like this.

All the attention made my cheeks burn hot as I

sank even lower into my chair. Seeing myself on television was a humbling experience. First thing next week, I was going to make an appointment with my hairdresser. I noticed my chestnut locks were looking a little faded. And why had I chosen to wear short sleeves? Did my arms really look that big or was it just the camera angle? What I liked to think of as my curvy, Rubenesque figure looked a bit, well, plump on camera. But cameras did that . . . didn't they always say that? In those few seconds I decided that maybe one less caramel latte a week might be a good idea.

Thank goodness, I was only on the screen for a minute, otherwise who knew what other decisions I might end up making! The rest of the segment focused on the project and featured Damian, who appeared quite relaxed on camera. I admired the way he spoke with ease and seemed to make it all look so simple. The final shot showed the finished project, which I was very happy with, and added one more plug for the upcoming event.

As everyone applauded, Bentley flipped off the television and faced us with a beaming smile. "That seals it! This weekend's event will undoubtedly be sold out. I predict a successful book launch and record sales. To the James Joyce Pub—drinks on me!"

Everyone jumped up from their seats and started for the door. I grabbed Flora and pulled her aside. "How are you doing, Flora? I haven't had a chance to talk to you since your interview with Sean."

"And I have to thank you for that." She scooped me into a quick embrace. "It's like a burden has been lifted from my shoulders. Oh, the wonders a good confession can do for the soul!" she added dramatically. "Can you imagine that after all these years, I've finally decided to go to counseling? Had my first session yesterday afternoon and I swear, it was absolutely enlightening." She laid a hand on her chest. "This conflict that I've kept bottled up all these years. Why, it's just been eating away at me."

"I'm so happy to hear that. I only want what's best for you. All your friends do."

"I know that now. I'm just so sorry for the way I've been behaving."

I shook my head. "Please don't apologize. It's understandable." I hesitated, unsure if what I was about to ask was appropriate under the circumstances. "I wanted to let you know I'd been planning to head over to Dunston this evening to visit Peggy Cobb."

Flora eyes popped. "And?"

"And, well, after we finish our celebration it'll probably be too late, but I'm wondering if you'd like to go with me first thing in the morning. I want to take the photos I found at Fannie's and see if she can identify any of the children. The police already tried with no success. You see, Peggy's mind isn't always clear, but I thought I'd give it a shot. Maybe if someone other than the police approached her . . ." I shrugged. "It's probably a long shot since many of them would have been placed in other foster homes. But it might be the only way to identify the remains of the young woman in my yard." Flora hesitated, biting her lower lip. I continued, "Just think about it. I don't want to upset you in any way and it was only an idea, you know, in case you felt you might find it therapeutic."

"Aren't you two coming?" Damian was standing in the doorway, his eyes gleaming intensely. "You can't miss the celebration, Lila. You were the star of the show tonight."

I tipped my head back and laughed. "Hardly. It's just a good thing I've got a job, because I'm definitely not cut out for television."

Damian stepped between us and looped his arm through mine. "Ah, now. I thought you were terrific. But I'm glad you're not planning on pursuing a career in television. Because you're a damn good agent. Now let's go celebrate."

We laughed and walked arm in arm down the hall, stopping short in the reception area when Vicky ran over to us. "Lila!" she hissed. "Detective Griffiths is here."

I immediately dropped Damian's arm. "Sean?"

He was seated in one of the waiting-room chairs, arms folded across his chest and blue eyes sparking with anger, clearly in view of the hallway. "Lila?"

The atmosphere went from jovial to icy cold. Grabbing Eliot and a diaper bag that she'd started using to transport Eliot's toys and food, Vicky bid us a quick good night. As soon as she exited, I turned to Damian and Flora. "You guys go on ahead. Make my excuses to Bentley, please. I'll lock up the place."

Flora nodded and grabbed my arm with a quick whisper. "I'll go see Peggy with you first thing in the morning. How about I come by your place at nine. I'll tell Bentley we'll be in late tomorrow."

I squeezed her hand and managed a small smile. "Thank you, Flora."

After everyone had gone, I moved about the office, turning off the lights and checking in the break room to make sure the coffeepot was turned off. Sean remained in the waiting room, silently watching me as I completed the end-of-the-day tasks. When I was done, he stood and walked to me. "I just stopped by to follow up about the, ah . . . incident last night."

"Incident? Sounds like you're even more convinced now that Mama was imagining things."

He shrugged. "We checked the hospital in Dunston and they haven't treated anyone with a buckshot wound. And, with that much glass being blasted out, anyone nearby would have been cut. There should have been some blood at the scene." He placed his hands on my shoulders. "Is everything okay?"

I didn't quite know if he was really referring to my mother, my window, or us. Truth was, at the moment I didn't much care about my shotgun-blasted window or anything else, for that matter. All that mattered to me was telling this man just how crazy I was for him. I drew in my breath and looked directly into his eyes. "I know what you've been thinking, but I have no feelings for Damian York, whatsoever. It's you that I love."

His blue eyes glistened. "And I love you."

I moved to him, wrapping my arms around his waist and holding tight. "I'm so sorry, Sean. I led you to believe that I had feelings for Damian because I was angry that you never have time for me. You see, I overheard you that night at my house, asking Trey for my hand in marriage and I've been waiting for your proposal. When it never came, I got impatient."

He pulled back and tipped my chin upward. "What? You overheard that?"

I nodded. "I'm sorry, but I did. And, ever since then, I've been waiting for you to ask me and when you didn't . . ."

"Oh, Lila. I'm so sorry. I had no idea."

My head bobbed up and down, tears sliding down my cheeks. "It's all I've thought about. But you never asked, so I assumed it just wasn't as important to you. I was hurt. That's why I let you think those things about Damian. I was hoping to make you jealous. It was wrong of me."

"Lila, our future together is the most important thing in my life. Come on, let's head over to your place. We've got a lot to talk about."

The next morning I rose from bed, padded across the room, and spread my curtains wide. A hazy heat was hugging low on the horizon, causing moisture droplets to form along the edge of my windowpane. I knew without taking a single step outside that the heat would be unbearable. But I didn't care. Not the heat, my messy schedule, blown-out window, or even the still-unanswered questions about the body in my yard could dampen my mood this morning. Sean and I had spent most of the evening snuggled on my porch swing talking things through, and all was right with the world again.

The first scent of coffee brewing wafted into my room and drew me from the window and out to the kitchen, where I found my mother and Trey sitting together at the table. On the floor, next to the table, was Mama's old brown traveling bag. "Going somewhere, Mama?"

"Home. I've been thinkin' 'bout what you said about Mrs. Peabody being in jail and all. My feelin's aside, seems the police have their killer. The only danger left around here is me, so I best be headin' on home."

I threw my arms around her shoulders and placed my cheek alongside hers. "Oh, Mama. Please stay. I love having you here."

"I know, sug. But you two have your own lives and there's no sense in me hangin' around and gettin' in the way."

Trey got up, put his plate in the sink, and grabbed a banana off the counter. "But we're still on for tonight, though. Right, Nana?"

She shot him a thumbs-up. "You bet. Lookin' forward to it."

I waved good-bye to Trey and turned back to Mama. "So, did I miss something?"

Her smile lingered after he left. Trey and my mother had a special bond. Sometimes I envied it, mostly I was just grateful they had so much in common. After my divorce, my mother stepped in and filled the void Bill had left. She's always had a way with Trey. While I was more of the authoritarian, laying down the rules and making sure they were enforced, she provided the occasional lapse in protocol, the impulsiveness that I lacked, and a wonderful sense of adventure that encouraged Trey to explore and take on new challenges. Together, Mama and I made an awesome parenting team.

"Trey is goin' to start comin' to my place a couple nights a week for cookin' lessons. He wants to know all the family recipes."

My jaw dropped. "He does?"

My mother's head bobbed up and down. "Bet you didn't know that he wants to be a cook, did you? Seems he's been savin' all his extra money to open a restaurant one day. He's got all sort of dreams. Good ones, too." The lines around her eyes deepened as her smile spread wide. "Yup, that boy of ours is goin' places. Just you watch and see."

My mouth was still hanging open. I was absolutely shocked. I had no idea Trey was considering a career in the culinary arts. How had I missed that?

A knock on the door interrupted me before I could ask any more questions. I rushed to let Flora in. "You're right on time. Do you want a bite to eat before we go? Some toast or tea?"

"No, but thank you. Brian fixed me a three-cheese omelet before I left this morning. I'm so glad I married a man who likes to cook. Oh, hello, Althea," she called out, peering over my shoulder. I was smiling and trying to make small talk, but my mind was stuck on Trey and his new career choice. I couldn't believe he hadn't discussed this change of heart with me. Did he want to leave college at UNC Wilmington and study at a culinary school? Where would that be and, pray tell, how much would it cost? Not to mention the restaurant business is one of the most difficult to make a living at.

"Lila?" Flora interrupted my thoughts. I noticed

Mama had her bag in hand and was already heading out the back door. "I was asking your mother about your front window. I think something I said must have upset her."

I waved it off. "Don't mind Mama. She's been in a mood lately." I glanced toward the window, wishing the glass people could have fit me into their schedule earlier. As it was, they couldn't come out until Friday, which meant I'd have to tolerate the eyesore for another day.

"So, what happened to the window? Neighborhood kids?"

I nodded. "You could say that," I answered, letting her think what she wanted. I didn't want to embarrass Mama by telling the real story. I grabbed the box of photos from next to the recliner and joined her by the door. "Ready to go?"

Despite a quick detour through Dunston's donut shop drive-through for an extra cup of coffee, Flora and I made it to the group home before ten o'clock. Either the extra caffeine had given Flora the jitters, or she was exceptionally nervous, because by the time we walked up the flowered path and reached the front door of Dunston Manor, she was shaking like a leaf. Guessing it was the latter, I pulled her aside and gently asked, "Are you sure you're up to this? I can go in alone."

"Don't be silly," she admonished, removing her

handkerchief and dabbing at her forehead. "This will be good for me. I need to face down my past and come to terms with my fears. Besides, Peggy Cobb was always the sweetest woman; it was that no-good drunken husband of hers that was so mean to me. Why, I think she was half afraid of him herself."

"It could be. Perhaps she wasn't as brave as you."

"What do you mean? I wasn't brave. I ran away."

"That's exactly what I mean. You thought enough of yourself to get out of that situation. If Peggy was, in fact, abused by her husband, she never had the courage to leave him. That's really sad."

She paused, her eyes searching the ground. "I never thought of it that way. Leaving, and facing things on my own, did take courage."

"That's right," I agreed, hugging the box of photos to my hip and hooking my arm in Flora's. I eyed her closely. I could tell facing down this terrible memory from her past was difficult. Her normally rosy cheeks appeared pale and sallow. Her lower lip was trembling. "Come on. It'll be okay."

I rang the bell. After a little wait, the door was opened by the director, Janet Martin, whom I'd met during my last visit. Only today, she didn't appear quite as happy to see me.

"Hello, Janet," I greeted. "I've come to see Mrs.

Cobb again. We spoke on the phone about my visit," I reminded her.

The woman's features remained somber as she opened the door and motioned for us to come inside. I quickly introduced her to Flora. "I'm sorry you've made the trip over here for nothing. I tried calling you this morning, but I must have just missed you."

"I don't understand. Is there a problem?"

"I'm afraid Mrs. Cobb isn't up for visitors today. She's not feeling well."

Flora's hand flew to her chest. "Oh no! She's taken ill?"

The woman shook her head. "Not exactly. She's terribly upset, that's all."

"Upset? About what?" I asked.

"We haven't been able to determine what exactly is upsetting her, but she was so distraught last night, the nurse administered a sedative. She's sleeping soundly now, but she was awake most of the night."

My mind reeled as I processed this new turn of events. What would have caused Mrs. Cobb to become so upset? "Did she have a disagreement with one of the other residents?"

Janet shook her head. "Not that I'm aware of, anyway. Mrs. Cobb usually gets along well with everyone."

Another thought jumped to mind. "Did she have a visitor, perhaps?"

"Oh, I didn't think of that. Although, it's unlikely. She's not really had many visitors since she moved in."

"Well, that's terrible," Flora lamented.

I leaned in. "Do you keep a record of visitors, by chance?"

Janet straightened. "Of course. We keep a record book of visitors in the office." Flora sat in one of the foyer chairs and I placed the box on the table by her as I followed Janet.

In the office, Janet opened the book and glanced at the latest page. "No, in fact, the only visitor we recorded last night was Mr. Cartwright's son. He came by at about eight thirty. It doesn't show that Mrs. Cobb has had any visitors recently."

My shoulders fell. I was disappointed that I wouldn't find any answers today. "Thank you for checking," I said, heading back to retrieve the box of framed photos. I found Flora holding one and staring at it with a bewildered expression.

"Flora?" I asked, looking over her shoulder at the picture she was studying. "What is it? Do you recognize that girl?" The photo was of a dark-haired teenager with large, solemn brown eyes on a too-pale face.

Flora squinted and shook her head. "She looks familiar, but I just can't place her."

I took the picture from her and gently opened the back of the frame. "Maybe there's a name written on the back of the photograph." But no such luck. I sighed and replaced the photo in the frame and gathered the box before following Flora toward the door. "How about you keep these overnight?" I said, putting them into the backseat of her car. "Maybe if you had a chance to take a closer look, you might recognize someone or at least remember why that one looks so familiar."

Flora shrugged. "I'd be glad to, but don't get your hopes up. Your best bet is to wait for Mrs. Cobb to settle down so you can show them to her."

She was right. Only who knew when that would be, if ever. But I would have to let it go for now. Besides, the fact was that Sean and I had already reconciled how our busy lives had catapulted our relationship into a negative spiral. Both of us were determined not to let that happen again. So solving this cold case for him at this very moment was no longer quite so necessary. As Sean said, this was a decades-old case and it could wait a bit longer.

I sat back in my seat, watching the scenery flow by as Flora drove me back to the agency. I noticed the wild chicory along the roadside stood straight and strong, refusing to bend even under the recently oppressing heat. I could take a lesson in perseverance from this formidable plant, I thought. Raising my eyes to take in the beauty of rolling green hills dense with Carolina pine, my mind wandered to all that had happened these past two weeks. It was time for me to push the negative aside and take stock in the positive. My yard was no longer bordered with yellow crime scene tape and looked better after Damian's makeover. That, plus Alice was in jail. Of course, there was the intruder incident. Still, now even Mama was admitting that she probably just imagined seeing someone coming through the window. Probably a few nights sleeping in her own bed would give her some much needed rest. Rest. That's what we all needed. We'd all been under so much strain lately. It was time to let all that go. All I needed to do was get through the next couple of days of planning, then I could simply sit back and enjoy.

Chapter 17

LATE THURSDAY MORNING, I ENTERED MY office with an attitude of determination. Damian's event was only a couple of days away and I still needed to attend to plenty of last-minute details. Luckily, my teammates rallied and were helping to pull me through the final stretch of preparations. Jude and Zach, angels that they were, sold off the last of the dinner tickets, making for a sold-out event. They'd even organized a shuttle service to transport garden walk participates to Damian's signing and dinner. Flora, although still a bit unsettled herself from all the stuff with the Cobbs, managed to pull together a selection of pies that would tempt even the most self-professed health nut. And Vicky, in her ever-so-efficient manner, sweet-talked the other garden club members into accepting a replacement for Alice Peabody's garden. Since brochures had already been printed before Alice's assault escapade had disqualified her yard from the garden walk, Vicky was able to simply reroute walkers from Alice's yard to the neighbor's with only the slightest inconvenience.

The rest of the day went by quickly. I had just finished a phone call confirming a few details with the party rental company in Dunston when something tumbled into my mailbox, spurring my spirits even further. An email with a subject line that read: "Re: *The Barista Diaries*." When I'd first read Makayla's manuscript, I was impressed with how each cleverly crafted tale provided a personal peek into the lives of the café's customers and gave the reader witty narratives of love, heartbreak, and human triumph. I knew Makayla's book would delight readers as much as it had me. The tricky part, of course, was finding a publisher. After a few minor revisions, I had submitted it to a list of editors. So far, we'd received several rejections, but I was hoping this one would bring some good news. I clicked and anxiously leaned forward. Holding my breath, I scanned the email. "Yes!" I screeched, throwing both hands into the air and tipping my head back. "Yes! Yes! Yes!"

The editor loved *The Barista Diaries* and wanted to extend a publishing offer to Makayla. They were even offering a small advance and a request to see more of her work. Reaching across my desk, I snatched up my phone receiver. *No,* I thought, replacing it with a thud. This was something I wanted to tell her in person. Selfish as it was, I wanted the thrill of seeing the joy on her face when she found out she was going to be a published author. I glanced at my watch. It was her closing time, but if I hurried, I'd be able to catch her before she left.

I was skipping down the back steps when my cell rang. "Hello?" I answered, stopping in my tracks when the caller identified himself as a Dunston police officer.

"Is this the mother of Trey Wilkins?" he asked.

I nodded, my heart sinking to my stomach as my mind flashed back to the last time an officer had called about Trey. That time had cost me several thousand dollars in repairs to the Dunston football field. But that was back in Trey's rebellious stage. Certainly he hadn't gotten himself into trouble again.

"Hello? Ma'am?"

"Yes," I blurted into the phone. "This is Trey's mother."

"I'm calling because your son's been in an accident."

"An accident?" I shrieked.

"He's okay, ma'am. Just a little banged up. He's been transported to the Dunston hospital emergency room as a precaution. He gave me your number to call."

I disconnected and ran the rest of the way down the steps, toward the back entrance of Espresso Yourself. The door was already locked, but I banged on it anyway. "Makayla!" I yelled, peering through the window in hopes of seeing her still inside. I banged again. "Makayla!"

I caught sight of her moving across the floor with a mop, her hips swaying in beat with the music playing through the earphones she was wearing. I banged again and waved my hands. She finally looked up, pulled the earphones off, leaned the broom against the counter, and came running toward me. She fidgeted with the lock for a second before throwing open the door. "Lila! What is it?"

"Trey's been in an accident. Can you take me to Dunston?"

Her hand flew to her mouth. "Oh no!" She hesitated a second as the news registered in her mind, then she kicked into high gear. In a matter of seconds, she retrieved her purse, locked the shop's doors, and got me to her car.

A quick twenty minutes later, we were making our way into the emergency room when I heard Sean's voice. I'd tried to dial both him and my mother en route, but hadn't reached either of them. Mother, of course, didn't have a cell phone or an answering machine, but I'd left a message on Sean's voicemail. He caught up to us just as we were nearing the emergency room entrance.

"Lila," he called out, running up to us and pulling me into a quick embrace. "He's okay, Lila. I called the responding officer on my way here. They just sent him here as a precaution."

"I need to see for myself," I said, pushing past him and heading through the sliding double doors, Sean and Makayla following closely behind. Sean flashed his badge at the woman managing the ER front desk and spewed Trey's name. The woman immediately directed us toward another set of large glass double doors and pushed the entrance button allowing us to proceed. Makayla stayed behind in the waiting room. "I'll be right here if you need me," she said.

Directly inside the entrance dividing the waiting area from the actual ER, we encountered the nurses' station. Once again Sean showed his identification and the nurse calmly pointed us toward a hallway of curtained rooms.

I sped off in the direction she'd indicated and threw back a curtain only to stop short when I encountered a nurse bent over and adjusting the IV of an elderly gentleman. I stood staring in frozen confusion for a second before Sean came up behind me and drew the curtain closed. "Wrong room, Lila. He's next door."

I rushed into the next room and found Trey sitting on the edge of a bed. Next to him was a young nurse, reading over his chart.

"Mom! How'd you get here?"

Crossing the room, I threw my arms around my son and pulled him close, relishing the feel of his scruffy hair against my chin. "Trey! I was so worried!"

"Easy, Mom. That hurts," he said, squirming out of my grip.

The nurse touched my shoulder. "He's going to be sore for a while, but everything checks out okay. No broken bones and his brain still seems to be intact," she added with a chuckle. She was probably trying to insert a little humor to ease my worries, but I didn't find anything humorous about my son being involved in an accident.

"What happened? You weren't texting and driving, were you Trey?" I paused as Sean's phone buzzed and he stepped to the other side of the curtain to take the call. I turned back to Trey and kept on him. "Is that what happened? Were you on your phone?"

Trey shook his head. "No, Mom. Honest. I don't know what happened. I was just on my way home from work when the car started acting funny. Next thing I knew I couldn't control it. I went off the road and ran into the utility pole. Oh man, is my car bad?"

"Your car?" I sank down next to my son, suddenly feeling bone-tired. "I don't care about your car, Trey. We can always get another car, but you . . ." Tears started spilling down my cheeks. I couldn't help myself. He was okay, but what if things had happened differently?

The nurse reached over and touched my shoulder. "It's okay, ma'am. All the X-rays were clear and the doctor said he's good to go." She passed a clipboard full of papers toward us. "We'll just need him to sign a few papers and then you can take him home."

I asked Sean to find Makayla in the waiting

room and send her home. Everything was fine, so there was no need of her spending the rest of her evening at the emergency room. For the next half hour, Trey signed paperwork and received instruction for taking a mild pain reliever for any discomfort he might feel. We were just wrapping things up when a familiar voice rang through the hallway. "Don't tell me I'm not allowed back here—I'm the grandmother!" I could hear curtains being ripped open, one by one. "Trey!" my mother's gravelly voice bellowed.

I rushed to the hall just as Sean flagged her down. "Mama!" I called out, running to her outstretched arms. "I couldn't reach you on the phone—how'd you know?" Had she sensed it? Certainly when you're as close as Trey and my mother are there must be a bond that transcends conventionality and taps right into the psyche. I'd heard of similar phenomena between twins. When one was injured, the other immediately knew, even felt their pain in some cases.

"No, Makayla just called me about twenty minutes ago. I rushed right over." She patted my back. "It's okay, sugar. I'm here now. Where's that grandson of mine? Some uppity nurse out there told me I couldn't come back here, but I've just gotta see Trey with my own eyes."

I led her to Trey's bedside, where she immediately began fussing over him. Sean followed close behind and stood next to me, shifting from one foot to the other. I turned to him and saw a deep scowl. "What's wrong?"

The room grew quiet as we all sensed his tension. "There's something I need to tell all of you. This was no accident. The officer at the scene just called. The power steering line on Trey's car was cut. Someone fully intended to cause this accident. His car's been impounded for further examination. There're a couple of officers on the way here. They'll have some questions for Trey and a report for him to fill out."

As it turned out, the whole process took the rest of the evening. By the time we finally left the hospital, ran through a fast-food drive-through, and arrived home, it was after eight o'clock. Once there, I settled Trey in the family room recliner with his supersized meal and the television remote before joining Mama and Sean at the kitchen table, where they'd already started eating their own meals.

"I'm not sensing this act of evil was aimed toward Trey," my mother started. While Sean and I were sipping sodas, she'd rooted through my cabinets until she'd found her old friend. Jim Beam was the only one that could quiet her prickled nerves. "I think there's somethin' more going on."

The emotional toll of the day had left me famished. I swallowed a humongous bite of burger and took a quick sip of soda before replying, "Why do you say that? What do you think is going on?"

Mama took a long sip. "I think whoever did this was after you, darlin'."

Sean's head snapped and he paused, French fry midair. "Why's that?"

"Yeah, why's that, Mama? If the accident was aimed for me they would have sabotaged my Vespa."

She shook her head. "No, you've been borrowin' Trey's car a lot lately. I'm thinkin' that whoever did this thought the car was yours."

I paused for a second, taking another bite of burger, thoughts spinning through my mind. Maybe she had something. I'd used Trey's car to go to Dunston to Peggy's senior home and then out to the Walker farm. Had Alice seen me in Trey's car? I couldn't remember. She was in jail, though, so it couldn't have been her. But Grant had seen me. I looked to Sean for an answer. "If she's right, that puts Alice in the clear. Since she's still in jail, she couldn't have sabotaged Trey's car."

Sean shook his head. "She's not in jail, Lila. Her lawyer got her out this morning."

"What!"

"We couldn't hold her for murder—there wasn't enough evidence. As far as the other charges, she'll have her day in court."

"She's out?" I reiterated, thinking back to

something Matt from All Creatures, Feathered and Furry had said about Alice's husband owning the building before he did. I explained my theory to Sean. "So, there's your evidence," I finished. "Her husband used to be a mechanic, she probably learned about things like power steering lines from him."

Sean held up his hand. "Hold on. You're really jumping to conclusions now. I'll definitely look into it, and admittedly she's nutty enough to do something as drastic as murder. But I'm not sure."

"Me, either," Mama chimed in. "It just wasn't in the cards."

I glanced her way, noticing she'd polished off her glass and was fixing to pour another. "Take it easy, Mama. I don't want to have to carry you home tonight."

She pushed the glass aside. "You're right, hon. Just such an upsetting day, that's all," she added, folding her hands on the table and nodding for us to continue.

I turned back to Sean. "Is Grant still on your list?"

"He's not only on my list, but he's moved up a notch. Think about it: He was there the day you received the threat letter and you drove Trey's car when you went to give Damian a second opinion on his land, so he would have seen you in it and, not knowing better, assumed it was yours alone."

"Don't forget about the man I saw trying to get through your front window," my mother added.

"I thought you only saw a leg." I paused. "And, you said you might have been dreaming about that." I shot a look toward Sean. We'd all been going on the assumption that Mama had just been seeing things. Were we all wrong?

"A man's leg," she maintained. "And I'm starting to think it was no dream."

Sean moaned and rubbed his forehead. "Walk me out?" he asked, standing and pushing back his chair.

I left Mama in the kitchen and followed Sean back through the cottage. He turned to me as soon as we reached the porch. In one sudden swoop, I found myself in his arms, his lips on mine. I melted into the warmth of his embrace, cherished the feel of his lips against mine. When he came up for air, I started to say something, but he placed a finger on my lips. "It's all going to be fine. I'm going to make sure an officer is posted outside your house again tonight. First thing in the morning, we'll bring in Alice and Grant for questioning. We'll get this figured out, Lila, I promise." He kissed me again. This time even more passionately, his grip tightening around my waist. For a second, the strength of his kiss frightened me, then I relented, leaning in and surrendering myself to the comfort of his strong arms.

• • •

Back inside, I found Mama rummaging through my linen closet, knocking down a few pillow cases and mussing my orderly stacks of sheets. I moved in next to her, straightening her mess as she went along. "What's going on?" I asked. "Does Trey need another blanket?"

"No, sug. I'm just gettin' my bedding ready."

"Decided that you're coming back to stay here again?"

She paused. "If it's okay with you, that is."

I nodded and smiled. "Let me help you." We carried the bedding to the living room sofa. Trey was already snoring in the recliner, wiped out from his day.

"Will you look at that?" my mother said, staring warmly at Trey. "Why just yesterday it seems he was taking his first steps. Now he's gone and grown into a man."

A little ache pulled at my heart. I stopped tucking the sheet and looked directly at her. "I feel the same way, Mama."

"Whoever did this to his car may have it out for you, Lila, but he almost killed our boy." She glanced around. "Where'd Rusty go?"

I tried to shrug off her question, but my eyes betrayed me by sliding back toward the linen closet, where I'd hidden the darn thing. Attempting to cover my ocular blunder, I dropped the sheet and went to her side. "Sean is placing an officer outside our house tonight. We're safe; don't worry." I offered a little smile, but deep down I knew she was right. Our family had been targeted—nothing was more personal and urgent than that. I just didn't know how to go about doing something about it. But I didn't need Mama worried as much as I was. And trusty Rusty in Mama's hands after her nightcap with Jim Beam surely wasn't the answer!

Chapter 18

I TOOK FRIDAY OFF TO STAY HOME AND fuss over Trey while he rested and recuperated from his accident. For a day off, it was busier than a workday. The phone rang nonstop, my fellow agents calling to check on Trey's condition and express their concern. Then, around mid-morning, Makayla sent Zach over to our house with a much-appreciated delivery of hot coffee and scones. Just as he was leaving, the glass guy showed up to install my new front window, which took the rest of the day and cost twice as much as I'd anticipated. What's more, just before suppertime, the doorbell rang again. This time it was Flora and Vicky dropping by with carryout from the James Joyce Pub. Which was wonderful and so appreciated, since I hadn't had a chance to cook a single thing all day.

Despite everything going on, Saturday had finally arrived and I found myself at the Secret Garden, setting up and decorating for Damian's dinner. As I stood, surveying all our preparations, I felt in awe of all that had been accomplished. An event of this magnitude could have never happened without team effort. Not only after Trey's accident, but even now, my friends and fellow agents were by my side, helping me put the final touches on the dinner decorations. Over and over again, my coworkers amazed me. Not only were they the best people in the world to work with, they were truly caring friends.

"I can't believe how well everything has come together," Franklin said, using a pair of tongs to gently lower a white pillar candle into a blue-tinted mason jar. Next to him, Makayla twisted a dark grapevine along the center of the table, interspersing it with galvanized containers filled with bundles of snipped lavender and fresh herbs.

"Lovely, just lovely," Flora complimented her.

At the other end of the pergola, Zach and Jude were busy shuffling a tall stepladder from beam to beam, adhering strings of tiny white globe lights. They were so intensely dedicated to covering every single beam with lights that they reminded me of Chevy Chase in *Christmas Vacation*. "You missed a spot," I called out, pointing to a beam above Zach's head.

"Where? Where?" he inquired, twisting his head like an inebriated owl.

We all laughed and continued along with our separate jobs. Once again, I had to admire how well we worked together, like the parts of a finely tuned engine, each person performing their task to make the whole event run smoothly.

"Is everything ready for the signing, Franklin?" I asked, my head turning as Jay pushed by with a wheeled cart stacked with old doors. His tables made from farmhouse doors were the focal point of the entire setup. They set the tone and added just the right amount of rustic flare.

"Oh yes. We're set up by that grand magnolia tree near the gift shop entrance. Bentley is there now, making sure everything's in tip-top shape." He glanced down at his watch. "My goodness, it's almost three thirty." The garden walk was scheduled to finish around four, allowing people to make it to the Secret Garden's gift shop and purchase their books in time for Damian's five o'clock appearance. We'd estimated the timing would allow a couple of hours for the book signing before everyone would need to be seated for the dinner. Since dinner wasn't going to be served until seven o'clock, Paul Cohen had arranged for drinks and appetizers to be served at the signing while patrons waited in line to meet Damian. All of which would help in the sales, too.

Franklin excused himself. "I should head over there to see that everything is on schedule. Can you manage the rest of the decorating?"

"Of course," Makayla's sweet voice chimed in. "We just have a few final touches." She and Jay had been stealing glances at each other all afternoon, almost like schoolkids. I was finding it increasingly difficult to not spill the beans over Jay's pending proposal. I wondered if he'd thought of a romantic way to pop the question yet. Considering he'd serenaded her with musicians and roses just to ask for a first date, his proposal would have to be over-the-top romantic.

A while later, I stood next to Makayla at the garden gate, looking over our handiwork. "It's absolutely stunning," I observed, taking in the beauty of it all. A late-night thunderstorm the night before had brought relief to the unbearable mugginess of the week, lifting depleted foliage from its heat-induced slump and inspiring sleepy flower buds to burst open with color. I inhaled, filling my lungs with the post-rain freshness as I watched the crisp linen runners flap in rhythm with the humming of tree locusts. I'd never seen the Secret Garden so beautiful; it practically sparkled in the midday sun. "It's like a magic kingdom awaiting the arrival of the prince," I declared.

"Speaking of the prince"—Makayla chuckled—"maybe we should walk to the gift shop and see how things are coming along with Damian's signing."

"Let's do," I agreed, taking one final look before turning down the path and heading through the gardens toward the gift shop. Franklin had had the great idea of lining the nursery paths with tiki torches, which Jay and the other guys would light near the end of tonight's dinner event. That way, guests could depart the dinner and follow the lit path back through the nursery and out to their cars. All in all, the whole setting was so wildly romantic that, once again, I found myself thinking about the possibilities for my own wedding—that is, if Sean ever got around to proposing. Our long talk the other night had not broached the subject of marriage, even after my admission that I'd overheard him tell Trey he intended to propose. We'd spoken for hours, discussing the importance of our jobs, our mutual reluctance to open up, the pressures of our careers, and how we felt about, well, nearly everything. Everything, that is, except if we felt marriage was right for us two career-intensive types. I'd ended up relieved that we could talk so freely, assured of our love for each other yet unsure just where that really left us as a couple.

"Looks like they're right on time," Makayla said, bringing me back to the moment. I followed her gaze and caught a glimpse of several white catering vans pulling into the service entrance.

"I can't believe things are actually coming together so well," I commented. "There's no way Franklin and I could have pulled this off without your help."

"Hey, let's not count our chickens before they hatch. Or in your case, books before they're sold. The real test of success tonight is going to be proven with book sales. I have to confess, I've been daydreaming about what it would be like to have my book published one day. Oh, I know it's a long shot, but could you imagine the way it must feel to know that your words have reached people all over the world, maybe brought a moment of joy or laughter to their lives?" Her whole face lit up as she spoke. "It would be my dream come true."

I slowed my pace and paused, pretending to admire a border of daylilies, my lips practically twitching with anticipation. I'd been on my way to tell Makayla the good news before Trey's accident and hadn't had a chance to do so yet. Now seemed like the perfect time. "So, if I were to tell you an offer came in for *The Barista Diaries*, your life would be complete?"

She hesitated midstep, turning to me. "What are you saying?"

I grinned and nodded. "You have an offer from a small press, but they have great distribution, especially to libraries. And they want to know if you can write a sequel."

Her hands flew to her mouth as she tried to unsuccessfully contain a sudden burst of happy squeals. I noticed joyful tears forming at the edges of her eyes. "Are you serious?" she managed to ask.

Placing my hands on her trembling shoulders, I slowly repeated the terms of the offer.

"This is the most wonderful thing that's ever happened to me!" Her words came in breathless spurts as she wrapped her arms around me in a giant bear hug. "Thank you, Lila. Thank you!"

She released me and gasped. "I've got to tell Jay! He's going to be thrilled!" With that, she took off back down the path the way we'd come, half running, half skipping, and giggling all the way.

My heart soared as I continued toward the gift shop. I couldn't honestly think of anyone else who deserved happiness as much as Makayla. She was always there for everyone: her friends, her customers, and especially me. It's wonderful when life rewards kindness and hard work with good fortune.

Still grinning like a fool, I rounded the corner and was surprised to see an enormous crowd already gathered in front of the gift shop. Under the magnolia tree, a tent was set up with a long table prominently displaying a full-color poster of *Perfect Outdoor Spaces*. At the end of the table, Damian was sitting, pen in hand, flourishing his signature inside one book after another, stopping only to strike an occasional pose with an eager fan. I wasn't sure which line was longer, the line to meet Damian or the line leading into the gift shop, where his book was available for purchase.

A little ways down from the signing area, Franklin had set up another tent with café-style tables where guests could linger, sip wine, and sample appetizers until it was time to be seated for dinner. Just for fun, he and Addison, the nursery manager, arranged additional tables with design displays for container plantings. Everywhere I looked inside the tent, there were pots over-flowing with the most vivid flower combinations: spiky pink salvia paired with rambling white petunias and trailing black sweet potato vine; fluffy pink geraniums peeking out of a sea of blue velvet petunias and purple sorbet violas; or my personal favorite, a pot stuffed full of dwarf sunflowers, yellow snapdragons, and marigolds the color of melting Dreamsicles. Each display was accompanied by a customized container recipe card, which guests could take for replicating the container design at home. I picked up a few myself, thinking how fun it would be to put together a couple of pots for my front porch.

I mingled with a few guests as they enthusi-astically perused the displays with signed books under their arms and champagne flutes in hand, snippets of their conversations ranging from gardening to food talk and almost everything in between. As people finished getting their books signed, the crowd grew and cheerfully spilled out of the tent and onto the nursery paths, where Damian's fans anticipated dinner while admiring the rest of the nursery gardens.

"There you are, Lila!" I turned around to find Bentley scurrying toward me, looking ever-so-professional in a crisp white suit and red patent platform heels. Her signature reading glasses dangled from a ruby-embellished chain, comple-menting her shoes and, although she must have tucked it temporarily away in a safe spot, I imagined a matching purse—perhaps a rich red leather or even a deep scarlet fabric accented with rhinestones to jazz up her ensemble. "A smashing success!" she enthused. "For certain, we'll sell out tonight." She glanced at her watch. "Is everything set for dinner?"

"Yes. When I left, Jay was just mounting speakers and setting up a microphone for Damian's speech and the announcement of the van Gogh winner." After speaking to Paul Cohen, I'd mentioned a little of Damian's backstory to Franklin and he'd convinced the author to speak about his rocky road to success. According to Franklin, Damian had prepared a moving speech that was sure to inspire the audience. I glanced over to where he was charming one of his readers now, a young woman blushing with pleasure as he stood and placed an arm around her shoulder, posing for the camera. I silently wondered how a man like Damian had made it to his thirties without being snagged by a beautiful woman.

"Damian may be one of our biggest successes yet," Bentley was saying, her eyes sparkling as she watched him in action. "I plan to do whatever it takes to make sure I've secured his representation for many years to come. That man is going somewhere; I'm sure of it."

Something about the emotion in her voice caused me to do a double take. It wasn't often that

Bentley showed her softer side. Had Damian actually charmed my ever-cool boss? Was "secure his representation" some sort of Bentley code-talk for her desire to be in a relationship with the man? I volleyed my head back and forth between the two of them and shrugged. Why not? They'd make for an interesting couple, that's for sure. "Do you need any help here?" I offered.

She glanced at her watch. "No. Actually we'll be finishing within the hour. Maybe you should head back and make sure everything is in order with the caterers." She looked pointedly at me and added, "So far, everything's gone according to plan. Let's just make sure it continues that way."

So much for the softer side of Bentley, I thought, turning and heading back down the path. I didn't let her directives dampen my spirits, though. After all, things were going well so far. All we had to do was get through the dinner and I could mark this event down as another accomplishment in my book of agent events.

Chapter 19

JUST BEFORE SEVEN O'CLOCK, THE FIRST of the dinner guests started arriving to be seated. Vicky and I stood at the gate, greeting and collecting tickets while Jude, Jay, and Zach were busy escorting groups of guests to their tables. I kept my eyes peeled for Sean. He'd promised to arrive in time to eat dinner with me.

It was easy to get caught up in the joviality of the event. Guests' faces beamed as they entered the gate and took in the enchanting scene set for them. Whispers of astonishment, happy giggles, and throaty laughter carried over the flower-scented breeze as they settled at the tables and eagerly awaited the guest of honor.

As soon as the tables were full, the waiting staff started making their rounds, filling water goblets and delivering the first of the dinner courses. I took my seat at the agency's table, where Bentley, Damian, Zach, and Jude were already involved in a lively discussion about the evolution of ebooks and whether or not they would eventually outsell print books. Bentley, always a champion for print books, was holding her own in the debate. I sipped at my water and listened with interest, trying to focus on the conversation and not glance at the empty seat next to me. I was just about to speak up and express my opinion on the convenience of electronic reading devices when I felt a tap on my shoulder and glanced up to find Brian and Flora. Brian rolled his neck and drew in a deep breath. "I want to apologize," he started.

I reached up and touched his arm. "No need, Brian. Flora explained everything and I completely understand."

"Still, I want to tell you how grateful we are that you . . . uh . . ." He glanced around self-consciously, realizing that Damian and the other agents were listening. "Helped us face this issue. It's been a good thing for us." I nodded and bit back a smile as they exchanged one of those looks shared only by couples deeply in love.

Once again the sparkle had returned to Flora's eyes. "It sure has," she agreed, grazing his shoulder with her cheek. "Oh, by the way, Lila. I forgot to tell you I still have that box of photos in my car. I looked back through them like you asked, but I'm afraid nothing stood out to me."

I felt deflated. I'd been grasping at straws, hoping Flora might recognize one of the girls in those photos. "No, that's okay. I'll get them from you tonight. I should make sure they're returned to Fannie's house this weekend, I guess."

Across the way, I saw Jay and Makayla, sitting at one of the long tables, their heads bent together in conversation. Although there were other couples seated around them, they seemed to have eyes only for each other. I wondered if they were discussing Makayla's pending book contract, or something even more important, like their own future story.

With another longing glance toward the gate, I decided to try to push Sean's absence out of my mind and enjoy the evening. After all, along with a lot of other people, I'd worked hard to make this evening happen; I wanted to enjoy it.

"This food is awesome," Zach commented, finishing off his caprese salad with zest.

"You can thank Lila for that," Flora spoke up. "She arranged the entire menu with How Green Was My Valley."

Jude tipped his glass my way. "Excellent menu choices, Lila. I'm sure your boyfriend would agree, if he were here," he added with a glint in his eye.

Everyone's head snapped to the vacant spot next to me. My mind flashed back to that night a couple of weeks ago when I sat alone in Voltaire's waiting for Sean to arrive. A familiar feeling crept over me—impatience, tinged with a bit of worry and covered in a whole lot of ticked off. Suddenly, I felt like the odd one out. But I swallowed back my pride, along with the last forkful of my salad, just as the second course was served. I'd opted for the hickory-encrusted pork, while a couple of my tablemates chose the vegetarian plate. According to the general consensus, they were both delicious. I picked at mine, trying to enjoy it, despite the still-empty chair next to me and the little empty feeling that was growing in my heart. I did understand that Sean's career, like my own, was important to him; his time was not his own when it came to the inconvenient hours when crimes were committed. I just had to accept that as part of our relationship and trust his love for me. So why did my skin prickle whenever I turned toward that empty seat?

Finally, halfway through the main course, I folded my napkin and placed it by my plate. "I think I'll go check on the caterers. I want to make sure they got the updated instructions for serving the pie." Nell and Flora had come up with the idea of serving the pies family style. So instead of having waiters serve individual slices, several pies would be placed on each table, allowing guests to help themselves to their favorite flavors. I thought the idea was ingenious and lent itself to the bucolic, down-home feel of the evening.

Across the table, Flora started to rise. "Let me take care of that, Lila."

I motioned for her to sit back down. "Don't be silly. Stay here and enjoy the rest of your dinner with Brian. I'll be back shortly."

I wound my way through the tables and spied Paul on the other side of the pergola, dishing out orders to his waitstaff. They'd set up a food tent, complete with food warmers and a fully stocked bar. I couldn't imagine how much went into pulling off the food for an event of this magnitude. The whole process amazed me.

I caught up to him just as he was finishing directing one of his waitstaff. "Paul! Hold up a sec."

"Lila," he answered with a tentative expression. "Everything's okay with the food, I hope."

"Oh, it's wonderful, Paul. I just came back to tell you so. Everyone is singing your praises."

He clapped his hands together. "Oh joy! I'm so happy to hear that. You'll be glad to know that the pies have been sliced and we're preparing to deliver them to the tables now." He cupped his hand over his mouth and leaned forward. "I have to admit, I sampled a piece or two. That Nell is one amazing baker. By chance, is she single?"

I tipped my chin up and laughed. "I'm afraid not," I replied, knowing that Ed from Catcher in the Rye and Nell had been seeing each other for some time. "But I'll tell her you approve of her baking skills." I waved my hand toward the tables. "Everything's gone so well this evening, Paul. Thank you."

"I'm glad you think so. If you were on this side of things, you'd see how many little things have gone wrong. But I'm glad it hasn't been noticeable to the guests."

"Not at all. In fact, everyone, including Damian, is dazzled by your food."

"Good. I was hoping to catch up with him after the festivities this evening. Maybe rehash the old times."

I thought back to when I'd mentioned Paul to Damian. He didn't remember ever knowing him. "You know, Paul, it's been a long time since Damian grew up here. He might not remember all his childhood friends."

Paul shook his head. "He'd remember me. We were both 'C,' so we always ended up seated by one another. Alphabetical seating charts, you understand."

I blinked. "But York starts with a 'Y.'"

Paul cocked his head to one side. "York? No, didn't I tell you? York was his mother's maiden name. His last name was the same as his father's name, Cartwright. He must have taken his mother's name as a stage name. Damian York does have a better ring to it, don't you think?"

My mind was working overtime. *Cartwright? Where have I heard that name before?*

Paul went on, "I can't wait to ask him if he remembers the crazy pranks our class used to play on Mr. Stevens, the math teacher. I swear, that man had the patience of a saint. All the crazy stunts we pulled and he never once gave us detention."

I couldn't help but smile as Paul went on to describe a few of his adolescent shenanigans. All this talk about pranks reminded me of Trey's middle school years. Too bad his teachers weren't as understanding as their Mr. Stevens. I'd fielded more than my share of calls from irate teachers.

"There you are!" We both looked up to see Flora quickly approaching. "I've been looking for you," she said, completely out of breath as she reached us.

"You have?"

She reached under the neckline of her blouse and extracted a lacy handkerchief and began dabbing at her face. "Yes, it seems your beau has arrived. He was going to come find you but I told him to sit and eat his dinner. Besides, I wanted to meet the man behind all this delicious food." She eyed Paul. Realizing the two probably hadn't met yet, I made a quick introduction.

She gestured to the other end of the pergola. "He's back at the table, waiting, dear. Go on. If there's anything to do here, I can take care of it," she added, turning her focus back to Paul. I excused myself while they started chatting about the success of the dinner and Nell's delicious pies.

Now I could really enjoy the evening, I thought, making my way back toward our table, my steps a little lighter than before. I was looking forward to sitting back and enjoying a slice of Nell's pie and listening to Damian's speech with Sean, finally, at my side.

Only . . . I was passing the stage when I spied Damian slipping down the service path and heading toward the catering vans. What was that all about? He was due to announce the van Gogh award and give his speech anytime now. "Damian!" I called out, but he kept going. I took off after him. Maybe he'd lost track of time or was confused about the schedule. I broke into a jog, trying to keep up with his pace. He walked past the catering vans and started for a group of cars parked in the back lot. As I saw him approaching his rental car, I slowed down my pace, thinking he must have left something in his car, probably the notes for his speech. Still, I should remind him he was scheduled to speak very soon.

Then he did something that shocked me. Instead of unlocking his own car, he stopped and peered inside Flora's sedan. "Damian?" I asked, catching up to him. "Is there something you need in there?"

He wheeled around, surprised to see me. "Lila! Uh, no. I was just coming back here to get something from my car." He seemed embarrassed by being caught snooping around. Looking down, he shuffled toward his rental, extracting his key fob and hitting the button to release the locks. "I'm afraid I left my speech notes out here."

I'd figured as much. I glanced at my watch. "You're on in about fifteen minutes, you know?"

"No problem." He opened his door, leaned in, and stretched across the driver's seat, rooting around in his car's glove compartment. I glanced down and noticed a white bandage, instead of a sock, peeking out from under the hem of his pants.

"Oh my. Did you hurt yourself?"

He glanced down at the bandage. "Oh, that? Gardening injury." He chuckled. "Those thorny bushes out at the Walker place got the best of me."

I laughed. "A great showing tonight, huh? Looks like you sold out of books at the signing."

He shoved the piece of paper into his suit pocket. "I did. Bentley was thrilled, to say the least."

"I bet. She lives for the bottom line."

Damian relocked his car and turned to me. "We should head back to the party," he said, motioning for me to walk in front.

I scooted ahead, turning sideways to squeeze between a station wagon and a compact that were practically sharing paint, they were parked so close together. Zach and Jude, tonight's parking directors, must have been snoozing when these were parked. "Say, were your ears burning a while ago?" I teased Damian.

"What?" he asked from behind.

"Paul Cohen and I were just talking about you."

"Really?"

"Yeah, he's the catering director from How Green Was My Valley. I told you about him the other day. Anyway, he's done a wonderful job with the dinner menu, don't you agree?"

"Wonderful."

"It's funny you don't remember Paul. He has strong memories of you from junior high."

"Well, that was a long time ago. And I'm afraid I'm not good with names."

"Oh, speaking of which, he said you changed your name from Cartwright . . ." I paused, suddenly remembering where I'd heard the name Cartwright—the spunky speedster from the group home. The same home where Peggy lived. The same man who had seen the only visitor the night before I'd come with that box of photos to talk with Peggy. A visit from his son, Janet had said. I slowed my pace and turned toward Damian, my mind slowly making connections.

"What is it, Lila?"

I forced myself to look him in the eyes. "When we first met, you'd told me your father was still in the area but that you two weren't close. But there's a Mr. Cartwright living in a senior group home in Dunston. Your father? Did you visit him at the Dunston Manor the other day?"

He didn't respond, but simply stared at me with a strange expression. I shifted my stance and cleared my throat. My eyes moved to his leg as I thought about that bandage I'd seen a few minutes ago. Was this the leg Mama had seen coming through our window? "I don't recall any thorny bushes at Grant's house. How'd you really get that cut on your leg, Damian?"

He glanced down at his leg and then back at me. This time his expression was anything but charming. "You really should have minded your own business, Lila."

I gulped. The threat note. Of course. I'd been so sure it was from Alice, maybe even Grant, but I'd never considered that Damian was also in the office that morning. Why would I? He'd been there off and on all week, discussing the signing with Franklin and Bentley. What's more, he knew Grant had been in that morning and he'd timed the threat to frame Grant. Then my gaze went to Flora's car. He was after Fannie's photographs. But why?

I backed up a couple of steps. There was something else, too. Damian was at the Walker land the day I was driving Trey's car. He would have assumed it was mine. He was the one who cut the power steering line on Trey's car!

I watched in horror as Damian's expression changed to a look that scared me all the way to my toes. I backed up a little more, then turned to make a break for it, but suddenly Damian lurched forward, latching on to my arm. "Come with me, Lila," he ordered, his voice low and menacing.

I protested, struggling against his hold. "You almost killed my son," I accused, lashing out with my free hand and digging in my feet. I started to scream, but his other hand came out of nowhere, hitting me so hard in the face that I tipped backward, my legs giving out under me.

He grabbed me by my neck, wheeled me around, and jerked me against him, clamping his hand over my mouth. For a second, we stood there, pressed so closely together that I could feel his heart pounding against my back. I struggled, trying to reach my hands over my head and connect with his face, all the while my eyes scanning the parking lot, searching for help. Off in the distance, over the high-pitched buzz in my ears, I could hear the faint drone of laughter and the clinking of dishes. I knew Sean was there. Sitting at our table, waiting for me. Would he get tired of waiting and come look for me?

"You really are Novel Idea's own version of Nancy Drew," Damian hissed into my ear. "I suppose that's what happens when you spend all your time reading mysteries." He was pulling me along, dragging me between the cars and toward a storage shed at the back of the nursery property. "You just wouldn't give up on those stupid photos of Fannie's, would you?"

We'd reached the shed and he threw open the door. Dragging me inside, he shoved me up against the far wall. Before I could even react, I felt the chill of steel against my throat. I slid my eyes down to see a pair of pruning shears pressing against my skin.

Damian shook his head over and over, his features morphing into a sinister expression. "If it weren't for you I wouldn't have had to go have a little talk with the old woman, make it real clear that she wasn't to talk to you two. I couldn't take the chance that she'd point out my sister."

His sister?

His nod was slow and mechanical. "Yes, my older sister, Rachel." His eyes took on a faraway gaze, his words tumbling out, devoid of emotion as he spoke of his childhood. "When my father left us, things got tough for my mother. She was so desperate she embezzled money from her employer and was arrested. There was no one else to take us. So the state intervened and placed us kids in foster homes. They split us up."

"And Rachel was placed with the Cobbs?" I whispered, hoping to keep him talking while my eyes searched the shed walls for some sort of weapon.

Suddenly his eyes took on a wild expression. "Fannie Walker put her there," he bit out.

"I don't understand." Although a horrible picture was starting to come together in my mind. The body in my yard—it was Rachel, his sister. And Fannie placed her with the Cobbs. Did Damian kill Fannie out of revenge?

"All these years, I thought she'd run away. Left us like my father did. I've been searching for her ever since." His voice cracked. "I never gave up."

A little piece of my heart went out to Damian. All these years, searching and hoping, just to

331

find his sister had been dead all along. "But the night you brought me home from Voltaire's you recognized my house as the home where they'd placed your sister."

His face was screwed into a sinister look. "Yes, and you told me about the skeleton you'd found, and I knew. I knew Doug Cobb had killed Rachel. Everyone in town knew he was a mean old drunk. And Fannie made her live there."

"You blamed Fannie. So you killed her."

"I didn't mean to kill Fannie. It just happened," he stated, his voice taking on a panicked tone. "I called and told her who I was and what I suspected about the skull in your yard. We arranged to meet at her house. After I called, she'd gone back into the social services office and snuck out her old file on Rachel. She kept showing me the paperwork, telling me about all the background checks she'd run on the Cobbs. She just kept saying she didn't know, she didn't know that Doug Cobb was an abusive drunk. But she should have known—that was her job. She acted so sorry, so righteous, so sincere, like she couldn't have known, like she wasn't responsible. All those types are the same, all sweet smiles and saying the right words but never, ever responsible. She even said she'd be willing to go to the police and make things right." He shook his head back and forth and let out a low chuckle. "Make things right? There was no making things right. My sister was dead!" His eyes desperately searched mine for any sort of compassion. "The spade was there on the ground," he explained. "I don't know what happened. I just hit her." I felt the steel blade gnawing on my skin as he broke down crying, his hands trembling as his shoulders shook.

"But then, you got scared," I whispered. "And you were afraid I was going to find out so you sabotaged my car and tried to kill me." My eyes caught sight of a nearby shovel, propped up in the corner.

He shook his head. "No, no. I just wanted to scare you. Distract you so you'd quit snooping around. I didn't know it was your son's car." He was sweating profusely, his eyes wide and crazed. He raked his free hand over his brow and through his hair, causing it to jut out at weird angles, making him look even more sinister and deranged.

"It's not too late to turn yourself in, Damian. Anyone would understand how you might have lost control and snapped. You can't be blamed. It was Fannie's fault really, Fannie who did some-thing dreadful." He blinked as if considering that and I plunged ahead. "Everyone will understand, everyone will rally round you. Everyone loves Damian York."

At those words his features softened and I felt the blade slide off my neck. Seeing my oppor-tunity, I shoved him as hard as I could, grabbed the shovel, and swung, thwacking his shoulder with a *thunk!* As he stumbled, I started to run. Only he was too fast. I'd barely made it outside the shed when he snatched the back of my shirt and with one fierce movement, slammed me against the outside wall.

Instantly, I realized how foolish it was to try to escape. My bold move had sparked his rage and now there was no stopping him. I watched in frozen horror as he raised the shears over his head, their points aimed for my chest. I screamed and turned away, pressing my face against the rough wood of the shed. Then a large cracking sound pierced the air. I flinched and pressed harder against the rough wood.

"Lila!"

I managed to turn my head. It was Flora! She was standing over me, wielding a heavy gilded serving tray and staring in disbelief at Damian's crumpled body. I heard footsteps and voices in the parking lot.

"Over here," I called out, taking the tray from Flora and pulling her away from Damian.

She looked at me, her face flush and her eyes wide with shock. "Oh my! Are you okay, Lila? He didn't hurt you, did he?"

I stared down at the shears on the ground and shook my head. "No, Flora. Thanks to you, I'm okay."

"Lila!" Sean yelled, reaching the area with Brian

on his heels. He immediately kicked the shears out of the way and bent to feel for Damian's pulse.

Flora's hand flew to her cheek. "Oh my goodness! I didn't kill him, did I?"

"Unfortunately, no," Sean mumbled. "What happened?"

I quickly explained, "It was Damian who killed Fannie. I figured out some of the pieces and Damian went crazy, tried to kill me with those shears. Flora knocked him out." Flora offered a little gasp at her own part in the scenario.

Sean was already pulling out his cell and calling for backup.

"You did the right thing," I assured Flora. "But how did you know?"

Her voice wobbled as she attempted to explain. "I got to talking with Paul about things and, you know, we went to the same school in Dunston. He was several years younger than me, of course, so I didn't know him back then. But then Paul mentioned that Damian was his classmate and told me his name used to be Cartwright. That's when it clicked. That girl in the photo. The one who seemed familiar. It was Rachel Cartwright. She was closer to my age. Thinking about it now, I recall there was some discussion when she disappeared. But everyone assumed she'd just taken off. She was eighteen, an adult in the eyes of the law, so I don't think much effort was put into finding her." Flora paused for a second, then rambled on in a shrill voice, "So, I thought to myself, What if Rachel was really Damian's sister? If so, I wanted to ask if he knew where she was and how she was doing. I decided to get the picture from my car and show it to him. Only, when I got to the lot, I saw Damian manhandling you and got worried. I called Brian on his cell and told him to come help."

"That's right," Brian interjected, placing a calming hand on his wife's shoulder. "I was just getting ready to eat some pecan pie when the call came. Sean and I got here as fast as we could."

I rubbed at my chin. I was going to have a heck of a bruise on it tomorrow. "Damian believed his sister was the girl found in my garden, placed in foster care with the Cobbs who used to own my home. Damian blamed Fannie for placing her in an abusive household and confronted her. Then when I put it all together . . . If it weren't for you, Flora, I'd be dead, too."

Her eyes fluttered. "I swear, I don't know what got into me. I've never hit a soul in my entire life. It's just that I followed you two and hid over there." She hitched her thumb toward one of the catering vans, its cargo door wide open. "When I saw him throw you into the side of the shed, I just grabbed the quickest thing I could find and came after him."

"What's going on here?" came a stern voice

from behind. "Damian!" It was Bentley, stomping toward us on her platform shoes, fists clenched as if she was ready for round one. "What's happened to Damian?" She made a move toward the crumpled figure on the ground.

Sean stepped in front of her, blocking her way. "Stay back, ma'am. He's all right, just out cold. He'll come to in a few minutes."

"Well, I would hope so. He's due to announce the van Gogh winner at any moment."

"I'm afraid that won't be happening," Sean informed her. "As soon as he comes around, I'm arresting him for murder and attempted murder."

Bentley stumbled backward, her mouth agape and her face turning ashen.

I stepped forward. "It was Damian who murdered Fannie Walker." *And almost killed my son,* I thought. "He was trying to kill me, when Flora came to my rescue."

Bentley squinted at me, then at Flora, then back to Damian, who let out a little moan and was starting to writhe on the ground. The distant sound of sirens cut through the air as we all awaited Bentley's reaction to my news. For a second, I thought I noticed a crack in her usual ironclad façade as all the hopes and expectations she'd placed on Damian's rising stardom—and perhaps a few personal hopes of her own—were shattered. Then again, when they coined the phrase, "you can't keep a good woman down" they most undoubtedly had Bentley in mind. Because, after just a couple of slow blinks, she threw back her shoulders and lifted her chin. "Detective Griffiths, search that man, right now."

Sean's eyes popped. "What?"

"You heard me. Search him. I need the sealed envelope that contains the name of this year's van Gogh winner and I need it now." Then, looking at Flora and me, she said, "We'll need to improvise a bit. Gather the rest of the agents and meet me behind the stage in fifteen minutes."

"Whoa!" Sean protested. "Flora and Lila will need to answer a few questions before they leave."

Bentley narrowed her gaze, giving Sean a glaring once-over. "I'm sure, Detective, that your questions can wait; they certainly aren't going anywhere. And I have hundreds of guests antici-pating the announcement of the van Gogh award as well as Damian's speech. Now that I'm forced to come up with a different speaker, I need *all* my agents on hand. And the envelope." She held out her hand, palm up.

Sean grimaced, but didn't offer any objections. Instead, he bent down and searched inside the pockets of Damian's blazer, coming up with a small white envelope. Bentley snatched it from him and motioned for us to follow her. "Come with me, ladies."

I sent Sean a searching look, which he answered with a smirk and a shrug. "The boss has spoken. Go on, I'll come find you in a little while."

I scurried along, catching up to Bentley and Flora as they reached the stage. Bentley tapped the envelope against her hand. "All right. I'm going to get up there and attempt to sugarcoat this entire ordeal. What I need for you two to do is rally the other agents. See if any of them can come up with something to fill tonight's entertainment void. Anything."

With a quick adjustment of her blazer and a curt nod, she took to the stage. "Ladies and gentlemen," she started, adjusting her glasses on the end of her nose. A hush fell over her crowd. "In my hand"—she flourished the card for all to see—"I have the winner of this year's coveted van Gogh award. Unfortunately, Damian York is . . . um . . . temporarily indisposed." Her words were punctuated by the sharp wails of sirens as the police arrived to take Damian away. An excited murmur started through the crowd. "Please pay no attention to the sirens, ladies and gentlemen. I'm afraid there's been a minor emergency, but everything is under control. Now if I can have your attention." As she waved the envelope, bringing the crowd back to silent anticipation, Flora and I took off in search of the other agents. We hadn't made it far when I heard Bentley's voice bellow out from the speakers, "This year's van Gogh winner is . . . Ms. Vicky Crump!"

Chapter 20

"I JUST CAN'T BELIEVE THIS," FRANKLIN lamented after I recounted the lowdown on Damian's crimes. Flora and I had found the entire gang, including Jay and Makayla, back at our table polishing off their pieces of pie. "And I'm all to blame," Franklin continued. "I told him all about your sleuthing endeavors." He buried his face in his hands. "If anything had happened to you or that dear boy of yours . . ."

I placed my hand on my friend's back. "Please don't blame yourself, Franklin. No one knew."

"We all should have expected it, though," Zach blurted. "Lila here attracts murderers like flies to honey."

"That's bees to honey, Zach," Makayla corrected him. "And now's not the time to bring that up." She started tapping her fingers on the table. "What we need to do is put our heads together and come up with a plan. The show must go on."

Not so easily appeased, Franklin continued, "But what about all the money our agency has riding on his success? I'm responsible for signing him." He shook his head. "Oh my . . . I can't believe I signed a murderer for a client."

I sucked in my breath. Bentley was going to take

a hit on this one. She'd invested a lot of money into Damian in hopes that his future dividends would pay out. Once word got out that he was responsible for murder, sales were sure to plummet. Or maybe not. I recalled Bentley saying there was no such thing as bad publicity.

I was teetering between optimism and pessimism when Jude stepped forward and threw his arm around me. "I think the important thing is that Lila's okay. If it weren't for Flora, things could have turned out much differently. There'll be time later to rehash the business ramifications of tonight's events. Let's focus on the positive now and figure out how to move forward."

I eased out from under Jude's arm. "Jude's right. The guests were expecting Damian to give a speech tonight about his rise to success. We have a void to fill."

"The solution's right in front of our eyes," Jude said, pointing at Jay. "We have a future best-selling author right here."

Jay shrank back into his chair as all eyes settled on him. "Of course!" I agreed. "Jay, would you mind taking the mic and reading an excerpt from the next installment of *The Alexandria Society*? The crowd would love it."

Makayla squeezed his arm. "Do it! You'd be wonderful."

Before agreeing, Jay stared for a second into Makayla's eyes. "But I don't have a copy here."

"Zach to the rescue!" Zach chimed in. "The office is only five minutes from here. I'll go get a copy and be back in a flash." With that, he took off jogging, disappearing down the torch-lit path, headed toward the parking lot.

"I'll go inform Bentley of the plan," Jude declared, taking off in the opposite direction.

The rest of us stayed behind, rehashing the plan and preparing an anxious Jay for his first reading. To my right, I spied the Dirty Dozen, seated together in a cluster of three round tables. Vicky was seated there, amongst her fellow gardeners, basking in the limelight of her recent victory. Of course, the ever-nervy Alice Peabody was also there, all traces of her former superior attitude gone as she stared, sullen-faced, at Vicky. I wondered if once the other club members found out about Alice's attempt to steal Fannie's prize rose, she might find her presidency . . . what was the word she'd used that day at lunch? Relinquished. Anyway, I considered it poetic justice that Vicky won the coveted van Gogh award, despite Alice's attempts to thwart her. Perhaps with the prestige of the award as a boon, Vicky would even take Alice's position as president of the Dirty Dozen. I hoped so. Vicky, with both her talent for organizing and her love of gardening, would be the perfect club president.

I turned my attention back to my own table and tried to focus on the conversation. However, after a few moments, I excused myself to search out Sean. There were a few things I needed to tell him.

I finally located him by the catering tent. "Damian's on his way to be booked," he told me. "After he came to, he started confessing. We don't have the full story yet, but in addition to killing Fannie, it seems he was the one behind Trey's accident and your threat letter."

"There's something else," I started. "Right before he attacked me, he admitted to being the one who tried to break into my house." I relayed seeing the injury to Damian's leg. "Mama will be glad to hear she got a piece of him, that's for sure." I sighed. She'd be relieved about something else as well. To think she'd been doubting her abilities all this time, and, truth was, my mother was more on top of her game than ever.

"If it were just Fannie, I'd almost feel sorry for the guy," I continued. "He'd just found out about his sister's death and cracked, killing Fannie in the heat of the moment. But sabotaging the car and almost killing Trey?" I shook my head. Then a thought hit me. "Oh, I'm not sure, but I think I know what happened to the missing file from the social services office." I told him how Fannie showed it to Damian right before he killed her. "When Damian called, it prompted her to get the file from the agency. She might have snuck in and pulled the file herself, or gotten a friend to do it, I don't know. It's likely that Damian destroyed it after he killed her, in an effort to hide their connection."

Sean nodded. "I'll check into it." He moved closer. "I'm so grateful Flora acted the way she did."

I cracked a smile. "Who knew she had it in her?" I sobered. "Poor Peggy Cobb, though. When she finds out what happened to her foster child . . ."

Sean shook his head. "First of all, we'll need to run some DNA testing to verify that it *is* Rachel. And if it is, I don't think she needs to be told. While I was waiting for you, Flora told me how much better she felt after facing her past, giving me her statement for the record. She mentioned that she's anxious to go back to Mrs. Cobb's group home and talk to her now, get to know her. I think letting the old woman have a chance to reconnect to a still-living child all grown up might be nice for Mrs. Cobb. She doesn't need to know about the one who didn't make it."

He wrapped his arms around me. I nodded, then recalled, "Oh, there's a man at the group home named Cartwright. I think he might be Damian's father. Someone should break the news to him about . . . Rachel." I'd almost said "Helen," the name I'd used to make this girl real to me, but part of me felt relieved to finally have a name to give the poor young woman. Now maybe she could receive a proper burial in a real cemetery and some closure for her life.

"Shh . . . it's okay, Lila." He tightened his hold, pulling me back into his body, nestling me, spoonlike. "It's all over now."

I exhaled, feeling my body relax against his. The sun had finally dipped below the horizon, the strung lighting twinkling above, casting a warm glow over the tables below. In the background the clinking of dishes mingled with the constant din of guests' conversations as servers refilled coffee mugs and removed dessert plates.

He started kissing the back of my neck, just as a crackling sound emitted from the mic. Bentley took to the stage again, this time introducing Jay and his sequel to *The Alexandria Society*. The crowd clapped politely, but I could tell the applause was somewhat reserved. I felt an instant kick of nerves for Jay. Standing in for a celebrity like Damian York wouldn't be easy.

But as he read, something magical happened. The impatient crowd quieted, spectators quit squirming in their seats and sat silently, listening intently to Jay's eloquent flow of words. They floated over the air like magic, captivating the crowd and drawing them into the story. When he finished, a wild applause rang through the night air.

Modestly, he took a quick bow and then held up his hand for silence. "If I may indulge you for a minute longer," he addressed the crowd, "I'd like to read something else I've been working on. It's probably the most important piece I've ever written, and I'd be honored to share it with all of you this evening." He looked out to the audience. "Makayla, will you come up here, please?"

Bentley's eyes grew wide with surprise. In fact, the whole audience seemed to be sitting a little straighter, hanging on the edge of their seats as Makayla slowly walked to the podium. Knowing what was coming, I snuggled in closer to Sean.

"What's he up to?" Sean asked, his breath hot against my neck.

My whole insides gushed with joy. "You'll see."

Makayla reached the stage and stepped up to the podium, her eyes sparkling with a questioning look. Jay removed a piece of crumpled paper from his pocket, unfolded it, and held it up for the crowd to see. "Many of you know Makayla as the girl who serves your morning coffee. I've been lucky enough to get to know her as much more." A few people in the audience chuckled. "This is a letter that I've written to her and I'd like to share it with all of you." Silence fell over the assembly as he drew in a deep breath and began to read. "My dearest Makayla, do you know what makes me happy? The little crinkles that appear around your eyes when you laugh at my corny jokes. That it takes you almost an hour to do your hair in the morning." A collective chortle rose from the crowd as everyone stole a glance at her close-shaven head. "It makes me happy that you own a coffee shop, but you prefer to drink organic tea. That you care so much about your customers and you give so much of yourself every day. Your laugh, your smile, your beautiful green eyes— They all make me happy. You see, Makayla, there are so many ways to be happy in this life, but for me, there's only one . . . you. I'm happiest when you're the first person I see in the morning and the last I see at night." We all watched in awe as he came out from behind the podium and pulled a box from his pocket. "Makayla, will you give me a chance to make you as happy as you've made me? Will you marry me?"

It was as if the entire world held its breath, waiting for her reply. When she nodded and said yes, everyone burst into cheers. I squirmed out of Sean's arms and waved my hands in the air, cheering with the rest of the crowd. When the excitement finally died down, I turned to him, brushing a tear from my own cheek. "Wasn't that the most beautiful thing you've ever seen?"

Sean cleared his throat. "It took nerve, that's for sure. Asking her in front of all these people. What if she said no?"

"What do you mean? She loves him, you know that."

"Yes, but loving someone and committing to spending the rest of your life with them are two different things."

My jaw dropped. Where was this coming from? We'd talked through all this, hadn't we? That we loved each other. And that, with time, with better communication, we could make it work. Right? Or was this the way he really felt? I started to ask when we were interrupted by Bentley swooping onto the scene. "Well, I'd say we covered well for Damian's absence, don't you think?" She waved her hand toward the stage. Apparently, she'd recovered from the shock of seeing Damian arrested for murder. "People will be talking about Jay's proposal for years. A great publicity move on his part."

I shook my head. "I don't think publicity is what Jay had in mind."

Judging from Bentley's blink-blink reaction, she didn't quite understand what I was getting at. I didn't bother to try to explain, though. Her mind ran on only one track, the business track. "Still," she continued, "from a publicity standpoint, it was a brilliant move. It got me thinking . . ."

I squeezed my eyes shut, waiting . . . waiting . . .

"A wedding expo!" she let drop.

My eyes popped open. "A what?" Next to me, Sean let out a little groan.

She dragged her hand across the air as if spelling it out. "The Novel Idea Wedding Expo. It's perfect timing! Flora has two new releases this winter, *The Billionaire's Bride* and"—she cleared her throat—"another release from that bestselling erotic series she represents, what's it called? The Reluctant Brides of . . . of . . ."

"Babylon," I finished for her, casting a sheepish grin Sean's way. He raised a brow and smirked.

Bentley kept going, "Oh, and Franklin represents the author of *Strong Women, Strong Marriages*. Speaking of which, did you by chance sign the author of *Murder and Marriage* yet?"

"Lynn Werner? Um . . . I sent the contract this week. She's completely on board, though."

"Good. If her book is as good as you think, this will be the perfect little venue for her to gain some name recognition. You know how much editors love it when authors have an established platform." She waggled a finger my way. "But you'd better brainstorm a better title. *Murder and Marriage* isn't going to cut it."

I nodded.

Bentley's tone rose an octave as she continued brainstorming. "Anyway, it'll be fabulous! We'll host a bridal fashion show, cake design contest, maybe even a wine tasting." She waved away the final suggestion. "Actually, we can work all the details out at Monday's status meeting." She glanced around. "Where's Jude? I want to run a few of these ideas by him," she said, turning to tromp off to find him before I could even offer an answer.

"Reluctant Brides of Babylon?" Sean teased as soon as Bentley was gone. "I'm shocked, Ms. Wilkins."

I flushed and tried to explain. "Hey, reading books is part of my job description." Although, truth was, I preferred to read the books that Flora represented over the sport-centered books Zach signed or even the thrillers written by Jude's authors. But Sean didn't need to know that. "You know how I like a good love story," I added.

He moved in, clamping his arms around my waist and pulling me close. "Do you now?"

"Do I what?"

"Like love stories. Especially those with happy endings."

I nodded.

"How about our love story? Does it end happily?"

The edges of my lips twitched with excitement. "I don't know, Detective. Why don't you tell me?"

His eyes grew wide and I could feel his heart kick up a notch. "I know this probably isn't as romantic as you wished. I'm not reading prepared notes in front of a throng and I don't even have the ring yet . . . but, Lila, I love you and—"

"Yes! Yes!" I collapsed against him, pressing my lips against his.

For a long time, we simply stood there—contentedly holding each other under the twinkling party lights—watching the guests depart by torch-lit paths and listening to the distant chatter of our friends. After a while, I slipped off my shoes, letting the cool grass soothe my tired feet. Then, leaning back against Sean, I let my thoughts run their happy course. All I could think was how much my life had changed since moving to Inspiration Valley. Here I was with an amazing family and friends, the job of my dreams, and now the man I love to share the rest of my life with. "Our love story," Sean had said. He was right. Life was like a story: each day a new scene and every event a new chapter, the many words and pages depicting a lifetime of memories. What would the rest of my life's story bring? I wondered. New authors with fresh voices and captivating plots? An array of exciting literary events to plan? I nestled in closer to Sean. No matter the twists in the plot, I'd be satisfied just as long as the pages of my life story included an eternity of nights in the arms of the man I love.

Center Point Large Print
600 Brooks Road / PO Box 1
Thorndike, ME 04986-0001 USA

(207) 568-3717

US & Canada:
1 800 929-9108
www.centerpointlargeprint.com